The Ginger Tom

Booklocker.com, Inc.
2008

The Ginger Tom

Oscar Robinson

To Shae with best wishes —

CHAPTER ONE

FEDERAL CORRECTIONAL INSTITUTE
MARION, ILLINOIS

At one minute past midnight, Senior Guard Walter Kendall opened the heavy steel cell door and admitted the warden and two other officials. He locked the door behind them, left the keys in the lock, and stood outside listening intently with four other guards. If the prisoner became violent or otherwise uncooperative, the door would be unbolted and these additional men would rush inside and restrain him.

Counting the prisoner and the young watch guard, there were now five men in the sparsely furnished fifteen-by-fifteen-foot cell. The prisoner, dressed in a denim shirt and trousers, did not move from his place at the small card table that he had been sharing with his overseer. The watch guard, however, immediately stood to attention in the presence of the senior officers.

Warden Superintendent Robert Proxmire nodded to the larger of the two men who had accompanied him into the cell. This man now spoke evenly and without emotion to the prisoner. "Please stand up, sir."

The prisoner was of medium build and height and had weighed 178 pounds when examined three days previously in a routine visit by the prison doctor. He was helped gently, almost reverently, to his feet.

The larger man then said in the same even tone, "Please put your hands behind your back, sir." After a moment of fumbling, the prisoner's wrists were positioned behind his back and locked there with government-issue stainless steel Smith and Wesson handcuffs. A three-inch-wide canvas strap was placed around his lower chest and tightened with a buckle in the back, pinning his elbows to his side.

The warden turned and tapped sharply on the gray-green wall opposite the entry door to the cell. Instantly, the entire panel slid aside silently on well-oiled tracks.

The prisoner was moved quickly and firmly into the adjacent room. The larger of the two men was on his left, the other man, the one who had fastened the strap around his chest, was on his right. The prisoner's legs did not function well, so he was half carried, half dragged into position on the square steel plate. This trapdoor was positioned directly under an iron girder. A one-inch diameter hemp rope hung from the girder behind the prisoner's back and almost touched the floor. At its end was a hangman's noose with the thirteen traditional looped coils. Once the prisoner was in place, the watch guard bound his ankles together with a short woven belt.

The larger man released his grip on the upper arm of the prisoner and was immediately replaced by the watch guard. The prisoner did not struggle. The larger man stepped in front of the prisoner, reached in his coat pocket and withdrew what looked like a black knit ski cap. Holding the death hood in both hands, he stood in front of the prisoner at a distance of perhaps five feet.

The supervising warden spoke the last words the prisoner would ever hear. "Do you have a final statement that you would like to make?" He then activated a small tape recorder and held it forward.

The condemned man made no response.

The warden clicked off the recorder and replaced it in his side coat pocket. He nodded, and the hood was placed over the prisoner's head. Smoothly, the noose was placed over the condemned man's head and adjusted snugly with the knot on the left side of his neck. The man patted the prisoner lightly on the shoulders with both hands and stepped back. The other men that had been holding the prisoner stepped aside, releasing their grip.

The warden nodded, a handle was pulled, and the prisoner dropped immediately through the trap door. A dull snap was heard as the rope tightened and the neck broke cleanly.

An eerie silence prevailed as the body swung at the end of the rope. There was only the muffled creaking of hemp against steel.

The procedure was complete.

Clicking the button on a stop-watch, the warden spoke. "Seven minutes, twenty-two seconds, start to finish. Not bad, but not good enough. I want it to be six minutes or less. There was a bit of fumbling with the handcuffs at the beginning. We have to practice until that part runs more smoothly."

Turning to the smaller of his companions, the warden asked, "Comments?"

The weathered man spoke with a thick Cockney accent. "Well, I once hanged eight in one night in the old days in Rhodesia," he responded. "But the way you do it we'd still be here at Christmas! That bloody noose, for instance, what do you want to muck about with that for? I tell you, half-inch India hemp, with beeswax for the bottom three feet is what you should use. Put a steel-insert loop in the end and thread the rope through the loop. Then tie the bitter end to the beam and push a bit of extra beeswax into the open spaces of the loop to hold it open. Now you've got a proper way to hang a man quickly and easily."

"And coil the rope, don't let it just hang there! You coil the rope above the slip-noose and tie it with a black cotton thread. Adjust the height of the slip-noose so that the prisoner walks right into it, by God. Face him, look him in the eye, ask for his last words, step forward, put the hood on, tighten the slip-noose behind his left ear, step back, pull the lever and Bob's your uncle, lads. He breaks the thread in the first six inches of fall, the rope uncoils perfectly, and the whole thing has the precision of a dance recital. That's what my old Governor used to call it, the precision of a dance recital, he said. And, in his time, he dispatched over four hundred people to the great beyond."

This was obviously a man who had loved his work. Retired for many years, this bright-eyed little English hangman had executed more than three hundred people himself during his career. The warden winced at the man's enthusiasm for his job.

Another man asked the warden, "Do you think that Navy bastard could hear us?" He gestured vaguely in the direction of the nearest cells.

The warden smiled grimly. "He may not have been able to make out all the words, but he damn well heard the trapdoor let go." The others smiled at the thought of the terrified man in his cell, listening to what he surly would have believed was an execution.

"What about his friends? Do you think they'll try to break him out? They're a mean bunch from what I've heard. Real fitness freaks and the like. I'd hate to have to shoot at our own people," a large man commented.

"That'll never happen," the warden said emphatically. "I spoke with the Navy and told them in no uncertain terms that if an assault was mounted here, we would kill the prisoner without hesitation. They'd never rescue him alive. That's why he's the only inmate with an armed guard outside his door twenty-four hours a day."

"Preemptive killing of a prisoner. God, that's against every federal regulation on the books." the large man replied. "That's even against the Geneva Convention, I'll bet. We would be in a lot of trouble if the word got out."

The warden snapped at him. "Quit your pissing and moaning, Rogers! There are a lot of hard feelings about what this guy did and why he did it, and I can understand their anger. But I'm not going to allow anything to disturb the orderly running of this institution, no matter how much I agree with their anger. I would have preferred to have had the former Lieutenant Gurney, U.S.N., on the scaffold tonight instead of Burt. But we can't hang him because that was the deal when he was transferred here from England. But by God, we can remind him every waking hour of every day for the rest of his natural life what a completely cowardly piece of crap he is. And that's exactly how long he's going to be here: for the rest of his natural life. I intend to make it as miserable as I can within the law. I only hope that somehow we might be able to ease the sorrow of the families of those fourteen kids that he murdered."

That said, he turned and walked away.

In cell D-115, Tom Gurney tried to return to sleep. One night each month since he'd been here, there had been this thumping and slamming of doors and talking. It lasted about ten minutes, and then he could go back to sleep. He couldn't make out the voices or identify all of the sounds. It was almost three months now since his arrival. He looked at the piece of paper that he'd been given when he was brought here. It was a list of rules. Those rules indicated that he would get a visit from a lawyer soon. He replaced the paper underneath his pillow.

The prison staff didn't like him, and he didn't care.

His own goal was a simple one. He would get out of this prison, find the colonel and kill him for setting the whole thing up. The colonel with his snotty manners and his stinking French cigarettes. But before he killed the colonel, he would try to find out why he had been chosen to be framed. The true reason was not actually that important, but if it could be learned, then other men might be able to avoid a similar fate. Over and over, he reminded himself of what was important. Work against the situation, don't hate the people. The people were only doing what they had been instructed to do. Hate destroys a person. Planning, logic and work make you strong.

At least, he was alive.

The rules on the piece of paper said that he had to serve the first year of his sentence in isolation. He was to have no contact with the other prisoners. If he was cooperative, the list said that after his first month of confinement he could have some of his personal belongings back. It did not elaborate, it just said that some of his personal belongings would be returned. The item that he wanted the most was his wristwatch. He had become fixated on the time. His diver's watch was a symbol of what he had once been.

At his first monthly meeting with the guards in an interview room, they returned the clothes that he had been wearing when he was arrested. They had handed him a brown cardboard box about one foot long on each side. He was told to open the box, examine the contents and sign for the returned items. It had contained one pair of black cotton socks, two Navy-issue tee-shirts, and a pair of black Navy shoes with the laces removed. There was also a cheap plastic Timex watch. He had held the watch in his hand and looked at it, wondering if he should complain. A guard had smiled and said to the other guards, "He doesn't seem to like the watch, does he, men?" The man was grinning and he made a point of checking the time on the Navy-issued diver's watch with the Rolex movement on his wrist. It was a painful insult, but he did not complain. A watch was a watch. He would not give them the satisfaction of making a fuss. He would only lose the argument.

Another guard had asked, "What's the matter, Gurney, don't you like your new watch?" and had snatched it out of his hand. He had stared straight ahead and replied, "Yes, sir. I like the watch just fine. May I have it back, please, sir?" The grinning guard had handed it back, then snatched it away, then finally returned it to his hand for good.

It was a sadistic game, and the man had terrible reflexes for a person who appeared to be in his mid-twenties. The slowness came most likely from too much smoking and drinking. Gurney could smell the cigarettes. The alcohol odor was of vodka. Drunks always assume that no one can smell vodka on their breath. He could see the small dilated surface blood vessels on the man's left cheek. Cirrhosis and slow reflexes. Gurney was also in his mid-twenties. He knew that he could snap the man's neck before anyone could react, but it would just get him killed by the other guards.

After a second month of good behavior, he was to be allowed a choice of either some books or paper and pencil. It was to be his choice, they said when he was brought to the interview room that day. He chose the books, asking for a copy of the King James version of the Bible and any of the plays of Shakespeare. Laughing at his confusion, they returned him to his cell with nothing, saying that he must have misunderstood. He was only allowed to request the books that he wanted. He was not guaranteed to ever get them. A guard snickered and told him that he should have taken the paper and pencil, which were right on the table in front of him. He would have been given them right on the spot, he was told. It was too bad, the man had chided.

Perhaps this month's meeting will go better, Gurney thought. Maybe they would let him have a haircut and a shave. He had not had either one since he had been here and had begun to look like a vagrant. The prison staff knew that he would prefer to be short-haired and clean-shaven. They were doing this on purpose. He accepted the harassment, because he had no other choice.

But inside his cell, he got to make all the rules as long as he was quiet about it. It was ten feet by ten feet, with an eight-foot ceiling and a light set flush in the overhead behind a clear plastic cover. There were no windows, only a peep-hole in the door. A metal frame bed was bolted to the floor next to the wall by the door. It came with a thin gray mattress, two sheets, one wool blanket and a pillow with no pillowcase. The floor was smooth concrete painted in navy gray. The walls and ceiling were painted in a pea-green enamel, very shiny, and the paint both looked and smelled recent.

He did three hundred sit-ups a day and four hundred pushups a day. Twice a day, he was escorted to an eating area and fed processed food, nothing fresh. Everything was overcooked and mushy. He never got any milk or coffee, only water that tasted of chlorine. He was always the only prisoner in the small dining room. One day he saw one of the guards drink from the same pitcher that was used to fill his cup, proof that there were no drugs in the water. That was good news, at least.

During his first days of confinement, he had examined his cell minutely, foot by foot. On the fifth day, he found a small hole in the wall opposite the door. It was just an indention, where an air bubble had been formed as they poured the concrete bulkhead and tamped it down. It was near the back corner of the cell, about two feet from the floor. He had then formed the habit of sitting on the floor with his back to the door. With a straightened piece of steel wire from one of the bedsprings, he began to dig at the concrete, as the navy had taught him in SERE school. Survival, Evasion, Resistance, and Escape. He was digging to get his mind free from the confinement. If his mind could get free, perhaps the rest of him could stay sane.

A metal flap was fitted over the peep-hole in the door. It had a hinge that squeaked. The men who stood watch in the corridor were older and even slower that the other guards. He could hear them fumbling against the door seconds before they raised the squeaking flap to peer inside and check on him. He had plenty of time to stop digging and pretend to be picking at something under a fingernail or sitting on the floor in hopeless boredom.

In forty-five days, he had managed to dig a half-inch diameter hole through the concrete wall. He could now see into the next room. It was empty, but he could see the window on the opposite wall. Outside the window, he could see a tree's leafy limbs tossing in the breeze.

In his mind now, alone in his cell, he could feel the breeze on his face, filled with the remembered smells of newly mowed grass and laundry hung outside to dry. And for that moment at least, he was carried him away from his caged existence.

This month, the third month, he would take the paper and pencil and begin to write. First he would catalog all his photographs from

Northern Ireland. Although no one had ever said it, the photographs had to be the problem.

Would he ever be free again? Would he ever be allowed to go back to his SEAL team? What had really happened to him? What had he done?

Tonight, after the evening meal of mushy rice and overcooked beans with ham, after the strange monthly noises outside his cell, he turned over and went back to sleep in the windowless concrete gray-green container.

There had never been an execution at the Federal Correctional Institution at Marion, Illinois. Tonight's exercise had been the standard monthly familiarization procedure required by the Federal Bureau of Prisons to maintain and assure operational efficiency.

The anatomically correct "prisoner" (known as "Burt" to the staff) that had played the role of the condemned man, was a federally supplied training aid that could accommodate lead bars in the midsection to vary its weight. The full-sized dummy also had a unique compartment in its upper part that was built to hold a length of beef backbone in simulation of a human neck. After the procedure was over, the prison medical staff would remove this test sample from Burt and give it a thorough postmortem examination to make sure the hanging had gone as planned. Their report would confirm whether the executioner had done a proper job with his calculations. These calculations of weights versus the lengths of drop were obtained from the US Army Manual on Execution Procedures (the 1959 seventh edition, still the latest available).

Then the medical staff would chop the backbone into individual vertebrae and use them to make a pot of oxtail soup. It was a monthly treat that they all looked forward to with great anticipation.

CHAPTER TWO

DALLAS

Oh to be anywhere else now that August had come to Dallas. The days were hot and humid and breezeless. Piper prayed every day for relief from the sameness of the heat, and also that the air conditioning in his 1966 Mercedes sedan should not fail. London, for example, would be nice this time of year . He thought of England a lot when the weather was like this. England, with its cool nights and sunny but temperate days. And he thought of the black-haired, blue-eyed English woman with the peaches-and-cream complexion who drank Scotch with him and smelled of lavender in the morning.

His consulting business was suffering from the heat as well. There had not been a decent contract for two months, and all his business contacts seemed to have dried up and gone on extended vacations. He worked out of his home-office, making a decent living as a Security Specialist, helping small and medium-sized companies with their various problems with employee theft, burglary prevention and protection of intellectual property rights. Lately, his life had been composed of just him and Daniel, his black Siamese cat.

Because of their forced confinement, they were beginning to get on each other's nerves. Daniel was never allowed outside, because the neighborhood was awash with dogs on the loose and stray teenagers driving too fast down the street. And Daniel was his only companion.

So he thought of Nancy in England.

It was Sunday, and he was trying to think of a biblical spice in eight letters for 14-across in the New York Times crossword. "Myrrh" didn't have enough letters; "frankincense" had too many. It was that kind of day. A Japanese pine tree in his back yard stood motionless, trying to conserve its energy in the choking humidity. The central air-conditioning in the house cycled on every two minutes. Maybe it only seemed that often.

Daniel sat on the back of the sofa, looking into the backyard. His green eyes studiously ignored the pullet-sized blue jay eying him from the back patio. Two great egos were at work. The blue jay making it clear that he would peck the living daylights out of Daniel if he ever came outside. Daniel lazily thinking about the fun of tearing the bird to pieces and then eating all the pieces. There would never be a meeting between the two if Piper had his way. But if there ever was a meeting, then his money would be on Daniel.

Not two weeks before, a small gray field mouse had appeared in the house from God-knows-where. Piper had seen only a blur in his peripheral vision. It was around seven in the evening, and he had been reading a book and listening to Vivaldi on the stereo. Daniel had come storming into the living room, tail in the air, eyes snapping this way and that. Inconceivable as it might be, he must have heard the mouse's footsteps on the carpet from the far corner of the house. Daniel had slowed, treading warily as he searched the room. Perhaps he had smelled the mouse from where he had been sleeping. Yes, that made more sense. The air-conditioning had filtered some mouse-odors to the north bedroom, where Daniel slept atop the single bed.

In the Intelligence world it was called exception processing. You simply memorize the terrain, be it a floor plan, a sound pattern, or accounting figures or whatever, and then watch for any changes.

To Daniel, the house smelled like, well, Daniel. And Piper, and food, and sometimes a cigar, and Kirin beer, and Scotch, and once in a while soap or carpet cleaner or Formula 409 or Clorox or Lysol. That was it. No mouse smells. Ever.

Piper had quietly closed his book and watched with interest. He turned down the volume on the Vivaldi with the remote control. That was for him, not for Daniel. The big cat's ears had already tuned out the sound of the music. Daniel lay down, stretched out on his belly. The mouse appeared, climbing the folds of the drawn living room drapes. That meant Piper was going to have to buy new drapes, because Daniel was going to tear the current ones to shreds. He would be up them like a streak, with his claws flying about like razor blades.

Daniel spied the mouse climbing the drapes. The mouse saw Daniel see him. Casually, the cat stood up and stretched, yawning widely so the little gray rodent could see his teeth. Then he sharpened his claws on the carpet. The mouse continued to climb for freedom.

Daniel strolled slowly to the drape and waited for the mouse to make a mistake. The ruffle at the top of the drape trapped the mouse and he could climb no higher. Out from under the ruffle, tiny pink paws with sharp toenails reached to catch an outstretched edge and lost their grip. He fell right at Daniel's feet, almost hitting him in the process. Bravely, the mouse ignored the 12-pound Siamese and proceeded to clean and groom his whiskers. Insulted, Daniel whacked him a nine-iron shot into the adjoining kitchen.

From then on, Piper sat in his chair and listened. If he went into the kitchen, it would interrupt the play. And he wasn't particularly interested in the details of the play because he knew what the final score would be: Daniel: One, Mouse: Zero.

The tinkle of glass suggested that something had decided to enter the Forest of the Empty Kirin Beer Bottles where Piper kept them until the trash man arrived. Another set of muffled sounds indicated that the chase had progressed to the lower levels of the pantry among the cans of food.

Then, a sharp yip from Daniel signified that the mouse had decided to bite.

Finally a lot of growling and thrashing signaled that Daniel was through screwing around.

Time to take a look, he thought. Getting up and peeking warily into the kitchen, Piper got a view of Daniel gnawing on a decapitated mouse head like a gray-and-red radish. Time to sit back down, he decided, not wishing to be an intimate part of the affair anymore.

Five minutes, and much too many crunching sounds later, Daniel strolled through the living room back to his bed.

The house was safe from intruders again, thanks to his vigilance.

Now it was two weeks later, and Daniel was bored again. Thinking of a favorite treat, Piper said softly in the direction of Daniel's back, "You want some dried shrimp?"

Cats cannot understand English. With rare exceptions, circus mutants as an example, cats will not obey vocal commands unless punctuated by shouted threats or gunfire. Ask any cat owner.

A cat lover, however, will tell you without hesitation that cats are able to understand spoken commands quite well. They just don't care, that's all. Your wishes are of no interest unless they coincide with one of the cat's wishes. It's just that simple.

And dried shrimp, the oriental taste treat of tiny desiccated crustaceans, was at the very pinnacle of Daniel's num-num desires. He loved them to distraction. He could not get enough. It was like Piper and guns, or fast cars, or war stories. There was no enough.

Which is why Daniel turned from looking out the window, got down from the sofa, strolled over to Piper's feet and figure-eighted through his legs, looking up and making his strange purr-yowl-meow that Piper called yodeling.

Getting the cellophane bag of dried shrimp from its secure hiding place (it had to be well-hidden, because while Piper slept, Daniel roamed the house looking for ways to get into mischief), the game began. Daniel took his place about eight feet in front of Piper. Individual shrimp were tossed in the general direction of the big cat's mouth. He caught the good throws in his teeth like a retriever; the bad throws he batted down with vicious accuracy and immediately devoured on the carpet. When Piper thought that Daniel had eaten enough (Daniel never thought he had eaten enough), he got up and replaced the bag in its hiding place in the otherwise unused latchable bread box that had belonged to his grandmother. Daniel quite happily grazed the carpet for remnants for another five minutes.

The phone rang. Late for a call. Probably a salesman pitching carpet cleaning. Before the answering machine could pick up, Piper said hello into the phone.

"How much have you had to drink tonight, Lew?" a sultry English voice said.

"Nancy! I was just thinking of you."

"Liar. You never think of me. All I am is a plaything for your libido. Who was Frances Gumm?"

"Judy Garland, of course. Discovered by George Jessel teamed up with her two sisters in a vaudeville act as the Singing Gumm Sisters. Amateur stuff. You ought to be ashamed of yourself. What are the Christian names of the current Prince of Wales?"

This was their game, trying to stump each other over the names of show business celebrities and public figures.

"Charles Philip Arthur George, naturally. Easy for you. You were reading the paper over your morning coffee when he was born, whereas I had to painstakingly research the fact from the ancient newspaper archives of the British Museum. How would you feel about a holiday in England?"

"Maundy Thursday, how's that for a holiday?" he quipped, pleased with himself. He knew what she meant, of course. She meant 'vacation,' not 'holiday' in the American sense.

"Well, you're too good for me, as usual. Talk to you again soon. Toodles." And she hung up.

Wait! He was only joking! What was her phone number? He jerked upright, and in the process knocked the ashtray off the end table. He tried to grab it before it fell, but missed and only succeeded spilling magazines everywhere. Daniel immediately headed for another room, because his master had obviously lost his mind.

Piper was trying to pick up the mess when the phone rang again.

"Hello," he said absentmindedly, sweeping up ashes with a copy of Time magazine.

"You be sweet with me, you big bully," came the English accent, "or I will forget you completely."

"I'm sorry, I thought I was being amusing."

"Really? So did I. Didn't you think I was funny?"

Why was life so complicated? "Of course you were funny. I wasn't lying. I had been thinking of you. I swear it. I was just about to call you back."

"Its oh-double-one, double-four, oh-eight-three, don't dial the 'oh' at the beginning, remember . . . "

"Don't torture me. You said holiday. I am ready for a holiday, believe me."

"Well, yes, so was I, here in this house all by myself, the kids gone to be with their father for a fortnight. How is the weather in Dallas, by the way?"

She knew the truth. There was no use attempting to lie. "It's terrible, it's blazing hot and humid like the tropics without the beaches." Please invite me again?

"Yes, I can imagine," came the melodious accent. "It's been in the seventies here south of London. A real heat wave for the UK. But it cools off in the evenings with the rain and all, so you still have to sleep under a blanket. Unless you have a man to keep you warm, that is." A short pause, then, "The old man who used to be my neighbor is a now a caretaker at Ealing Studios, you know, where all the great movies were made in the nineteen-thirties through the sixties. He's offered to show me around the sound stages before they are torn down to make room for a television company and some new council flats. If you'd like to come over, I think I can find warm accommodations for you for a week or two."

His toes curled at the thought.

"And perhaps you can help my brother with a problem that he has."

"What problem?"

"He's a career officer in the army with medals and all that from Northern Ireland. He wants to contact an American officer that served with his unit. I think it's the chap that blew up the school bus. Anyway, I'll explain it all when you get here."

"I'll do what I can, Nancy, you know that." School bus? What the heck was she going on about? No matter, he could sort it out when he got there. Her brother could just drop a letter, addressed to whoever the guy is, off at the nearest American embassy and ask them to forward it along. They do it all the time. It's part of being an embassy.

"And, Lew?"

"Yes, Nancy?"

"Do us a favor and leave all your emotional baggage in Dallas when you come. I know that you have problems with your ex-wife and your children, but if you come over and tell me your troubles, I'll tell you mine and we'll both be miserable. Just come over and I'll rub your back and we can just forget the rest of the world for a time. Is that a deal?"

His toes were curling again.

18

"Are you still there?" she asked.

"Yeah, I'm still here," he smiled. "I thought of you and those blue eyes and all the blood left my brain for other parts, that's all."

"Let me know your arrival time, so I can see that you are properly met," she whispered softly in his ear.

CHAPTER THREE

ENGLAND

With Daniel tucked safely away in the cattery with Dr. Beamer and his staff, he packed for the trip. He set the air conditioning up to eighty-five degrees so the inside of the house wouldn't melt in the sweltering heat, then turned on all the alarms and stopped the mail until further notice. Daniel had made his normal howling complaints about being taken to the vets, but it was all a load of rubbish. The staff spoiled him rotten each time he was boarded there by hand-feeding him special treats and talking to him endlessly. After he returned from his trip, Piper understood that he would be in charge of reversing this behavior. It was always a chore, but it came with the territory of being a cat owner. Cats frequently complain no matter what goes on around them. Anything different in their lives makes them uncomfortable. A cat's attitude is very similar to the military wife who never likes where her husband is stationed at present, but always prefers the duty station they just left behind. It would take a week of ordinary life at home to get Daniel to stop pouting and demanding the type of service that he had so recently become accustomed to. But that was what made Daniel a valued member of the family. He had personality.

The last step before leaving on a trip was always to call Calvin Tucker, his friend in the Dallas Police Department.

"Sergeant Tucker," the bored voice answered.

"Watch the store for me, will you, Calvin? I'm catching a plane to London today."

"Business or pleasure, Mr. Rich Consultant?"

"Pleasure. At least I hope so. I'll let you know when I get back."

"This the Lavender-scented lady you met in a bar a few years back?"

Piper, you talk too much. And Tucker listens to every word, darn him. "Yep, that's the one. And it was a Pub, not a bar. There's a difference."

20

"Don't get too many Lavender-scented ladies down at The Cabin, you're right about that." The Cabin was the local Cop bar near police headquarters. "I'll keep an eye on the place and keep the alarm company on its toes. Bring me back a present, OK?"

"What do you want, a little Bobby helmet to wear to work and impress your friends?"

"No, what I want is for one of our loudmouth councilmen to tone down his rhetoric so he'll stop getting death threats, a promotion to Lieutenant, a different Mayor, a new Police Chief, higher pay, better benefits, a new house and a wife that doesn't get together with her mother and stereo-bitch at me." Calvin was stressed-out, as usual.

"I'll bring you a Bobby helmet."

"Have a nice trip, you lucky bastard."

Leaving his old Mercedes 300SEL locked safely in the garage, he took a shuttle-cab to the airport to begin the familiar bad-food, no-sleep, eight-hour flying adventure to London. After check-in at DFW Airport, he squinted at his plane through the tinted glass of the boarding lounge. The view told him nothing, as usual. The shiny American Airlines plane squinted back at him blankly. Airline baggage handlers dressed in shorts and tee-shirts could be seen loading the metal cargo containers into the underbelly of the plane.

Soon the familiar boarding refrain sounded: "Passengers accompanied by small children and those requiring extra time for boarding may enter the aircraft through Gate 22B." The college-age passengers in the boarding area frowned disapprovingly as the nervous young families with children formed a queue at the gate. Why should they board first? Why are they traveling with their brats anyway? They'll probably scream the whole way to London. The frowning glances continued as a gray-haired man with a cane was helped along by his wife, followed by a woman in a wheelchair. Youth is uniformly impatient with the handicapped because the young are insulated from death and infirmity. As they get older, however, the skeletal figure with the scythe and black cloak would stand closer beside them, and they would become more tolerant. Bury a few of your friends, and see what it does to your outlook, Piper thought as he watched their impatient twitching.

21

The flight departed on schedule and was only half full. This offered him the opportunity to move to a seat with no one alongside, fold up the arm rest and spread out a bit. His seat pocket yielded a copy of yesterday's Times of London that the aircraft cleaners had missed. An article on the second page caught his eye because of its typically British phrasing: Failed Businessman Sentenced. A man whose company was sliding into bankruptcy had attempted to raise some new capital by importing cocaine from the Far East via Marseilles, France. He got caught when he tried to sell the narcotics to an undercover police officer. He also got a one-day trial and five years in prison. It was the phrase "Failed Businessman" that had caught his eye. In his case, he assumed that the phrase would have read "Failed Intelligence Officer". He had tried his best to fit in, he had loved the work, he had even been very good at it, and still he had been fired. And the failure still gnawed at him, despite everything he could do to make it go away.

The in-flight beverage service and the meal were over, and a spy movie was about to begin. People were starting to settle down, trying to digest their leaden meals. He drank two Scotches and took a fitful nap.

The flight made an on-time arrival at Gatwick, the airport to the south of the City of London. He scurried through a rather efficient immigration procedure (Purpose of your visit to the UK, Sir? Tourist. Thank you. Stamp placed on passport. Told to Please go to the Luggage Hall.).

There he got tangled up with the Customs and Excise men. Since he was on vacation, he wasn't thinking about how he would get through customs. His usual method, a holdover from his days with the government, was to put his luggage on a cart and stroll around the baggage claim area looking for a scapegoat to follow through the inspection area. "Scapegoats" were anyone that the Customs people would want to stop and question.

In the US, it was the young and disheveled person coming in on a flight from the Far East, particularly Thailand or Hong Kong.

In Brazil, it was citizens coming back into the country with too many undeclared luxuries purchased on their shopping spree in Miami.

Here in the United Kingdom, the safest scapegoats had always been the East Indians. They may have blended into the population in Calcutta or Delhi, but in England they stood out a mile. They might as well have been dressed in clown suits. Customs people were drawn to them like lawyers to malpractice suits. They would draw them aside as they attempted to go through the Nothing To Declare line, and search every square inch of their belongings. There would be a great scurry of probing, questioning, disassembling, untying, and prodding of every square inch of their belongings. While Customs people were doing this, they would have no time or personnel available to search the people directly behind the Indians, so he invariably walked through unscathed.

But this morning, he was breaking all his old rules by relaxing and disengaging his mind. Actually, he had his mind on other things. Like blue eyes and black hair and lavender-scented sheets. He bumbled along through the customs line.

"Would you place your luggage here on the counter, sir?" the polite, accented voice of the Customs inspector asked.

"But, I don't have anything to declare," he heard himself say stupidly.

"I realize that, sir, but if you wouldn't mind, I would appreciate your placing your luggage on the table here." The man was serious and extraordinarily polite. Piper hefted the three-suiter off the cart and onto the counter in front of the man with the blue uniform.

"And the shoulder-bag as well, please, sir."

He set the carry-on bag beside the suitcase.

"Is that your magazine in the basket, sir?" the man pointed. Piper's thoughts had drifted away.

"I said, is that your magazine in the basket, sir?" The words were a little sharper this time.

He was acting like an idiot. The overnight trip from DFW must have robbed him of his smarts. "Yes," he finally managed to answer. "It's a free magazine called *Touring London* that they have in the Customs Area."

"Would you place it here on the table, please, sir?" the polite customs man asked, then added, "And, just as a point of reference, sir: you got the magazine in the immigration area, not the customs area.

This is the customs area, and you had the magazine with you when you entered. Isn't that right, sir?"

Obviously, his jet-lagged brain had lost its ability to communicate. As a result, this man was going to strip him naked and poke long, slim rods into each of his body orifices if he didn't get his butt organized. They would want him to open his carry-on bag first, of course, because that was where you kept the things most precious to you. They were placed there so you could keep them close by and protected from harm.

The Customs Inspector was idly leafing through the pages of *Touring London*. What was he looking for? Whatever it was, he didn't find it. No slim packets of cocaine or pornographic photos or seditious literature advocating the abolition of the Customs and Excise Service. Bored, the inspector set the magazine on the table.

"Would you open . . . ?" he began. Piper immediately unzipped the top of the carry-on bag that contained his notebook computer, some toiletries, writing paper, a well-used Comoy pipe, a tamp, a disposable lighter, and a pouch of tobacco.

"What I was going to say sir, was would you open this large case for me please?" the blue-suit continued with just the tiniest sign of amusement. The man was having fun with him. He deserved to be made fun of, and it was happening. Piper was acting like an amateur, plain and simple. Extremely simple, nose-picking simple, as a matter of fact. Tediously, he started to close the carry-on bag, but the inspector said, "No, just leave that there and open the large one in addition." While he fumbled about searching for the microscopic key to the worthless lock on his suitcase, the inspector was able to step over to the left side of the jumble and probe through the carry-on bag. Just like a military drill-team: Piper went to the right, the inspector went to the left. Piper unzipped the suitcase, the inspector moved to the right and began to feel about among the shirts and Levis and underwear. He showed no interest in the decoratively wrapped box of perfume for Nancy. Satisfied, he closed the lid on the suitcase and said, "Thank you for your assistance, Mr. . . . " The rest blurred away as Piper replaced the bag on the cart, picked up the magazine, shouldered the carry-on bag, and headed out the door with the sign that read "ARRIVALS

HALL". Wait! What had that inspector called him as he handed back his passport? Piper fumbled in his pocket, found the little blue book and confirmed that it was, indeed, his. But had that man just called him "Mr. Healy"? That was the name on the Irish passport, the one hidden in the suitcase lining. He looked back at the inspector with a question on his lips, but the man was busy with someone else and did not look up.

He searched for Nancy among the milling crowd, but did not see her smiling face. It was a delight to arrive at an international airport and not be greeted by a hoard of outstretched palms wanting to carry your luggage, get you a taxi, sell you their sister, or drive you into the mountains and rob you. He had spent too much time of late in third-World countries. He needed to visit England more often. They were civilized, these people.

He didn't see Nancy, but he did see a neat-looking middle-aged man wearing brown corduroy pants, an open-collared dress shirt and a dark blue cardigan sweater. He was bareheaded and wore what appeared to be desert boots, something Piper hadn't thought about for years. He was holding up a white sign about the size of a piece of notebook paper. The sign read "Mr. L. Piper". Nancy hadn't mentioned this to him. Why not? He walked past the man and moved about twenty feet away against a wall to observe. Old habits die hard. Was this someone looking for him, who doesn't know what he looks like? Or was it someone looking for him who does know what he looks like, and remembers him from the bad old days? This might be one of those people from out of his past that he had inconvenienced by his tenacity and abrasiveness.

To his credit, the sign-man had passed the first test. Piper had looked him straight in the eyes as he pushed the luggage cart past, and then continued straight on to where he now rested. He had gone very slowly past the man, as though having trouble with his cart. The man had glanced up at him, then tried to see around him, and finally had maneuvered so as to display his white sign with the name on it to the trailing queue of passengers. Which was exactly what someone would do if they had no idea what the person that they were meeting looked like. From the distance, Piper watched the man to see if he looked around to see where he had gone. The man might be an expert. He might have recognized Piper and never changed the expression on his face. But he knew that Piper had seen the sign, and the man would eventually tire of the game of let's-pretend, and look around to try and spot him. Or he would look at his backup man and pass him a querying look. Good spooks always worked with a back-up man.

But the man in the dark blue cardigan did none of these things in the fifteen minutes that Piper watched him, and now he was tired of playing games. So, he pushed the luggage car ahead of him into the rest room, seeing if anyone would follow. He relieved himself, washed his hands, and then ran water over the stubble of yesterday's shave. He looked in the mirror and admired himself. He was doing all the things that he had seen other people in his position do in all the spy movies. Nothing happened. No one else came into the rest room. He dried his hands and went back into the Arrivals Hall, and looked at where the man had been.

And he was exactly where he had left him, still holding up his sign with the "Mr. L. Piper" on it. Finally accepting that he had been wrong, he walked against the flow of the outgoing luggage carts over to the man. "I'm Lewis Piper," he explained. "Sorry I missed you the first time, but I had to go to the bathroom. My bladder was bursting, and I didn't even see you." Test Number Two: Will he be dumb enough to say, "Oi, I remember you! You looked right at me!" No, all he said was, "That's all right guv. I was beginning to wonder if I had the right flight number."

As the man took over the luggage cart and led him away to the mini-cab, Piper gave him Test Number Three: He asked, "Who made the arrangements for the mini-cab, please?" These guys, if they were real, always had a sheet of paper resembling a computer printout, that said who they were to meet, where they were to take them, and who had ordered the cab. That was how they knew who to bill for the service. As soon as Piper asked him, the man stopped and turned the white sign over. The reverse side was a clipboard. He read from the sheet of paper.

"Ordered by a Mrs. Nancy Carpenter, 14 Beechamp Close, North Cray, Sidcup, Kent, DA14 5LY, phone: Six Three One Double-Three Seven Six. Is that her, mate?".

That was her, all right. The man had now passed all the tests. Piper was paranoid, but he was still alive.

In the early morning hours like these, all the traffic on the M25 was going the other way, so the beige little four-door Wolseley, or whatever it was, zoomed right along. The driver did not engage in any small-talk but instead concentrated on driving smoothly at ninety miles an hour. Piper read Touring London. "To get from the Houses of Parliament to The Tower of London, get on the District Line at Embankment, go through Temple, Blackfriars, Mansion House, Cannon Street, and Monument and get off at Tower Hill. From there, it's just a short walk . . . " Rubbish! On a day like today with the sun shining in all its mid-fifty-degree glory, you simply walk along the Thames east from Big Ben for about two miles and you're there! No reason to ride the underground at all! What idiots! It was a beautiful view, past Cleopatra's Needle and the three ships docked in a row farther down, whatever their names were, and then you were at the Tower! He felt very superior about all his detailed knowledge.

Whoops! Unless it was raining, of course. Then you'd get soaked to the skin and frozen stiff by the gale-force breeze off the Thames, and then probably die of pneumonia. The Underground! What an excellent idea! Inexpensive, relatively clean, and unaffected by the weather. Five minutes and you're there. Expert advice.

They arrived at 14 Beechamp Close, North Cray, Sidcup, Kent. He unfolded himself from the rear seat and watched as the driver set the suitcase on the sidewalk, said good-bye and was off to his next assignment. When the tip is included in the cost of the ride, and the ride has already been paid for, there's no need to hang about offering to help with the luggage, making stilted comments about the weather while the passenger fumbles in his pocket for loose change.

And here she came down the front steps, just as pretty as he remembered her. Three years later, and not a day older. She made him feel unkempt, but then, almost anything made him feel unkempt. And he must look terrible after spending all night on the plane. Unshaven and, oh! Why didn't he brush his teeth while he was in the rest room wasting time being a schizoid? He would kiss her and she would keel over from the smell of his breath!

As he opened the gate to the front walk, she came toward him like a vision from a nineteen-fifties movie. Donna Reed, June Allyson, Loretta Young, and other actresses. His mind wasn't working at all. He put the suitcase down just in time to have her put both arms around his neck, press her body tight against his and give him the kind of kiss where her tongue stopped just short of his left kidney. This woman was not even slightly fazed by Airplane Breath! He felt terrific. She felt terrific, as well. They both felt terrific. And they were standing in front of her house like idiots.

She looked deeply into his eyes, arms still around his neck, and said romantically, "Just stand here like this smiling and kissing until I can be sure Mrs. Broccoli has seen us, then we can go inside. OK, I just saw her curtain move. She's seen us. Now we can go. We've made the day for her."

"Who's Mrs. Broccoli?" he asked as they entered the neat front room of her home.

"She's an old woman who's been an old woman since we moved here when the children were small. Christopher and Amelia couldn't pronounce her real name, which is Broncksley, so they called her Mrs. Broccoli and it stuck."

A black and white shorthair cat stared at Piper suspiciously from behind the couch.

"Hello, kitty, " he said softly, trying to make another friend. The green-eyed cat looked at him blankly, then turned and went back behind the sofa. Typical cat.

"That's Pamela. I tell everybody she's named after Pamela Mason, the wife of James Mason the actor. But, quite frankly, until I had her spayed she was more like Anybody's Pamela. She'd come in season and have every Tom in the district howling outside the windows. She must have been an odoriferous little wench, because I swear one of the cats belonged to my newsagent, and his shop is over a mile-and-a-half from here! So I let her have a litter from her choice of boyfriends, and I found the multi-colored little cuties good homes and then she and I made a little trip to the Veterinary. It's been two years now, and I think she may be almost ready to forgive me"

Before he could sit down, a shadow appeared suddenly behind his back and a chill shot down his spine. He never liked surprises, particularly coming up behind him. Nancy's gaze shifted to his left, and she smiled. That meant it was OK this time. He relaxed as he heard her announce pleasantly, "Lew, I'd like you to meet my military brother, Major John Ross. John, this is Lewis Piper."

He turned and reached for the outstretched hand. The man was disgustingly fit and tan, and had an engaging smile that showed off the stylish creases at the corners of his eyes. He was dressed casually in a checkered broadcloth shirt open at the collar, khaki slacks and a beige pullover sweater.

"I wish she wouldn't always introduce me as though I were the Chief of the General Staff. Sorry about that. Nan tells me that you have friends high in the American government, Lew. I hope I may call you Lew, if that's all right?" He was still smiling as he applied a firm grip to their handshake. It was certainly not the sort of "limp fish" handshake that Piper had gotten from many British in the past.

"Nah, she's just trying to make me sound like a big shot so you won't be disappointed in her taste in gentlemen friends," he responded with a grin. "So what's this problem that she said you have with our government?" He could have waited until they knew each other better, but he was showing off for Nancy. A big sign flashed through his mind: "Lew Piper, Problems With the US Government Solved While You Wait." Piper, Master of the Universe.

Ross spoke hesitantly, seeming to pick and choose his words with great care. "There was an American that served a tour with us on my last posting to Ireland a year or more ago, a Navy lieutenant named Gurney, Thomas Gurney. I would like to get in touch with him. He was on an exchange visit, as it is called. It is a standard program, as you know, between our two countries. You send people to work with us; we send people to work with you. Even though he was an officer, he insisted on taking a turn at each of the field tasks, even the mundane and sometimes dangerous work that only the Troopers usually do. He was one of your SEALs, the Sea, Air, Land chaps that your Navy trains. He even volunteered to be a sniper on one of our Bunker Operations."

"What's a Bunker Operation?"

"I must ask you to treat this next information as confidential, because these things still take place, you understand. In a Bunker Operation, we would bring two lorry-loads of troops into a Catholic neighborhood very quickly, then have them get out and begin banging on doors and searching house-to-house as though looking for someone. One of the row-houses would be unoccupied. We would see to that even if we had to temporarily detain the family living there. We'd put twenty or so men through the front door, leave some lads outside to keep watch, spend some time inside standing around, then exit and go to the house next door. The difference was that in the empty house, we'd leave one of the lads up in the attic with enough provisions for two or three days. He'd have a two-way radio, water, food bars and special provisions for his personal hygiene. In addition, he would have a special night-sight equipped rifle fitted with a silencer. When he spotted one of the IRA through the roof vents, if the coast was clear, he'd shoot him on the spot, and no one was the wiser. It was very effective. Then the next day we would do the whole thing again in reverse and extract the man. The IRA never caught on to what we were doing. I am sure that if they had, they would have been happy to demolish a whole block of flats just to kill my trooper."

"Do you get a lot of kills with these operations?"

"No, they usually just ended up as reconnaissance patrols. Generally, we are just able to gather information as to what was going on in the neighborhood, that's all. Except the last one we set, just before we left Belfast. We had gotten information that a particularly dangerous IRA field commander had been seen in a certain neighborhood, so I laid on a Bunker Operation in the hopes of getting a shot at him. The IRA man we hoped to get was Nicolas O'Flynn, the man who was supposedly involved with Gurney in that school bus attack.

"This time, when I made my report to the colonel, he went into a towering rage. I was taken completely by surprise, because I had laid-on dozens of these Bunker Operations during my three tours in Belfast.

It was an expected part of my responsibility as the executive officer. I was never required to ask for permission, I just laid it on and that was that. All results went in the Morning Report to the Officer Commanding. Reeves-Benedict was a Lieutenant-Colonel then and I had been a Major for perhaps three years. But this time when he read about the operation, he sent for me immediately and cursed me roundly for what I had done. None of it made any sense at all."

"Was your field intelligence correct? That is, did the trooper in the attic actually see O'Flynn?"

"Yes, as a matter of fact he made a positive identification of O'Flynn on the second night, the last before he was to be extracted. But there was no chance for a shot, because a taxi drove up and blocked his aim. O'Flynn had squatted down, then he and the taxi-driver spoke to each other for a bit. After that some other civilians gathered around, and the whole opportunity simply evaporated. The taxi drove away, and our chance for O'Flynn was gone. Soon after, he turned himself in to the civilian authorities here in London. That was after the school bus incident."

"You have mentioned a school bus attack twice now. What is that all about?"

"The school bus incident?" Ross replied. "Oh, surely you read about the IRA attack on the busload of American diplomat's children? Fourteen of them died, I believe."

Piper had never heard of it, and said so.

"Perhaps it didn't get much publicity in America because of the tragic circumstances," Ross said. "Lieutenant Gurney and Nicolas O'Flynn were the ones that mounted the attack, you see."

An American Navy lieutenant that blows up school buses? That would have been on "60 Minutes". How had he missed this?

"Can you remember specifically what the colonel was so angry about?" he asked, trying to keep Ross talking while he put his thoughts in order.

Ross shook his head slowly and looked down at the carpet in thought. "He was so furious and profane that he rambled on a lot. It seemed to center on the fact that we were due to be relieved in a few days, and I had needlessly exposed the men to danger that was beyond

31

the scope of our mission. He ranted that I had not cleared the operation beforehand, which made absolutely no sense."

Ross stared into the carpet pattern in silence for a moment longer, and then looked up at Piper. "Sorry, I didn't mean to bend your ear like that."

"How did he end up in prison?" Piper asked. "I mean, who tried him for the crime?"

"He was tried and sentenced to life imprisonment without parole by a British court," Ross replied. "It was all very hush-hush. None of us were allowed to testify in person, only by deposition, even though he had been under my nominal command at the time of the incident. Because of the fact that he was a foreigner, our reciprocal law with the US allowed for his sentence to be served in an American prison. He's being held somewhere; I think it's called Marion, a prison in the State of Illinois. I believe it's a maximum-security place, much like The Maze in Belfast."

Piper winced at the mention of Marion.

Ross continued. "I understand that it is a waste of time to pursue this, but I cannot shake off my curiosity about this man. I ate in the officer's mess with him, we discussed field tactics together, he taught my men how to assess threats under a wide range of situations. His training saved many of my trooper's lives, and we owe him a large debt of gratitude. Terrorism is a filthy crime, I know, but I have grave doubts about his guilt and always will."

"And as a field commander, you want to know what signs he gave of his terrorist intentions, don't you?" Piper asked evenly. "And you want to know what signs you missed, right?"

Ross nodded.

Marion was the most tightly-secure Federal Prison in the US, reserved for only the most dastardly criminals or hardened prisoners. The former Navy Warrant Officer that had sold secrets to the Soviets was there, along with the former CIA officer that had supplied classified information to the Libyans. In addition, any 'uncooperative' Federal Prisoner would be found there. Every prisoner lived in solitary confinement without privileges. Even the simplest things such as television and phone calls had to be earned by good behavior. This was a place for the worst of prisoners.

"Whatever you can find out, I would appreciate it." Ross continued. "And you are right, Lew. I have had concerns ever since about my ability to judge people, and that is something that is an integral part of my job.. I have to know who to send on patrol in a dangerous area, who to assign to a Bunker Operation, and who is lying and who is telling the truth. I missed finding this man out, and my colonel loses no opportunity to remind me of that fact on a regular basis."

"I have someone that I can call to get that information, of course. He's in Washington, DC, so we would have to wait, let's see, it's Ten-Thirty in the morning now and he gets into the office at Nine AM, so. . ." Piper stumbled. Mr. Genius. A show-off that can't calculate Time Zones.

"One PM." Nancy said, smiling. "Nine AM in Washington is One PM in England."

"Yeah, that sounds right. I can call from here at One PM, John. Shouldn't be a problem in the least."

CHAPTER FOUR

BARKER

Lunch with Nancy and her brother was a blur because of his jet lag, but he made forced attempts at coherent conversation about nothing in particular. Finally, it was One PM and time to make his show-off call to Washington.

Nancy passed him the phone over to him. He was sitting on the couch where he had been chatting with her and her brother. He lifted the receiver and thought about his buddy Jim Barker at the Department of Defense. A college football star until one of his knees gave out, Jim had used his academic talent to get a PhD. in something like Physics or Chemistry. Then he had joined the federal government's mammoth bureaucracy at about the same time as Piper. A large, muscular man with a shock of uncombable hair and a pipe clenched in his teeth; that was the mental image that he had of Barker. How anyone could smoke a pipe at eight o'clock in the morning was beyond his grasp, but Jim could and Jim did. The spate of new federal no-smoking rules must be driving him right up the wall. The last time they had chatted was during the Christmas holidays, when he had called to wish the family a happy holiday. Jim was an eternally upbeat kind of guy, and always saw the best side of everything. He would have to remember to brag about Nancy.

Thinking for a moment, he dialed the phone number from memory. It wasn't a good idea to keep Department of Defense private numbers on a scrap of paper in your wallet.

"This is Dr. Barker," the gruff voice answered on the first ring. He could picture the curling smoke of the pipe and the clenched fist of coffee.

"Lew Piper here, Jim. How's your day starting?"

"Not any better than most of them have started lately. What's the matter with this phone connection? Are you calling from a submarine or something?"

"No, Jim, I'm calling you from London. I need a favor."

"It figures," he replied absentmindedly. "What have you screwed up now, Lew?"

His friend was obviously not in a good mood. Best not to waste any more of his time. "I need information on a naval officer convicted in the UK of terrorist activity who is serving time at the lock-up in Marion. His name is. . ."

"Thomas Gurney!" Barker snapped. Piper jumped at the force of his friend's outburst, hoping that Nancy and her brother hadn't noticed. "I know him, I hate the son of a bitch, and I hope he rots in hell. You still interested in classical music? I've got a CD that you'll like. Get a piece of paper. I'll wait."

Classical music? What the. . . Oh, cripes, it's a code string. "Start talking, Jim. I don't need a piece of paper.. What's the recording, Jim?" Piano meant personal, orchestra meant organizations, cellos meant callback, what else? I thought that I was never going to have to use this again, and now here it is all over again. Barker must think I remember every little. . .

"Oh yeah, I forgot about your memory. Age hasn't affected it yet, huh? Just too damn bad is all I can say. Wait a moment for us slower types to get organized."

Barker was right, of course. Piper's proudest possession was his memory. See it once, remember it forever. It had been both a blessing and a curse all his life. He smiled confidently at John and Nancy as he waited.

"You're always a problem, Lew, something is always wrong wherever you go. You're never doing anything that doesn't seem to stir up a stink," Barker grumped into the phone. Listen carefully, Piper, he's only going to say it once. "Tomorrow, go to the embassy and tell the front desk that you need directions to the Annex. They will tell you how to get there. When you enter, tell the receptionist that you want to speak with Dr. Michael Bohannon. He has the record I'm talking about. It's a Brahms cello sonata; I forget the name of it. If he's not there, ask to speak with his assistant, the one with the red hair."

Cello. So it was a callback. He was supposed to call him back on a secure phone. Asking for Bohannon and the redhead was a two-part entry code, useless to an eavesdropper unless you knew what to do with them. "You do mean the American Embassy in London, don't you Jim?" He should have saved his breath and not tried to make small talk.

"Of course not, you idiot! I meant the Danish Embassy in Tokyo. Don't waste my time." Then he slammed down the phone without even saying good-bye.

Piper smiled unconvincingly at Nancy and John. "My friend wants me to go to the American embassy tomorrow and pick up some stuff he's going to fax over for me. He was busy and didn't have time to discuss it with me over the phone," he lied unprofessionally. Lame, Piper, really lame. You sound like a teenage car thief. "Hey, a buddy of mine loaned me this car! His name? Paul something-or-other, I think." Really convincing, if you are a ten-year-old.

"What was that about classical music?" Nancy asked.

"Oh, he has a music CD with a Brahms concerto on it that he left here on his last trip. He was telling me who he had left it with in the embassy, so I could pick it up, that's all." Not lame, Piper, positively paralyzed. You talk too much. Change the subject quickly.

Major John Ross changed the subject for him. He stood up, saying, "I have to be getting back to the barracks, Lew. It was nice to have met you and I hope that you will have a nice stay here. Perhaps we can all meet in the City for dinner some evening. And I appreciate you looking into the matter about Lieutenant Gurney for me."

Piper wondered why life had to be so complex.

Later that evening, he and Nancy sat on the couch together and watched Eastenders, holding hands like teenagers. Then they went to bed together and Nancy rubbed his back with her strong hands until he fell asleep like he had been drugged. Nancy didn't ask any more questions about his phone call, and he was happy not to have to tell her a lie. He had no answers yet, only more questions.

They were both up early the next morning. He shaved and dressed while Nancy was downstairs fixing a breakfast of eggs, bacon, grilled tomatoes and fried bread. Eating and thinking, his mind was far away thinking about Lt. Gurney.

"Your brother has a unique accent," he offered as he ate. "I can't place it exactly. It's different from yours."

"It's different for a reason," she responded. "If you are looking for a similar type of speech pattern, think about Marion Morrison."

"John Wayne? What the heck does. . . Oh, wait a minute, you're right. He does speak the way John Wayne did. He speaks in bursts, then pauses in the middle of a sentence for a second, then continues. Just like the Duke used to talk."

"And the reason for that is that my brother was born with a stammer and went through years of speech therapy to get it cured. The mid-sentence pauses are all that remain of the problem. You have very good ears, Lew. And I appreciate the considerate way you phrased your question about John. He is not sensitive about his former problem at all, but I am. I remember how his schoolmates used to tease him."

She told him how to get to the American Embassy on Grosvenor Square. The train ride to Charing Cross station was very fast and uncrowded this time of day. With extra time to kill before the call at 1:00 PM, he stopped by the British Museum and went through the newspaper files for information about the school-bus attack. The Times had the clearest and most unemotional articles, as would be expected. It said that a bus carrying the dependents of American diplomats home from their school had been slowed by a sham road accident en route and attacked with explosive charges. Ten students had died in the attack, and twenty-seven more were injured. The IRA had claimed responsibility for the raid in a coded phone call to the police. The police believed that the leader of one of the provisional wings of the IRA, a man named Nicholas O'Flynn, had masterminded the operation.

He'd never read anything about in the US papers. Perhaps it had been too shocking a story for the American press to print. No, the press would have jumped all over this story. *US Navy Officer Convicted As Child Murderer*. Film at Eleven. The only way it didn't make the papers would have been if a security lid had been clamped tight. Otherwise, the TV news weenies would have delighted in telling us all how flawed our military establishment was. Obviously, they never knew about it. Maybe I should tell them and make myself famous. Yeah, right. And see your childhood bathroom habits debated on prime-time television.

He looked at he pictures. Sweet Lord. Children. The IRA had murdered children. Deliberately. A school-bus carries only children, nothing else. What complete monsters these people are.

Sickened, irritated and confused, he continued to read the archives. They were digital now, and the images were much clearer than the old microfilm spools he was used to. The following day's stories had been about the public outrage and the statements of sincere condolences from the Home Office ministers. There were stories about stepped-up police activities to combat this type of terrorism.

There was a tiny article, only five lines in all, headed "American Being Held". The text of the story said, "Anonymous sources told The Times today that an American citizen was being held in custody in connection with the recent terrorist attack. No further information was made available, but further developments are expected soon. Calls to the American Embassy and the Metropolitan Police were received without comment. The Home Office also refused comment and would not say if further information would be forthcoming." So this would be in reference to Lt. Gurney's participation.

He watched as the story slowly move from the top of page one to the middle of the page, then to the bottom, then to the inside pages, smaller and smaller and further back in the newspaper until finally it was gone. Displaced by stories of rising taxes and marriage troubles for two members of the Royal Family. The "American Being Held" story never got a follow-on. Obviously, the Home Office had place a news blackout on the subject.

The article had said that ten children were killed outright. Two died the next day and a third the following day. Later there was a small article on page 6 entitled, "Fourteenth Victim of IRA School-bus Attack Dies in Hospital". A young girl named Susan Jane Ashley, aged seven and a half years, had succumbed to massive internal injuries in spite of three operations to save her life. Four days. She'd struggled and fought for four days. And then lost the battle. All because some Irish maniacs wanted to claim a bit of territory.

Monsters.

Numbed, he continued to search through earlier editions of the papers. Three days after Susan Jane Ashley's death there was an article near the bottom of an inside page. "Nicholas S. O'Flynn, Rory McDougal, Ian Mathews and Thomas McCann, all wanted members of the IRA, were captured without a fight last evening at a flat in the Kensington district. Police are holding the men at an undisclosed location."

Why not more publicity? he wondered. If Nicholas O'Flynn was the man who had engineered the school-bus attack only a week earlier, why were the police not celebrating? It must not be the same Nicholas O'Flynn. That was probably the reason. There were undoubtedly thousands of Nicholas O'Flynns in the Emerald Isle.

On his way again, he grabbed a quick bite to eat from a sidewalk vendor who sold Genuine New York Style Hot Dogs. The small snack convinced him that this particular entrepreneur had never been anywhere near New York, but at least it killed his appetite. A short ride on the Underground and he was within walking distance of the embassy. Crossing the square he paused at the statue of Franklin D. Roosevelt, looking very noble in his Boat Cloak. FDR had meant a lot to the people of Britain in his time, and had taken outrageous chances to keep them supplied with weapons with which to fight the Nazis.

Entering the front door of the embassy, Piper told the Marine guard that he had an appointment in the Annex. The Marine, a Private First Class in Fleet Marine dress blues, asked to see some identification. He fumbled about his pockets, hoping that he had remembered his passport. While he searched, he repeated that he had a meeting in the Annex and asked for direction as to how to get there. Then a plump woman with a New Jersey accent eased the young Marine aside gently and said, "Go back out to the sidewalk, then walk to the left. You will see an iron gate with a sign that says PRIVATE on it. Go through that gate and follow the path." Then she returned to whatever she had been doing before he arrived. The Marine looked confused and a little irritated at being upstaged.

The gate was where it was supposed to be, and the path led to a four-story building behind the embassy covered in ivy and shrouded in shrubbery and trees. The air smelled of pine tar, just like most of southern Georgia where he had been born. He felt very much at home in the greenery. He took a deep breath and prepared to run the two-part code entry procedure.

Entering through the thick glass door, he asked the middle-aged female receptionist for Dr. Michael Bohannon. The woman stopped rummaging through her purse long enough to tell him that there was no one there by that name. He asked for the man's assistant, the one with the red hair.

"Are you sure you have the right place, sir?" she asked, squinting her eyes at him. "I have no idea what you are talking about." She shook her head slightly and resumed the search in her purse. He was about to ask again, but then he remembered the rules: Ask only once, then remain silent. He was working a security password exchange, and it had to be done exactly or not at all.

"I said, are you sure you have the right office, sir? We have no Dr. Bohaggan or whatever you said, and we have no one in this office with red hair," she repeated.

He remained standing and silent, looking at her with his blankest gaze.

"Look, you either answer me, or I'm calling Security," she announced, picking up the phone. She squinted at Piper, who didn't move or speak. She dialed a number and barked down the phone, "Security? I have a suspicious person in the K-4 lobby that is asking for people who aren't here, and now refuses to speak to me. Get over here on the double!"

Suddenly, she switched moods and asked him, "'You want some coffee while we wait?" He wanted a cup of coffee very badly and almost responded, but caught himself and continued to remain standing and silent. The woman peered around him, trying to get a better view out the front door. She went back to fumbling through her purse. Probably looking for her pistol, he thought.

Finally tossing the purse to the back of her desk, she said, "Come with me please," and led him to a door on the left side of the lobby. Opening it and pointing down the hall, she said, "Use Number Three on the left. You want some coffee now?" Piper went down the hall to the door marked with a '3' without answering. As he reached for the doorknob, he heard the snap as the receptionist released the concealed latch. He'd done it right! But he had no coffee for his efforts. Here in the embassy they would have genuine American-style coffee, not the terrible Nescafe instant slop that the British drank. Wretched coffee was the only thing he didn't like about Britain. Well, not the only thing, but it was high up on his list of dislikes.

He flopped behind the scarred desk and dialed Barker's number. When the phone was answered, he said hello.

"You made it, I see," came the dry answer from his friend. The caller ID box on his desk would have told him that they were on a secure line.

Piper was about to answer when the office door opened and the receptionist entered carrying a tray with a pot of wonderful-smelling coffee, some cream, a bowl of sugar and a plate of cookies.

"What's all that noise? What's going on?" Barker asked.

"Just the nice receptionist lady with a pot of coffee for poor little me," Piper explained.

"Tell Myrna hello for me," Barker replied.

"Jim Barker says hello."

She straightened up and said, "Tell him I said to screw off. He owes me a dinner!"

"She said..."

"I heard her, and I do not owe her a dinner. I won that bet fair and square."

"He says he doesn't owe you a dinner. He won that bet fair and square."

She snatched the phone from Piper's hand and yelled down the line loud enough to be heard in Washington without the phone wires, "You welsher! You bet me that Queen's Park Rangers would win that match, and they tied 4-4. A tie is not a win! You owe me a dinner."

She tossed the handset back to Piper and headed for the door.

"Jim wants to know if you still love him," he called after the retreating figure.

"He knows where I am. Tell him to call and ask me in person." She left the office, slamming the door with a bang.

"You need to do some fence-mending, my friend," he said into the phone.

"I got lots of stuff I need to do," Barker replied. "She's the least of my worries."

Barker was very high up in the DOD Intelligence division, so high that Piper had no idea of the altitude. But it was high enough that, if he wanted to, he could find out things that nobody else could even dream of coming close to. He also sounded troubled.

"Why the need for a clean phone line, Jim?" he asked. "Assuming the lines really are clean in here."

"Thomas Edison Gurney is the reason. He's an embarrassment to our government and a disgrace to the Navy. You asked about him, and I'm going to tell you. That bastard helped the IRA bomb a busload of children last year. It was such a sickening mess that the main IRA planner gave himself up in disgust and betrayed his whole group."

"You mean O'Flynn?"

"You've been doing your homework, I see. Yes, I mean O'Flynn. That school bus thing really made his little Catholic heart break, so he quit and ratted out the whole lot of them. And the head executioner was none other than Lt. T. E. Gurney of the US Navy. They found all kinds of schematics and plans and explosives in his luggage, plus a road map of the bus route marked in red pencil. When we went back over his navy records, it turned out that the bastard had always been a problem child. He barely made it through UDT School, and then he damn near washed out of SEAL training because he was such an insubordinate cowboy. Off duty, he once beat up a woman in a bar in Coronado when she told him to leave her alone and stop bothering her."

Barker was shouting. He was upset. Too upset.

"What's all this to you, Jim?" Piper asked.

"I'll tell you what it is to me, Lew. One of the children on that bus was my brother's little daughter. He worked for the State Department and was the Deputy for Agriculture at the embassy in London. She'll be twelve on her next birthday, Lew, and she doesn't have a left leg below the knee because of that animal. When I flew over to see her in the hospital she asked me why her Uncle Jim couldn't have protect her. She wasn't in Beirut, for God's sake, she was in London, and Uncle Jim didn't have an answer. That's what it is to me, Lew."

"Hate makes a terrible master, and an untrustworthy servant, Jim."

"Damn you, Lew, don't you throw one of my homilies back in my face! She's not you're goddaughter, she's mine, and I hate that bastard with all my heart for what he did to her."

"If he did it", Piper responded softly. True to form, the more people around him got upset, the calmer and more objective he became.

"You're pushing your luck on this, Piper."

So he had become 'Piper' now. He wasn't 'Lew' anymore. Calmly, he tried to reason with his friend. Barker wasn't an idiot. He was just hurting.

"Jim, ask yourself how this unstable cowboy-type, this guy that beat up a woman for brushing him off in a bar, get orders to Exchange Duty? We send only our best people on those kinds of assignments."

"Somebody in BuPers got a wire crossed, probably. An administrative foul-up. It happens all the time."

"Do me a favor, Jim, and get someone who's a friend of yours to go to Coronado and look at the private records on this guy. The UDT and the SEALs both keep their own records, records that are separate from the ones at the Bureau and at the Commands. They have a vested interest in making sure that one of their people doesn't go berserk or do something stupid and get his buddies killed in a fire-fight. Somebody could have altered the Master Records without knowing that these private ones existed, couldn't they?".

"Not a chance, Lew." Well, he was back to being 'Lew' again, at least.

One last try. "You didn't know these records existed, did you, Jim?"

"Of course I knew about them!" he snapped.

"Never try to out-lie a liar, Jim," he replied. "OK then, when the SEAL records were reviewed, did they match the ones in the Bureau of Personnel?"

"OK, OK, we didn't look at the SEAL records."

"Did you look at the Commanding Officer Rough Drafts?" Piper asked.

"What?"

"Every commanding officer in the navy who signs a Fitness Report is required to keep the rough drafts in perpetuity. That means forever. Did anybody review any of these CO's Rough Drafts?"

"OK, OK. Maybe I could get someone to ask around," he said softly.

"You got two days, old buddy."

"Two days? What the hell's the rush?"

"Hey, Jim, I'm on vacation here. I haven't got forever to wait for you to get off your behind." He pronounced it be-hind, like anybody from the deep South would.

"Yeah, OK. Call me at the same time day after tomorrow. I'll see what I can do in the meantime."

CHAPTER FIVE

HOMEBODY

Hurry and Scurry, Nancy called this morning ritual of shower, shave, brush teeth. Cute phrase. Nice to be around a woman for a change. Daniel was more reliable in the long run, but, after all, Daniel was a cat. Be realistic.

He was supposed to call Barker today for an update on the lieutenant. Maybe the guy really was a nut and just decided to murder children for the fun of it. Didn't want to see all that training go to waste. But what he had done made no sense, that was for sure

This was fun. Just like the old days. Then he remembered that those were the bad old days, not the good old days. Working on John Ross' question reminded him of just how much he missed the challenges of investigative work. But it was all for nothing. He'd failed. He'd blown it. And now he was too old to get back into it again. Anyway, he had this one challenge for now and he intended to make the most of it.

Dressed in the too-thin blue suit, but with a wool cardigan worn under the coat and the lined poplin raincoat on top of it all, Piper could barely feel the icy blast of wind as he turned the corner toward the bus to Bexleyheath. The warmth of Nancy's good-bye kiss lingered on his lips. She seemed to enjoy seeing him off to work in the morning; perhaps a re-living of better days in her life before her husband took off.

It was an uneventful fifteen-minute bus ride, then a ten-minute walk to the train station. There was the smell of fresh apples and cinnamon coming from one house along the way, and a housewife washing her front steps with a pail of water and a broom almost washed his shoes as well. The British in this area build the front of their houses right up against the sidewalk to give the maximum backyard space for the kids to play and for mom and dad to have a vegetable garden. Walk out the front door in this area of town, down three concrete steps, and you're on the sidewalk. You're on the sidewalk covered in a mass of people plodding their way to work, at this time of day.

He found a seat on the local to Charing Cross station, a welcome development. In the car were the normal morning mix of school kids in uniform, workers in suits and ties, unknown types in jeans and Dallas Cowboy jackets, and a few lads and lasses with purple and orange hair and Elvira eye-makeup. One aging biker in a Levi jacket with the sleeves cut off at the shoulders had a safety pin snapped through a hole pierced in his earlobe. With his arms covered in tattoos and his face buried in the Financial Times, he was just another anachronism on the 8:40 to London.

Exiting Charing Cross station, having deliberately planned some extra time, Piper walked to a little book store that he remembered from an earlier visit. The shop specialized in military manuscripts. On an earlier trip he had wanted to buy a four-volume set of the history of the Das Reich SS Regiment. It purported to show that Sepp Dietrich's bully-boys had not actually been responsible for the massacre at Malmedy, Belgium, in which captured American prisoners were machine-gunned to death in the snow. Watching how evil people attempted to rewrite history was another hobby of his. It taught him how to deal with the new generations of evil people. On his previous visit, the £125 price was too rich for his blood, but today he was feeling wealthier than usual.

It was wonderful to visit a city like London after an absence of years and find that most of the places that you loved were right where you had left them. St. William's Press was one of these places. Small by American mega-bookstore standards, nevertheless it had copies of books on military history that could not be found anywhere else that he knew of. Original copies of books on tank warfare from the thirties written by men with names like de Gaulle, Rommel, Patton and Horrocks. And a wonderfully knowledgeable staff that never talked down to the customer like so many of the other stores did.

Many years previously, he had inquired about a book on the Spitfire fighter plane of World War Two. The sixtyish clerk had inquired as to what purpose Piper required the book. More thin-skinned in those days, he had replied in the vein of. "What business is it of yours to ask a question like that?" Immediately, the man had apologized for the bluntness of his question and asked if Piper would join him in a cup of tea and a short chat. As they sat around a small table near the back of the shop, the man patiently explained that they had over two hundred different items in their inventory related to the Spitfire. He explained in great detail that these items ranged from modern-day full-color photo books of the various models, through individual volumes on each of the variants. They even had a few very rare copies of the original blueprints from the manufacturers, Supermarine. The latter would be rather more expensive, he had said. They even had two autographed copies of the autobiography of Reginald Mitchell, the plane's designer, for sale.

Finally he realized that these people were truly concerned about making sure that rare and limited-availability items would be bought by people who would show them the proper respect and not allow their children to use them for coloring books. Feeling a little chagrined by his defensive outburst, he had purchased one of the 1970's books showing the variants, their weights and measures, with black and white photos and production figures.

Today, the clerk was a man that he didn't recognize, but his manner was friendly, smooth and professional. "How may I assist you today, Sir?' he asked with a polite smile and a nod of his head.

"I am interested in purchasing a copy of the four-volume set on the history of the Das Reich SS Regiment. I'm talking about the one with the individual black and white photos glued to the pages, and the text in both German and English. I saw a copy here some years ago, but the price at the time was too much for my budget."

"I'm sorry to say that the price for the item you mention has now risen to £350, because it is no longer in print. The production costs, as I'm sure you can imagine, were horrendous what with each of the photos printed from the original negatives and such."

£350! That's almost $700, a totally outrageous price, he thought to himself. I can't afford this kind of money just for a hobby.

"Are you a student of Nazism, sir, or perhaps just the SS?"

"I am a student of historical revisionism", he responded. "I like to study how justice can be corrupted in the name of political expediency by people who have no morals."

"Rather than have you disappointed, might I suggest the four-volume soft-cover version? It contains all the original text and has all the photos, of course directly printed, not as individual hand-glued pictures. It is in a handsome display box and sells for only £60. I would be happy to package it and post it to the United States for you. And we do take charge cards."

His wish had finally come true, even if in altered form. He would always love this bookshop. He spent an additional hour rummaging through the displays in complete happiness. There were dozens of things he wanted to buy, but practicality forced him to leave them on the shelves.

He took an uneventful ride on the Underground, then a short stroll and he was at the American Embassy again. Since he knew the drill this time, Piper went directly through the iron gate marked PRIVATE, and told Myrna that he wanted to see Dr. Michael Bohannon.

She looked at him dejectedly. "Expired," she said. "You haven't spoken with Dr. Barker since your last visit, so you don't know there's been a change, do you?"

He greeted her question with silence. Myrna knew who he was because he'd been there only the day before. She knew that he could get a code sequence right, because she'd tried to get him to waiver the last time he was here. But this was a different ploy. Historically, the game was always played this way: I say this, then you say that, then I say something else, then you respond and it's complete. Myrna wasn't giving the proper response to his statement of *I would like to see Dr. Michael Bohannon.* If the code string had changed, Barker would have called and told him. Myrna was yanking his chain. When in doubt, stand still and keep quiet.

"OK, you were here before, and I know that you know Barker, the welshing jerk, so here's what I'll do." She removed a telephone from a drawer and placed it on top of her desk. It had a short cord with a plug on the end.

"Take this phone and plug it into that outlet over there on the far wall. Dial 121, wait for a second dial tone, and then dial Barker's number. Tell him you need the access procedure for today or I can't let you inside. That's the best I can do. And hurry up, because there's a Field Team due here in five minutes."

He was from the old school. They can break your bones, but only you can break your entry sequence. Step one, step two, step three, step four and done. Only that and nothing more. He had played step one. It was now Myrna's turn.

As he stood there in the reception area, Myrna's face assumed a scowl. "What a stubborn butthead you are. I've told you that you can't get inside with an expired passkey sequence, I've given you a chance to get the right sequencing, and you stand there like a zombie. OK. There is no Dr. Whatzit here. Now you want the redheaded assistant, he ain't here either, so follow me please, OK?" She moved to the door at the back of the reception area, opened it and looked back at Piper. "You coming, or are you welded to the floor?"

Step three, by the book. Myrna was trying to jerk his chain. "May I please speak to Dr. Bohannon's assistant, the one with the red hair?"

Myrna looked at him in disgust. She stood with the door open and replied, "There's no one here with red hair either." Now he could move. Finally, the sequence was complete.

"Now, are you happy? Are you going to come with me or not?" she snapped. Of course he was happy. He had beaten her cheesy little system and felt very pleased with himself. He entered the hallway, and Myrna told him to go to Room 5. The electric latch clicked just as he reached for the doorknob.

This room looked like any one of a hundred government offices that he had been in before. Pea-green paint on the walls and ceiling, a vinyl tile floor complete with an arc of dirt and wax build-up in the corners where the big round pads of the electric floor-polishers couldn't reach, a metal desk with seven empty drawers and a black push-button phone. He was early, so he idled away the time thinking about the games he had played and whether they really made any difference. The receptionist came in with the coffee and cookies just as she had done before. "You must be from the Old School, honey, because I just tried every trick old Myrna knows on you today, and you didn't budge an inch."

"Myrna?'

"What?"

"Stop calling me honey. I ain't your cotton-picking honey. You just about gave me a coronary, you old bat. Get a life, for Pete's sake!"

She flipped him the bird and left the room smiling.

He dialed Washington; Barker answered and began speaking immediately.

"We have a serious problem, Lew. I don't know how you manage to get yourself into the middle of these things, but it's no fun for the real professionals, I can tell you that."

"Carry on lecturing, Jim", he replied dead-pan.

"I sent Vice-Admiral Richter to Coronado to check on Gurney's records at the command, and they so much as told him to take a crap in his hat. They told him that the fix is in, and that all the records they turned over previously had been altered to say completely different things, and that guys that served with Gurney have been transferred to the ends of the earth where nobody could talk to them. They even hinted that they had put together a plan to get Gurney out of prison by force, but had to abandon it when they learned that he would be killed by the guards if an assault was mounted."

"Holy crap, Jim! You sent a Vice-Admiral to Coronado to look at the SEAL records? I said send somebody friendly, not overpowering. What the dickens were you thinking?"

"Never use a hand grenade when you have an A-bomb available. That's what I was thinking. Dan Richter is the highest-ranking man currently on active duty to qualify as a SEAL, and they told him to go to hell, Sir. We got serious problems, my son. Officially, the SEAL Commands, Atlantic or Pacific, claim to hold no more records relating to Lt. Gurney. No former commanding officer of his, from the time he left the Naval Academy, claims to have any copies of Fitness Report rough drafts. All men queried showed identical Xeroxed forms signifying receipt by the Naval Investigative Service of 'various written materials sought in connection with a Classified Investigation under Title 18 of the U. S. Code'. These SEALs are some of the best and bravest we have, and they're convinced to a man that Gurney was railroaded."

Good heavens, Piper thought. To burn the SEAL command so badly that they refuse to cooperate with one of their own people, and him a Vice Admiral, and then to admit that they had actively thought of breaking him out of prison in a cowboy operation. Something was definitely very, very wrong here.

"Backtrack. We have to backtrack. Jim, go through your diary from last year and find the first mention of Gurney. Use your personal papers, the stuff you keep at home, ask your wife, try to re-live the part where you heard that your niece had been hurt. Look for the people that gave you the news, look for the people that persuaded you to act the way you did. Somewhere in there is a lead to the person who set this up. He'll be the one at all the briefings, he'll be the one who pushed to have Gurney transferred out of UK control to a US prison. He's got to be in there somewhere."

"You're asking me to re-live some of the most painful parts of my life, Lew. I don't know if I'm up to it. I damn near went off my rocker having my brother calling me at all hours with medical updates on my niece. It really hurt my whole family to the core, man."

"Now I have to ask you to check the really bad part, Jim."

"Go ahead, I'm already starting to eat aspirin like breath-mints. It can't get much worse."

"Yes it can, Jim. Remember that you said your niece asked you something like, *why didn't my Uncle Jim protect me?* She was a ten-year-old kid at the time. That's an uncharacteristic question from a child, Jim. She doesn't know what you do for a living. Somebody got next to her in the hospital or in therapy or at the doctor's office, and told her to ask that question. See if you can find out who got her to say that to you, OK?"

Silence. He was walking on the razor-edge of disaster here, and he knew it. He was poking at a highly emotional area inside his friend. But there was nothing else he could do.

"Yeah, all right, I'll see what I can find out," came his friend's downcast voice. "Call me back again tomorrow, OK?"

CHAPTER SIX

SECRETS

"Sugar, do you have John's telephone number at the barracks? I want to call him before I go to the embassy," he asked in his best southern manner.

"So now I'm 'Sugar', am I? Why do American men call their lady friends 'Sugar'? Can't they remember their names?" Nancy was smiling as she spoke.

He was ready for this one. He gave her Uncle Harvey's answer, the one he first heard when he was six or seven years old.

"Women are called 'Sugar' for two reasons: they are sweet little things, and because too much of them can be bad for you."

She threw a dish towel at him and giggled.

"Phone number?" he asked once more.

She pointed to it in the little book by the telephone, and he dialed the number.

"Major Ross' office," came John's voice on the line. There was the recognizable pause in the speech pattern, just like John Wayne. He was having to answer his own phone these days.

"John? Lew Piper. I have a quick question for you. Can we talk about Belfast and Gurney one more time? I want to get some more details if I can."

"I'm sorry sir. Who are you looking for?" It wasn't John after all. Someone else speaks just like him. British accents all sound the same, I guess.

"This is Mr. Piper. I'd like to speak to Major Ross, please."

"Just a moment, please. I'll connect you," came the sound-alike voice.

"Major Ross."

"John? Lew Piper. Could I come by the barracks for a chat? I have a couple of more questions that I need answers to. If you have the time, that is. By the way, who was it that answered the phone? I thought it was you."

"That was Corporal Samuels. He's my batman, and he's assigned to office duties when we are in barracks. And, before we continue, I have some news that I must pass along. We were informed today all that the events surrounding the last deployment and any information relating to the school bus bombing have been reclassified as falling under the purview of the Official Secrets Act. No discussions are possible of any matters pertaining to these events. Apparently, there have recently been some rather indiscreet inquiries."

"John, did you tell anyone that you had asked me to find out about Gurney?"

"No, no, it has nothing to do with me. It appears that someone in the US has been asking around indiscriminately, you know, looking around for additional information. So, Whitehall simply decided that it was time to formalize the serious nature of the offenses, that's all. Nothing more than that."

And the Pope is Chinese, Piper thought. He arranged to meet Ross at ten that morning. Quickly, he changed into his suit, kissed Nancy good-bye, and headed for the train to London.

One hour later he was in front of the army barracks where John was attached. It was an arrangement of two story brick buildings that were well kept but obviously not constructed in this century, and possibly not even in the previous one.   It was bordered by a high chain link fence through which manicured lawns, rose bush hedges and a pea-gravel parade ground could be seen. He walked around the corner to the guard room and told the corporal at the desk that he had an appointment to see Major John Ross.

"Your name, please sir?"

"Lewis Piper."

"Yes, sir, your name is in the Appointments Registry. If you will just wait a minute, I'll have someone show you the way."

He pushed a button on the intercom and in a few moments a fresh-faced boy of seventeen appeared, all dressed up in khaki like a soldier. The corporal handed him a piece of white paper the size of a postcard, and the lad asked Piper to please follow him.

Across the pea-gravel the young man strode in carefully measured Queen's Regulation paces. Piper was taller than the boy, but the boy was faster on pea-gravel. It took a lot of catch-up to stay even with him. They entered a nearby building. At a door on the ground floor of the barracks, the young man knocked once, then entered. Another young man in khaki sat at a desk behind a number of discouraging stacks of paper.

"Mr. Piper to see the Major," his guide said, handing over the piece of paper.

Getting up from behind the desk while reading the small note, the second young man said, "This way, sir."

Walking to the door at the back of the room, the lad knocked once, opened the door, stood up very straight and announced, "Mr. Piper to see you, sir"

Piper entered through the open door as John Ross said, "Thank you, Samuels. Carry on."

"Sir!" the boy replied, leaving and closing the door softly.

Piper and Ross shook hands warmly. It looked very comfortable and cozy here in his office. Nice and big, that was for sure. About four times the size of a two-car garage, Piper reckoned. Eight Mercedes sedans would fit in here with no trouble. Fireplace in the middle of the wall to the left of Ross' desk, with its coal fire glowing away like a Bessemer converter making steel from pig-iron. Fire-guard screen at attention in front to catch any errant sparks. Mahogany bookcases neatly filled with important-looking tomes. Oriental carpet on the floor, covering the waxed wooden planks that had been there since they were installed in the 1850's, no doubt. There was pervasive smell of leather and floor-wax and furniture polish and tradition. Piper snuggled into a manly leather armchair at the side of the fireplace as directed by Ross' friendly gesture. Ross joined him in a similar chair at the other side. Samuels entered carrying a tray of tea and cookies. This is neat stuff, Piper thought. This is the way to run an army. Warm fires, hot tea, and an office the size of a tennis court. Not bad. The corporal poured tea and passed the cookies, then busied himself in a far corner of the room dusting and shifting books around on the shelves.

"My man in Washington is working on your request, John, but he has asked me for some additional information. I wonder if I might ask you some questions by way of clarification?" He was lying through his teeth, of course. The questions weren't from Barker, they were ones that he had thought up.

"Fine. Ask away. I'll answer within the bounds of what I mentioned before, of course."

"First, you told me before that you ran a bunker operation in Belfast to see if you might get a shot at an IRA terrorist named Nicholas O'Flynn. On the last evening of the watch, the sniper saw O'Flynn. But before he could shoot, a car came up, O'Flynn knelt down and spoke with the driver, a small group of people gathered, the car drove off and O'Flynn melted away into the night. The next day, you extract the sniper from his hiding place."

"Yes, Gurney was extracted without incident. He gave a complete verbal report of the operation just as I've told you. He also said that he believed that he had some more good items for our scrapbook."

There was a muffled thump as Corporal Samuels dropped some books on the plank floor. He was obviously flustered at his clumsiness and had trouble recovering. He would pick up three books, drop two, and then pick them up again. At this rate, he would never get done.

Ross saved him from further embarrassment by saying, "Just leave that for now, Samuels. Carry on with your office duties."

"Sir!" came the reply as he left the books on the floor and hurriedly exited the room.

Piper was instantly back to business. "You mean that Lieutenant Gurney was the sniper? You never mentioned that before."

"Sorry, it just slipped my mind, I guess. But now that I think of it, there was something else that I remember about what the colonel said to me. He seemed particularly angry that I had allowed Gurney to go on that operation. He went on and on about it, complaining about 'that bloody American and his cameras'. But he'd never objected to any of Gurney's assignments before."

"You're telling me that Gurney took pictures when he went on operations with you?"

"Oh, yes indeed. Gurney was quite the professional cameraman. He had one or two Minoxes, a Tessina wrist-camera and a couple of Leicas with some very expensive long lenses. He was quite good, actually. He gave some excellent after-operation photographic briefings that were quite well received by the command and the troops."

"Yes, but you said that Colonel Reeves-Benedict knew that Gurney carried cameras in the field with him. Had he ever told him not to do this kind of thing?"

"He didn't complain to me about it. Never."

Then why would he choose to make a fuss about Gurney and his cameras this time?" Piper asked.

"I have absolutely no idea why he was so upset. As I said, he seemed completely out of control. It was most unlike him."

"So, then you submitted your standard morning report concerning the results of the bunker operation to the colonel, in exactly the same manner as you had done many times before. He became furious with you. How soon after that conversation did the regiment return to barracks in England?"

"Let's see, two days later." John replied. "The officers and their batmen came back. . ."

"Batmen?" Piper asked quickly. "Clarify this for me, please. What are batmen?"

"Each officer is assigned a batman to assist him with his kit, his uniforms and such. It's an archaic word that come from Cricket. It refers to the chap who hands you your Cricket bat when you come down from the house to play. I am sure that in the more egalitarian American society, you would call them servants. But they are fully qualified Troopers, and the duty is a normal part of their course of learning in the army."

"Sorry to have interrupted. You were saying?"

"Yes," Ross continued, "the officers came over on an RAF aircraft, with the men following by ferry. We had a week's transfer time, so we formed up at the barracks about ten days later. By then all the men and equipment had returned, except one man who was delayed in Belfast with a personal problem."

"What problem was that?

"Trooper Delk, who was Gurney's batman, by the way, got himself involved in a fight at a local pub and was arrested. He was released a few days later and no charges were filed."

56

"So, after the bunker operation, you spent most of the time packing up and moving back to barracks in London?"

"Actually, I was basically at ease with a few turnover duties to the Fifth Gloucester chaps who relieved us, and that was all."

"Did you have any other problems with the colonel during these last days?"

"No, he had already departed for London. I was nominally in command of the regiment during this time."

"What about Lt. Gurney, did he have a substitute batman to pack his belongings, or did he do it himself?"

" I had Samuels pack his belongings in Delk's absence."

"After you returned to London, did you see Gurney?"

"No, only on the flight over. He told me that the Parachute Brigade had laid on some kind of a training exercise in Scotland. They had asked if he would be their guest, and he wondered if it would be acceptable for him to take a few days to attend. I gave him my approval, and he planned to go up there immediately."

"And while Lt. Gurney was in Scotland with the Parachute Brigade, that's when the school bus was attacked, correct?"

"Yes, I think that is correct."

"So the school bus was attacked, then security people came to the barracks and discovered a number of incriminating papers, maps, and explosives among Lt. Gurney's personal belongings, is that right?"

"The timing is right. They came the next day or the day after. I have no comment on the nature of what they found. Official Secrets Act, and all that."

"Were you present when the articles, whatever they were, were found?"

"No comment."

"Was Samuels present when the items were found?"

"No comment."

"Would it be possible for me to speak with this man Delk?"

"I'm sure I could arrange it, but I would have to contact him in Belize. He's on duty there with a Guards detachment."

"Where was Gurney taken into custody?" Piper asked.

"No comment. But here is another confusing thing about all this. I happened to run into the CO of Two Para later and we were commiserating over the sadness of the affair. He told me that there had been no training exercise scheduled in Scotland at the time that Gurney was arrested. It seemed that he must have manufactured the event to get the time away from the regiment. We were both puzzled."

"Where was Gurney tried?"

"No comment"

"Did you testify at his trial?"

"As I said earlier, I gave a deposition to a solicitor from the Ministry of Defence. That was all."

"And you never saw Lt. Gurney again?"

"No, I never did."

"May I speak to Samuels and ask him a few questions?" Piper asked offhandedly.

"I'm sure that would make him quite nervous, Lew. May I ask what questions you want to ask?"

"Oh, just a few unimportant things about what he did with Gurney's foot locker, that's all," he lied.

"I'm sure that would be all right. Just remember the information restrictions, if you would." Looking toward the office door, Ross spoke barely above a normal conversation tone, saying "Samuels?"

The door opened immediately. Not a good sign. Samuels had been listening on the other side.

"Sir?" he said as he entered the room. "Do you want me to finish. . .?"

"No, Samuels, it's not about that. Mr. Piper here has a few questions that he would like to put to you. I have told him about our recent information blackout, so you can be assured of his discretion. Come in please."

"Stand over by the Major, Samuels, if you would. That way he can come to your assistance if I touch on something that is improper. Is that all right, John?"

"Yes, that is an excellent idea, Mr. Piper. Come stand here, Samuels," Ross said, motioning to a place at his side. The young soldier quickly moved into position, much relieved that his officer would be nearby to protect him.

Now, young Corporal Samuels, I can watch your eyes and Ross' eyes at the same time as I ask my questions about who you gave the foot locker to. The question I have no intention of asking, by the way. Expect an explosion, Piper.

"Where did you get the items that you put in Lieutenant Gurney's foot locker, Samuels?"

"I am not required to answer that, sir!" he exploded nervously. "All the items found in that trunk are covered by the information blackout, and. . ."

"What on Earth are you going on about, Samuels?" Ross interjected. "He only asked you to describe where Lieutenant Gurney kept his uniform items prior to your packing them. Don't be so defensive, Corporal. It is a perfectly reasonable question, surely."

"Oh, sorry sir. I thought he was referring to the items found later when, well, you understand, sir."

"That is all I have for now, Samuels. Thank you for your assistance," Piper responded, quickly closing the matter. Ross never blinked, so he is not a part of the problem. Samuels had a fit, so he is definitely a part of the problem.

As Samuels left the room on being dismissed by Ross, Piper let him hear his parting shot. "Just in closing, John, I want to thank you for making this clearer for me. I'll keep after the thing with Gurney and let you know."

"With the information blackout, you won't have much luck, I'm afraid," Ross replied. "But thank you for trying anyway."

I wouldn't have any luck at all through ordinary channels, that's right. But Barker is not an ordinary channel.

"Would you care to join me for lunch, John? I don't have to be at the embassy until one." Maybe he'll talk more if I can get him outside the barracks.

"I wish that I could, but I have to prepare some remarks for a meeting of the British Veterans Society later in the week. However, if I might make a suggestion, there is a quite passable little restaurant about a fifteen minute walk from here. They have an excellent fish course at this time of year. I would recommend the Dover Sole, and although the place is rather small, I think you would enjoy the ambiance." Piper nodded in acceptance.

"I'll have Samuels make a booking for you, and then we can finish our tea and be off at the same time."

He punched a button on the intercom. "Samuels?"

"Sir?" came the quick reply.

"Make a booking for Mr. Piper at my restaurant for about twenty minutes from now and draw out a small map with directions for him, will you?"

"Sir," the voice replied. Sir. Always 'sir' and nothing else in the British Army, Piper mused. Since the answer to any direct question from an officer will always be Yes, Sir, they just shorten the answer down to one word.

"Enter," the colonel responded to Samuels' knock. Standing behind his desk with an ever-present Gauloise smoking away in its ivory cigarette holder, he looked at the young corporal coldly. "Well, speak up, corporal."

"It's the American, sir, this Mr. Piper. He's in Major Ross' office talking about the Naval officer."

"And what has Major Ross told him?"

"Nothing, sir. Only that there is an information blackout and that he can't assist him. He even asked me a question about the items that I packed in the lieutenant's trunk"

"And of course you told him about the maps and the explosives, is that right?" the colonel asked sarcastically.

"Sir, I told him that the information was privileged, as you instructed me to tell anyone who asked." He said the words with the straightest of faces, never betraying his nervous outburst. A true professional.

"Thank you for bringing me yet another problem to solve, corporal," the colonel responded acidly. "Do you actually have any duties, or is your major function simply to serve as an irritant to your Officer Commanding?"

God, he's in an even nastier mood than normal, Samuels thought. "Major Ross asked me to draw a map for Mr. Piper to direct him to his restaurant, sir. May I be dismissed, sir?"

"The restaurant over by. . .?" The colonel gestured in a general southerly direction with an idle wave of his hand.

"Sir."

"That is an absolutely ghastly pigsty with abominable food served by a staff that can barely speak English. I have no idea what Ross sees in the place. I wouldn't let my greyhounds eat there. Be that as it may, corporal, go ahead and draw the map as requested. Before you give it to the American, however, I have one more errand for you. Picking up the telephone, he dialed a number from memory, "Are you dressed?" he asked stiffly when the call was answered.

There was a murmured response.

"Excellent for a change. Get a taxi and meet Samuels at the corner. He will give you a document to deposit and some directions. Be there in ten minutes." He dropped the receiver back in the cradle.

The colonel studied a sheet of paper carefully. "Yes, this should do nicely, Samuels. Give this to our thespian friend, along with a copy of the map. And do it now!" he snapped.

The words MOST SECRET flashed before his sight for an instant as the colonel folded the paper in quarters.

Piper took the little hand-drawn map from Samuels. It was done on a piece of folded white paper, and the quality of the drawing gave no indication as to why it had taken over fifteen minutes to complete. Ross had become quite impatient, even going to the door to check on the corporal himself at one point. The other trooper had said that Samuels was running a quick errand for the colonel. Piper said his good-byes and made his way out onto the street.

Looking at map, Piper folded the paper in half again and put in his outside coat pocket. He found the restaurant, but the walk was more like 30 minutes than 15. He obviously wasn't as fast as a soldier. The place was named "The Bun Penny" after a rare English coin that had been embossed with a view of the young Queen Victoria with her hair done up in a bun. Entering, he was quickly seated in the velvet curtained, leather upholstered quietness and sipped at a white Rhone

Chablis that apparently had been had ordered when the reservation was made.

He was busy trying to separate a forkful of the Dover Sole from its backbone when a man quietly sat down at his table. He was about sixty, with a full head of neatly combed gray hair. The suit was a blue pin-stripe and quite obviously not off-the-rack. His tie was a regimental stripe worn with a French cuff white shirt.

His manner was direct, but soft. "Mr. Piper, I will take only a few moments of your time. I wish to convey to you that certain people have become anxious over the questions that you have been asking. You are on a dangerous course in uncharted waters, to use a metaphor not unfamiliar to a man with your naval background. I am here to ask you to relax for the rest of your visit to our country and continue to enjoy the companionship of Mrs. Carpenter. I most strongly request that you cease your inquisitiveness before someone is harmed as a result of your actions. Do I make myself clear?"

Piper stared mutely at the confident blue-eyed face with the un-British suntan. He had just received an official warn-off. In the Intelligence world there are always times when a civilian stumbles into a highly classified situation without knowing it. It is a standard procedure for these people to be given a chance to withdraw gracefully. Professionals have no reason to want to hurt amateurs. They just want them to stay clear of the action. If they don't take the hint, a bullet through the brain from a silenced pistol usually did the trick nicely.

He was obviously in way over his head.

Before he could respond, the man asked, "May I please have the piece of paper in your jacket pocket?"

Having no inkling of what it was about, Piper fished in the side pocket and handed him the map to the restaurant. The man slowly unfolded the paper to its full size with precise and dramatic movements that must have been designed to show the steadiness of his hands. He spread it out face-down on the tablecloth and pressed it flat with the back of his hand. Then he turned it over and showed the reverse side to Piper. On it were several lines of small print that he couldn't focus on and a diagram of some type, looking like a map, at the bottom. His gaze was transfixed on the two words stamped at the top and bottom of the page. They read, "MOST SECRET".

"You see, Mr. Piper, how easy it is to inadvertently run afoul of the law? You never even unfolded the paper, did you? And here you are, a guest in our country, in unauthorized possession of classified material. You see how easily someone could mistake your intentions? What if someone were to contact the police about this?"

Piper swallowed hard, understanding the implication all to clearly. Samuels had set him up, the little weasel. A snap of this man's finger and he would be in serious trouble.

"And Mrs. Carpenter, Nancy -- is that what you call her? Where is she now? Is she really safely at home, or has someone..."

He should not have said that.

Piper grabbed the man by the knot of his tie and drew him closer. The wine bottle fell over and a glass and silverware hit the floor. He hit the man directly in the face. The first blow broke the man's suntanned, aquiline nose with a satisfying pop. Still slightly conscious, the man turned his head to avoid seeing the second blow and it landed on his forehead above the left eye. This man's brain then realized that the situation was out of control, and issued a temporary shut-down command to his nervous system, rendering him unconscious. Piper hit him a third time just to make sure anyway.

He had lost his temper. He never lost his temper. Losing your temper meant losing control of the situation, losing the ability to think and plan rationally. On top of all that, the man was obviously an amateur, not an intelligence professional. A pro would never have threatened Nancy. A pro would have concentrated on Piper alone. This guy had talked too much.

Piper now became aware that the restaurant had become dead-quiet, and that everyone was staring at him. All the patrons and staff were gawking open-mouthed. Simply because he had beaten a man unconscious during lunch. How curious.

In the microsecond before each patron could recover their aplomb and begin to offer differing unsolicited opinions as to what should be done to resolve the situation before them, he got his best command voice to say, "Get me a taxi, please. This is a security matter." The head waiter nodded and went out the front door to find one. At that, the other patron's attention returned to their food, and soft conversation resumed.

Everything was back under control.

He quickly checked the bleeding man as his head rested face-down on the white tablecloth. Bleeding from the nose had almost stopped. Steady, even breathing, all good signs.

The waiter said who had nervously begun to dial a nearby phone when Piper began pummeling his table-mate said, "Never mind. It's all right," and hung up.

CHAPTER SEVEN

ANNEX

Amateur was all he could think of as he stared at the unconscious figure. The white-haired man appeared to doze peacefully, head down on the table. The breathing was still even, just a snort now and then as a bruised nerve ending tried to reconnect. The air passages were clear, and the man hadn't had a coronary. Yet. The day was young. A drool of blood coursed from the left nostril and began to form a dime-sized pool on the tablecloth. The few other patrons studiously avoided becoming involved in the battering of a fellow citizen, preferring instead to continue with their Cock-a-Leekie soup and truffles. Piper sat with his face close to the white-hared man's, studying the features and listening for signs of returning consciousness.

The head waiter popped back in the front door and said, "Your taxi is here, sir."

The unconscious figure was beginning to moan softly. Piper slung one of the man's arms around his neck and hoisted him to his feet. A second waiter held the front door open. Piper paused long enough to hand the headwaiter a £50 banknote. "Sorry for the trouble." he said, dragging the gray-haired figure toward the taxi. The driver opened the taxi door and Piper stepped inside pulling the man after him.

"Oh, my..." the man swooned, beginning to revive even more. Piper jammed a thumb firmly against the base of the man's neck, pressing against the correct nerve until unconsciousness returned. In a rush of words he told the driver, "American Embassy on Grosvenor Square. The annex entrance around to the side. And get there the fastest way, please." The black Austin diesel taxi sped off down the street toward the embassy.

"Wot's yer friend's problem, mate?" the driver asked, surveying both his passengers suspiciously in the rear-view mirror.

"He's had an accident." was the only reply that came to mind. Blood had run down the man's face onto his shirt front.

"We had best take him to the Emergency, then. There's one about three minutes from here."

Oh-oh! He's right, that's what honest, ordinary citizens should do, but that ain't who I am. Gotta think of something. . .

"This is a security matter" he lied. "This man's a courier for the IRA." Oh, poop! I shouldn't have said that. Look at the driver's name on his plastic ID on the sun-visor. "Kenneth M. O'Banyon". He's Irish, and I've just insulted every darn one of his relatives.

The driver squinted into the rear-view mirror again, then turned sharply down an alley so narrow and dark that it looked like a tunnel. Greenery and trees were visible at the far end of the alley, but that looked to be four blocks away. He dodged cardboard boxes and metal trash cans, racing along at breakneck speed. Cats and pigeons scurried for their lives. Bursting out the other end with a long blast on the taxi's horn, he made a quick right and then a sharp left turn, and they were at the annex. The iron gate with the word "Private" beckoned to them. His side was next to the curb. Piper opened the door and pulled the man from the taxi and out onto the sidewalk. He held the man with one hand and began to dig in his pocket with the other hand for taxi fare.

"It's free. I'll log it as a mercy dash." the driver said, and started to pull away. Then, he stopped suddenly, reversed the taxi and called out. He paused. The gray-haired man was beginning to moan and stir again.

"When you get him inside," the driver began.

"What?" Piper responded.

"Hang the Mick bastard, all right?" Then he sped away as fast as the clunking diesel engine would allow.

So much for Irish unity.

The man was able to stagger now, and he steered him up the path to the reception area door. Bursting inside, he gave Myrna such a fright that she dropped a lighted cigarette in her lap.

"Wha. . .?" she said intelligently.

"No time for formalities, Myrna!" Piper said, holding the bleeding man so she could get a full view. He moved to the door in the rear. "Come on, Myrna! Open the door and get us an interrogation room. Call security and find us a medic. I want this guy taken into custody and put on ice right now."

He was thinking of additional things to say, because he expected an argument from her. After all, she should not let him inside. He had no security clearance, and hadn't used the proper code string. And furthermore, he didn't care. He would drop the man on the floor and yell at her until she did what he wanted.

To his astonishment, she hopped up from her desk and unlocked the rear door immediately, leading him down the now-familiar corridor to a room whose door was ajar. It was larger than the others he had been using to call Barker, but it was the same musty green color. As they were making their way down the corridor, Myrna had been rapidly barking into a hand-held two-way radio. Scurrying footsteps could be heard approaching from the other end of the long hall. As he shoved the man into the office, a navy corpsman in a white smock and two young men with short hair and suits joined them. One was big, the other little.

"I want a policeman", the gray-haired man mumbled. He snuffled the blood in his nose, and looked surprised at the sound of his voice. Broken noses have way of making you talk funny.

"Sit down, and let me have a look at you, sir." the corpsman said.

"Who are you people?" one of the suits asked.

"My name's Piper; I don't know who this man is. He's probably IRA. He braced me in a restaurant and tried to warn me off. He also threatened a friend of mine." The old patter was flowing easily from his mouth. And it seemed to be working. He saw the gazes become less suspicious.

"What did you hit him with?" the corpsman asked. Piper clenched his left fist and showed it to the corpsman. The gray-haired man closed his eyes and shrunk back in the straight chair to get away from the weapon. The corpsman looked at Piper's fist in a detached, professional way, then said, "This guy's going to need a splint on his nose."

"First, empty his pockets," Piper ordered. The corpsman stepped aside, and Big Suit lifted the man bodily out of the chair while Little Suit attacked his pockets like a starving dog after a bowl of Puppy

Chow. As a small notebook was removed from an inside pocket, the man tried to take it back. Little Suit quickly thumped the man's sore nose with a snap of his fingers, then Big Suit spun him around and handcuffed his hands behind his back. The small notebook was tossed into the jumble of other items on the table. Little Suit pulled his hand slowly from the man's side coat pocket and stared at a piece of something that looked like transparent green putty.

"That's confidential" the man said. "I can explain it, however."

Big Suit shook the man and said, "Shut up, or I'll make you wish that you had." The tanned face flinched at the thought.

As they led the man from the office, Piper said, "Isolation. No calls until we talk to Security, OK?" The suits nodded, then said, "Oh, hello, sir" to someone in the hall.

A black man in a suit and tie came in the room. His collar was unbuttoned and the patterned tie hung loose. He was about forty-five and he glared at Piper as though he had just tracked dog shit into the room.

"I'm Wylie. I'm Security here. Who do you work for? No, wait a minute." He stuck his head out into the hallway and yelled after the departing figures, "I want a Class Three identification on that guy, and I want it in here in less than ten minutes, you got me?" Class Three is a complete life history. How could anybody be expected to accomplish that in ten minutes?

"Like I said, who do you report to?" Wylie asked again.

Piper put his wallet on the table in front of the black man. He told him who he used to work for in the old days. Then he told him the entire story. Everything. All about Ross wanting to write to Gurney, Corporal Samuels and his defensiveness and eavesdropping , the threat to Nancy's safety, and everything else that he could think of. Except the part about Gurney and his cameras and the Bunker Operation. Habit made him hold back a part until he was sure of his ground. He told him that the gray-haired man had been the last straw for him. He was fed up with this mess.

Wylie removed a small radio from his side pocket and spoke into it, telling the person on the other end to get a scientific technician sent to the room. He had an expression of I'm-better-than-you-and-you-better-not-forget-it written all over him. A typical government weenie's attitude. A young woman appeared, dressed neatly in a dark blue pants suit worn under a white lab coat. She was donning surgeon's gloves as she came through the door. Wylie handed Piper back his wallet after scanning the contents quickly, then pointed to the items on the table. "Full inventory and analysis in my office in ten minutes." he said flatly to the white-coated woman.

"It'll take at least a half-hour to go through this," she responded.

"I didn't ask you how long it would take, I said do it in ten minutes. Take any longer and I'll transfer you to Iceland before the sun rises again," he snapped at the figure disappearing through the door. Motioning to Piper, he said, "In my office. Now." He walked away without looking back. Piper almost turned the other way, figuring to go out the door past Myrna, and this guy could try to impress somebody else. But he fell in behind, realizing that he could do that anytime that he wanted to.

People in the hallway stopped their conversation and backed against the walls as they passed. At least someone was impressed. Wylie was apparently not the kind of person they wished to offend.

In his office, Wylie poured him a cup of coffee from a built-in coffee maker. The cup was Styrofoam and the brew was delicious. He sat down and sipped quietly in front of the man's desk, staring at the back side of a computer terminal whose screen was turned away. Wylie tapped on the keyboard and appeared to be reading something.

"He's a magician." Wylie said softly.

"A kidnapper?" Piper asked. Professional kidnappers were called "magicians" because they made people disappear.

Wylie corrected him. "No, I mean he's a magician, as in pulling rabbits out of hats. His name is Arlowe Peyton Cranmoore, and he bills himself as the Great Arlo. He started as a young man after World War Two in vaudeville, then went to television and nightclubs. Had a weekly kiddie show on Yorkshire Television for a few years in the seventies. Supposed to be retired now, doing a few acting jobs in movies and television. Apparently, he does a little work for other companies as well." Then he added, "You better give me that piece of classified stuff that you told me what's-his-name planted on you."

Piper dug in his pocket and produced the folded paper with Samuels' instructions to the restaurant scribbled on the outside. The little rat. Piper was still in a snit, still pumped up from the encounter. He thought about the nervous corporal. Samuels had planted classified material on him, and had done it right in front of a superior officer. He had obviously phoned the magician and told him where he could be found. He looked forward to an early opportunity to speak personally with the corporal about his conduct.

Wylie looked at the instructions to the restaurant, then slowly opened the paper and began to read. From the light coming through the window and shining through the paper, Piper could see the "Most Secret" stamp quite clearly in reverse, and the typing, and the diagram of whatever it was. He felt like an idiot for getting caught like that. Like an amateur.

"Did you read this?" Wylie asked.

"No, all I saw was the "Most Secret" stamp when the guy showed it to me. For all the good it does me.

Wylie scooted the paper across to Piper. "Go ahead and read it if you want." He read the paper once, then he read it again.

"Kinda hard to figure, isn't it?" Wylie said with the faintest hint of a smile. "I mean, to the ordinary layman, this would appear to be just an announcement about a regimental band concert to be held in Green Park this Saturday at 2 PM. It's odd that they would classify something like that as top secret, don't you think?" He was actually smiling now.

Now Piper was totally confused.

A knock sounded at the door, and the young woman who didn't want to be transferred to Iceland entered. She was still wearing surgeon's gloves, and carrying several clear plastic bags.

"Standard items, except for a single page from a classified Ministry of Defence document," she began without waiting for anyone's permission. Dumping the plastic bags on Wylie's desk, she continued. "His wallet contains a valid ID and a reasonable amount of money for someone to be walking around with. There's a bank card and a couple of credit cards, all in the correct name and all genuine. His keys have been duplicated and are on their way to the guy's house to be checked. We should hear within the hour on them. We're still checking the phone numbers in his appointment book, and a number of them are coming up MI5. There were a few restaurants, ordinary people, and some British Army personnel."

"What was that green plastic putty?" Piper asked.

"That's a transfer medium." she replied quickly. "It's a polyurethane-based putty that has the capability of picking up images from one place and transferring them to another document, as an example. Commonly sold as 'Silly Putty' in the US."

"Was it used to put the 'Most Secret' stamp on this document?" Wylie asked, pushing the paper across the desk in her direction. She sniffed the paper and then looked at it through a magnifying glass.

"Probably," she replied. Pointing at another piece of paper in a plastic folder on Wylie's desk, she said, "He had that single page of a document on him dealing with a new Russian infantry rifle, and it was stamped that way. Maybe he copied it across." Motioning to the paper with Ross' instructions she said, "You can see what is called the polyurethane 'sweat' from the putty's softener on the paper, plus the stamp doesn't smell like Limey ink. I could run some tests quickly and get back to you if you would like."

"That's OK for now, Alice. Thanks for the fast work." Wylie said, retrieving the document. "You can forget about Iceland for the time being."

Alice said thank you and left the room quietly closing the door behind her.

Wylie rested his hands on the desk. "You read the papers much?"

Piper nodded.

"Then you know that currently there is a truce between the IRA and the British. Sinn Fein, the IRA political wing, offered that truce in return for talks on the future of Northern Ireland. The Brits accepted, and they're circling and sniffing like dogs who have just met for the first time. Apart from the odd incident, the truce has held and the talks are continuing."

"My guess is that the thing you have become entangled with probably has to do with some of the unauthorized contacts made by people from all over the place. Everybody wanted to be a hero, a peacemaker, and lots of people got burned by the IRA in sting operations. There are a lot of incidents of blackmail operations being mounted against people who now wish they'd never gotten involved in the process. The major may be one of the people being blackmailed."

"It doesn't involve Major Ross," Piper stated flatly.

"You go home to Mrs. Carpenter in Sidcup, and we'll park a gray Ford Escort across the street to keep watch in case the people who hired Mr. Cranmoore decide to visit you again. In the meantime, we'll keep him as our guest and encourage him to speak freely about his involvement in the matter. Meanwhile, we will wait for the people who sent him on the mission to contact us."

"Is it OK if I call my friend at DOD now?" Piper asked.

"You the one that's been placing calls to Dr. Barker, by any chance?" Wylie asked.

"Yeah, I've been trying to get some information on. . ."

"I don't care about it. Make your call and tell Dr. Barker that you are getting wonderful cooperation from us, please. I don't need problems with him at this stage in my life, OK? And be back here tomorrow at ten, so we can do a formal de-brief on this mess."

Piper went to an adjacent office, dialed the restaurant and asked to speak with the headwaiter. Tightening his throat to make his voice a little higher, he introduced himself as Mr. Brown of the local American Express office. "One of our officers was involved in an incident in your restaurant today involving a financial security matter in our company. We are most anxious to see that this incident receives as little publicity as possible in order to keep it from reflecting on our company. May I ask if any of the local news media may have been in contact with you?"

"There was a call a few moments ago, sir," he replied. "But it was a personal inquiry as to whether we had seen an older man enter or establishment and speak with another gentleman. He was anxious to know if the older man was perhaps still here."

"And you replied. . .?"

"I replied that there had been a man here who fit the description, and that he had been taken ill and escorted from the premises in a taxi. Nothing more."

"Could you describe the caller's voice?"

"Young male, North Country accent with a slight hesitation in the speech. Certainly not a university man, would be my guess."

Corporal Samuels. "Thank you for your discretion in this matter, sir," Piper replied with satisfaction. "It was probably a clerk from his Solicitor's office. We will not forget your kindness."

"It is always a pleasure to be of assistance," the headwaiter replied courteously and hung up.

The evening with Nancy was pleasant and quiet. She asked no questions, and he gave her no answers.

The next morning he was back at the embassy at ten, ready to go through a formal debrief and resume his vacation.. But Wylie had a surprise for him. "I'm sure you don't remember me," he said.

He tried to picture the black man as ten years younger, with more hair and less weight around the middle. He drew a blank. That was unusual for him. He usually remembered everybody.

"I'll bet you remember Yolanda Pittered, though, don't you?"

Yolanda Pittered! Of course he remembered her. That was the black security officer that he arrested for smoking dope. That was the arrest that had ended his career with the Department of Defense. His gut cramped up just from thinking about it.

"Well, I was one of the young staffers that agreed with what you did," Wylie continued. "The shafting you got in the affair was just a power play, as I'm sure you've figured out by now. They came around to all the black agents and told us you were a racist trying to make your promotion over the body of one of the sisters. Real Huey Newton and Black Panthers rhetoric. I told them that if she smoked dope, she would ruin more African-American careers than any racist with some cooked-up story ever could. Anyway, for what it's worth to you, Yolanda kept up her wayward habits and was caught a couple of years later in a DEA sting operation when she tried to buy a half-kilo of heroin. That was too detrimental to the department for them to ignore, so she was dismissed. Then she was tried and sent to prison on the drug charge."

"I guess that's just tough cookies about my career,." Piper said bitterly. The whole thing just made him furious all over again.

"Get over it, Piper, and stop feeling sorry for yourself!" Wylie snapped. "I had to transfer to the CIA to get away from being called an

Uncle Tom and left to do office work. Given a chance at the Department of Defense, I would have stayed in Washington, DC. By now, my house would have been almost paid for. As it is, I move every two years, my wife divorced me eight years ago, I pay half my salary in alimony and child support, never see my kids, and when I retire she gets half my retirement pay. So, maybe you're the lucky one, huh?."

"Yeah, maybe," he shrugged. "Maybe I am the lucky one."

"Do you ever think about what it might have been like if you had not been shafted by the establishment?" Wylie asked.

"Of course I do," he replied quickly. "Why, in a few years I could have retired on a pension for the rest of my life if they hadn't screwed around with me!"

Wylie was laughing softly. "You don't even know what year it is, do you Mr. Piper? You and I became government employees within six months of each other, and I qualified for my twenty-year retirement pin three months ago."

He was stunned that so much time had gone by. Why, only last week he was thinking that he could have. . .

"Of course with your nice white skin, you wouldn't have had to transfer to the CIA to get the promotion opportunities the rest of us want, would you? And you wouldn't have had to go to the U.S. Navy Language School at Monterey, California for two years to learn Arabic so that you could qualify for a field assignment that would make you eligible for a promotion, would you? And you wouldn't have had to accept an assignment to Lebanon to pose as a local native in a white robe and a burnoose while you tried to find out which of the Islamic crazies were trying to destroy our fantastically moral friends, the Israelis, would you? Well I did have to do all that!"

Wylie was yelling.

Without thinking, Piper snapped, "You poor little tar-baby. It must have been terrible for you"

Unfazed by the insult, Wylie said, "The thing I remember about you was your memory for detail. In a class one day, you challenged the instructor's recall of the events surrounding the end of World War Two and told him the name of every German unit on the border between the Russians and the Americans in 1945 to disprove that his allegation that the American forces couldn't have lost no matter what they had done because of numerical superiority. Can you still remember the names of all those units?"

"Every one of them. And I also remember that I barely got a passing grade in the course," he grumbled.

"That's because you would rather be right than be popular. Well, try this one on for size, then. Can you remember who was killed in the bombing of the American Embassy in Beirut, Lebanon in the 1980's?"

"Of course right I can," he replied. "One of them was an American navy man, an Intelligence Specialist First Class who had volunteered for embassy duty because he wasn't married, and felt that unmarried men like him should take the chances in combat zones. I don't remember his name, but I served with him in Viet Nam. The other man killed was an Army Warrant Officer."

"Who happened to be my brother," Wylie finished. "I went to Lebanon to have a chance to serve beside him and only had the chance to phone him and tell him that I was there, and that was all. The next day he was killed when a van loaded with explosives tore the front off the embassy. So much for feeling sorry for yourself, Mr. Piper."

Wylie's eyes were smoldering with anger. Piper was stern-faced, clenching and unclenching his fists. The two men glared at each other, each seething with anger about their pasts.

It ended as quickly as it has begun. Piper lowered his eyes and said, "I'm sorry about your brother, Mr. Wylie."

Wylie drew in a deep breath. "Yeah, well, back to business." he replied softly, playing with some papers on his desk. "Mr. Cranmoore, or 'Arlo the Great' to some, had a restless night last night. It was probably the chemicals we put in his carafe of water to keep him disoriented. Shame on us for doing that."

"Wait a minute", Piper interrupted. "Why are you talking to me like this? You may remember me from the old days, but why would you open the kimono to me about what you're doing when I don't have a security clearance or a need to know?"

"Get real, why don't you? Where are you going to go with this story? I can have some men come in here from building security at the push of this button." He gestured to a place under the back edge of his desk. "They will escort you, willing or unwilling, down the path, through the iron gate marked "Private" and onto the sidewalk, telling you never to return. If you ever come back into this building, there will be no Myrna out front, no one will have ever heard of me, and if you get someone to open the door at the back of the reception area, it will be a closet. And remember, our roster of names is on the computer now. There are no directory books lying about that have to be collected and shredded. OK? You got the picture now?"

"OK, OK, don't get so fired up! I was just asking. So why am I here?"

"You showed good instincts yesterday. Your records indicate that you scored much higher than average as an interrogator, and had some useful experience when you were in the military."

"But the real advantage of having you question this guy is that it keeps my regular staff out of the line of fire, and it keeps it off the record. First indications are that this guy is a cowboy, and he wasn't hired by one of the regular security services. He had a few suspicious things sewn in the lining of his suit, a wire saw and some lock picks, but the key item here is the little memo book that he was carrying. It has a lot of very secure phone numbers in it, and no regular agency would have allowed him into the field with it in his possession. I mean, hell, he could get run down by a bus and it could fall into entirely the wrong hands. Hang on a second." He tapped on the computer keyboard, stared at the terminal, and then tapped some more.

"What are you looking at, if I may ask? Piper queried. The terminal's screen was still turned so that it faced away from him.

Wylie swiveled the screen so that he could see. On it were a series of phone numbers and a line or two of descriptions following. After one of the numbers it read "Technical Section, Home Office", after another there was written "Central Security Files, MI6, modem". These were very interesting phone numbers indeed!

"Our people have been working since yesterday to analyze the little book of numbers. So far, it appears that they were written in groups, that is, he would write maybe twenty phone numbers then stop.

Then at a later time, he would write twenty more. And, by the way, it is his handwriting. We checked that first off."

"He was reading them from some other source, memorizing them and copying them when he got in the clear. They're in groups of twenty because that's all his memory can reliably work with. Probably uses some kind of association system to remember them. Baby stuff," Piper sniffed.

"And you're some kind of professional, is that right?" Wylie asked.

"I've got a better memory than Cranmoore has," he replied matter-of-factly. "The first page of notes that you showed me, from the top down: The name Franklyn and the number 0227-99385, the name Garza and the number 0755-22908, the word klima and the number 230-05589-701, the word. . ."

"Third from the top, second page," Wylie said, clicking the computer terminal and staring..

"Different format," Piper replied. "Third from the top is a two-digit number, 31, then a name, Baan, then the number 788-2222, then the letters 'H. v.d'. The 31 is the Country Code for Holland, the 'v.d.' is the abbreviation for 'van der' and the 'H.' is the initial of the first name, probably Hendryk or something. Not very complex and not very secure."

"Its Henrietta van der Baan, the Dutch Minister of External Security's number. That's pretty impressive, Mr. Piper. How do you do it?"

"I have no idea, and I don't spend time thinking about it. I just do it, that's all."

After a pause, Wylie asked, "You ready to go to work?"

"Put Cranmoore in an interview room, and give me a few minutes to get prepared, OK?" Piper asked.

Wylie nodded, and stepped out of his office, closing the door behind him.

He read the folder on Cranmoore. Sixty-two years old, etc. etc., lives alone in a flat near The Strand, etc. etc., driving license but no car, etc. etc., had one hundred seventy Pounds Sterling in notes and two pounds sixty pence in coins. Just under $400. He was ready. He stood up, and Wylie came back in the office to show him the way.

As they walked down the pea-green corridor with its over-waxed vinyl tile floors, Wylie said, "Here's some more on the telephone numbers. This guy's really been around. These latest ones were very difficult to trace because they weren't in the computer. And they weren't in the computer because they were our numbers. We didn't put them in our computer because we never considered that we might have to trace one of our own numbers. He even had the ambassador's private line and the duty officer's number in the intelligence center. Not bad for a civilian, right?"

"Not bad for a Russian spy, even." Piper answered.

"They're our friends, now, sir. Don't pick on the poor Russians." Wylie chided with a grin. When they got to the interview room, Big Suit from the previous day was standing outside.

"This is Bob. Bob, this is Lewis Piper. He's going to do the first interviews of Mr. Cranmoore." Turning to Piper, he added, "Since he was kind of woozy yesterday when you brought him in, we kept him as close to that state as possible while we performed a routine physical exam and put the stitches in his cheek. Bob is most likely the only person here, other than you and the medic, that he could ID if he had to, and we want to keep it that way. There's no worry with him identifying you, because he already knows you. Good luck, and if we have any problems with the recording, we'll knock on the door. Just stop what you're doing and answer. If you have problems, just say so out loud, we'll hear you and be right there, OK?"

Bob opened the door to the interview room. It was a metal-covered door about three inches thick. No radio transmissions would leak into or out of this room, that was for sure. No sounds would, either. He entered and the door closed silently behind him with a soft clicking sound at the latch. Cranmoore was dressed in a gray sweatshirt and blue dungaree trousers. His silver mane of hair was neatly combed, but the bandage and swelling on his left cheek detracted somewhat from the handsome middle-aged features. He stood up in his white canvas tennis shoes as he entered and said, "I demand to see my solicitor this instant. You people have no right to. . ."

Piper barked, "Sit down immediately, Mr. Cranmoore! Do not so much as think of getting out of that chair again without my permission, or you will have matching stitches on your other cheek! Nod your head if you understand."

"I understand", Cranmoore stammered, "but you have. . ."

Piper slapped the flat of his hand on the table and glowered at the older man. "I will say this only one more time, sir. Do not speak unless you are given permission! I told you to nod your head if you understood, and I expect you to nod your head. Do you understand, Mr. Cranmoore?"

The gray head nodded in assent, eyes looking at the wooden table-top that separated them.

"My name is Lewis Piper, Mr. Cranmoore, and I am going to ask you some questions. You are going to answer them. When I am satisfied with your responses, you will be allowed to resume your life. If I remain unsatisfied by your responses, you will never be free again. You may respond if you wish."

The words began to tumble from Cranmoore's mouth like grains of rice from a broken sack. "This is all a terrible mistake. I have no idea who you think I am, but I am an ordinary retired person. I spoke to you in that restaurant believing you to be someone else, someone who has lately been a nuisance to a friend of mine. Before I realized that I was speaking to the wrong person, I was cruelly assaulted and dragged off here to the American embassy. Now, I really must protest. There is a very simple explanation for what has happened. The explanation is that I made a mistake in approaching you in a state of agitation, and I have more than paid for it. Now, please let me go this instant before there is a national scandal."

"Is that your response, Mr. Cranmoore?" Piper asked.

Cranmoore nodded in assent.

"The rules here are few in number and very simple, Mr. Cranmoore. I ask the questions, and you give me either truthful answers or silence. If you give me the truth, that is, if you give me a factual answer which can be checked out with the people concerned, then you will be set free and all will be forgotten. If you give me silence, we will then make a decision whether to inject you with drugs to make you talk or simply ignore you. Whatever decision we make, we will make it without any concern for your eventual health and well-being."

"Lying is not permitted. I will not allow it. You either tell the truth or stay silent and accept the consequences. I have read your record. You are a magician, a slight of hand artist. Your hands are slim, smooth and steady. You are proud of those hands, because they are very skilled."

Cranmoore let a small, proud smile cross his lips.

"On the other hand, no pun intended, I have small tremor in my left hand caused by nerve damage from getting shot in Viet Nam. I envy your manual dexterity, and would take great pleasure in destroying it forever. So, every time you lie to us, I am going to cut off the tip of one of your fingers."

Cranmoore was not smiling any more. His face paled visibly, and his hands were clasped to his chest for safekeeping.

"You called me by name when you sat down in the restaurant. There was no mistake on your part, except to get involved in this at all. You threatened to harm Mrs. Carpenter , and you threatened me as well."

Piper fished a small Kershaw knife from his pocket and locked open the longest blade one-handed. It was not even two inches in length, but he knew it would look like a sword to Cranmoore. He leaned across the table and continued menacingly, "So, you owe me the tip of one of your fingers, you lying little queer!" His left hand leaped forward and grabbed the prisoner's right wrist, pinning it to the table. As he moved the knife toward the man's fingers, he rotated the knife so that the dull back part of the blade pressed against the flesh. He put his weight against the man's finger as though he was using the sharp edge of the blade. Cranmoore screamed and thrashed like a fish on a hook, then fainted and fell to the floor.

The door opened and Big Suit popped in the room just as Piper folded the blade and put away the small knife. He knew that when he put on this violent act his face involuntarily twisted into some kind of crazed mask, because others had told him about it. As with many other things, he never spent time analyzing it, because it worked and that was all that mattered. He felt the little twitches in his cheek muscles and his teeth chattered once or twice. Bob was wide-eyed and holding his hands palm out towards Piper saying, "Easy, buddy, just take it easy. Everything's OK now."

Then the mask was gone until the next time.

"Just an act, Bob. I was pressing the dull side of the blade against his finger. It's an old trick, but it can be effective sometimes."

"Jesus, that guy screamed like you had just cut him in half." He was saying this as he looked at Cranmoore's hands to make sure all the pieces were there where they belonged.

"Couldn't have scared him too badly." Piper ventured.

"You're right, at least he didn't crap in his pants," Bob ventured, sniffing the air as he set the man back in the chair and laid his head on the desk. "We haven't got the guy's health records yet, Mr. Piper, so he may have a heart condition. Best go a little easier on him, OK?"

"If he has a heart problem, then he better not get me excited, right?" Piper glowered at Big Suit.

"Yeah, but why did you call him a queer. We have no indications that. . ." Bob started.

"Are you doing the interrogation or am I?" Piper asked with just a hint of a threat.

"OK," Bob replied.

"He's stating to twitch, so he'll be conscious soon. Leave us alone." Bob left, closing the door behind him with a wary look back into the room.

Cranmoore shook awake, and Piper poured him a cup of water from the plastic jug on the table.

"Mr. Cranmoore, I hope that you now realize how very serious I am about your telling me the truth," Piper began.

He began to babble, a good sign. He would make a mistake soon, just like every amateur always did. "But, surely you must understand. This is a matter of national security. I cannot any more betray my country than could any patriotic citizen! You must believe me!"

"Mr. Cranmoore, let me make some things very clear to you." he began. "You have no idea where you are. All you have seen are corridors and rooms. Earlier, you said that you believed that you were in the American embassy. You believe this apparently because I and the other man have American accents. If it makes you happy to believe that, then so be it. But you have now lied to me a second time. There is no national security question involved. That statement is simply a way for you to justify threatening a private citizen on behalf of your masters."

"I'm going to get you a pack of playing cards, Mr. Cranmoore, and let you practice your slight-of-hand alone for thirty minutes. Then, if you don't begin to answer truthfully, I'm going to do as I promised. You owe me the tips of two fingers now, and you can think of that while you play with the cards. You can begin to plan how you will perform your card tricks with two permanently shortened digits."

Piper glowered and snapped the knife blade open in the man's face. Cranmoore gasped, and his eyes rolled back in his head. Then he grabbed his chest, fainted and fell off the chair again.

CHAPTER EIGHT

GINGER TOM

"You can't keep scaring the wits out of this guy, sir! Every time he faints, he's one step closer to a stroke." Bob was grousing as he helped Piper raise the prisoner back into the chair for the second time. Only this time the scene was different. This time, the smell was there.

"Oh, Christ," Bob said. "Thanks for making my day, sir. Now I have to get the guy cleaned up. I don't even change my kid's diapers, and now I have to take care of a grown-up." They squished the man back in the chair and put his head on the table again.

"The smell will probably wake him up. Or maybe it will kill him," Piper observed laconically.

There was a knock at the door and a disembodied female hand waving a spray can of room freshener appeared.

"Get out of here with that!" Piper snapped. "Leave the smell alone. I was raised on a farm and spent eighteen months in Vietnam. I'm used to the smell of manure, and I don't care much about the prisoner's likes and dislikes right now.". Cranmoore started to make moaning sounds once again, so Piper sat back down in his chair as Bob left the room for some fresh air.

"Oh, my lord, what happened? Cranmoore mumbled.

Piper glared at him with his patented scowl. "You are such a pitiful little fruit, trying to play your children's games in a grow-up world," he said condescendingly

"Yes, but what. . .?" the man began, then said, "Oh, my God. I've . . . Oh, no! I'm so embarrassed! Please, can't I clean myself up and get on fresh clothes? Please?" His voice was soft and pleading.

"First, the truth. Then you can clean yourself up."

"I can't think like this. Please, I beg of you. It's only human decency!"

Piper took the pocketknife out, opened the large blade and began to slowly clean under his fingernails. The man's shoulders slumped in dejection.

He was beaten. It showed on his face. He had tried to resist and had fought off the questions as best he could, but it hadn't worked. There was no more courage left, and it had been a piteously small amount at that. The man's eyes looked old and watery and hollow as he realized the position he was in. He had overplayed his hand and disgraced himself.

All because of this dratted American. I will tell a little and hold the rest in reserve. I will begin by telling him only the things he already knows.

"It was Ginger Tom's idea. He called me and said there was this irritating American that was sticking his nose in the regiment's dirty linen and threatening the officers with public disgrace. He said that the regiment's name would be ruined forever because of the indiscretions of a junior officer, or something like that. He told me about you and Major Ross and your friendship with Mrs. Carpenter and about what I was supposed to say, 'Your questions have become an irritation', and 'think of the safety of others as well as yourself'. I have warned off people before, so I have some experience in the matter. You simply step into their domain, invade their privacy as it were, deliver the message and buzz off. I never expected to get assaulted. However, I should have expected it from a bloody American, if I'd been thinking. I was given a document that was marked 'Most Secret'. I was to plant it on you to be discovered by the police if it came to that. As you walked toward the restaurant, I saw you fold the other piece of paper and put it in your pocket. Simply for the challenge, I decided I would transfer the 'Most Secret' stamp onto that paper, confront you with it, then take your paper away with me. I would then have gotten something from you that might be of use to Ginger Tom. I simply never thought that you would attack me, that's where I went wrong."

"Who is Ginger Tom?" he asked.

There was a short pause, then he answered, "Colonel Reeves-Benedict, the colonel of the regiment. We always called him Ginger Tom when we were growing up together."

"Ginger, as in Cockney rhyming slang: Ginger Beer. In other words, Queer?" Piper asked.

"Not that I know of," the man continued, wincing at the reference. "I certainly fancied him and I let him know of my feelings on any number of occasions, but I guess I just wasn't his type.

Congratulations, Piper, you got that one right

"At least that's how I have comforted myself," Cranmoore continued. "No, we called him that because his hair had a reddish tint when he was younger, and he was quite a ladies man and was always 'tom-catting' about after them. And of course, Thomas is one of his Christian names."

A little shiver of distaste ran down Piper's spine at the thought of being "fancied" by another man.

"There is a batman that the colonel arranges to have assigned to anyone that he is concerned about. His name is Corporal Samuels. He's the one who gave me the secret paper to plant on you. He's really quite a lovely lad. Such soft hands. Reminds me of myself when I was younger. He could have a career in the business if he wanted it, but he's more the leather trade, I fear. At any rate, Samuels told the colonel about your lunch, the colonel phoned me on the little cellular that I was given as a gift, and I was off in a taxi, picked up the papers from Samuels and was waiting across the street before you went inside."

Samuels gave him the paper to plant. The colonel called him on the cellular phone. Pretty conclusive evidence, if it can be checked out.

"How many people have you warned off for the colonel in the past?"

"Well, let me see. There was the Spanish friend of Captain Mozier, the dancer who fancied Lieutenant Tuttle, the decorator friend of Lieutenant Mason. . . I think that is all, with the exception of yourself, of course."

"And these were all homosexuals, is that right?"

"I have no idea. I do not pry into people's private lives." Cranmoore was beginning to look pleased with himself now. He was reliving the breaking up of other people's love lives, and he seemed to be enjoying it. He would have to be stopped.

"Is everybody in the army a fruit?" Piper asked, getting as much venom in the words as he could.

"What an incredibly rude suggestion!" Cranmoore flustered. "There are many ways of expressing love without being crude and engaging in name-calling. And it always comes from the people who are too ignorant to admit that other possibilities exist."

"Or it comes from people who find the whole process so disgusting as to be beneath their contempt. You are dismissed, now, and will be escorted back to your quarters while I assess the truthfulness of your statements. You can tell me the rest later."

"But I have told you everything! There is no more to tell. May I go home now, please?" the man asked in begging tones.

"Twenty numbers at a time," Piper said.

"Pardon?"

"You read twenty numbers at a time from the list, assign one number to each of your fingers and toes, then copy them into your own book as soon as you are alone. There are better ways, of course, but you made quite an impressive list of your own in that little green book of yours. I assume that was to be your insurance policy in case one of your friends made a problem for you. A word of caution for the future, Mr. Cranmoore, assuming that we let you have a future. Never carry your insurance policy on your person at any time unless you want to invite disaster. We have you, and we have your secrets. Essentially, your life is of no value to us. Do you understand?"

Cranmoore nodded glumly.

"In the meantime, you will be taken to your room where you can get washed up and put on clean clothes. We will speak with you later."

"But I told you everything! Ginger Tom will be furious with me. Oh, please don't tell him I gave away his secret. He will never forgive me."

Bob led the little man away in tears.

Piper sat in the empty room and mulled what had just been learned. The colonel, Ginger Tom or Reeves-Benedict, was prepared to use violence to keep an unknown American from asking about Lieutenant Gurney. What had Gurney done to this man?

Bob poked his head around the door. "The boss wants to see you. Come with me please."

Back in Wylie's office, he came right to the point. "OK, so now we know that this colonel, Reeves-Benedict, is the one that sent the magician to warn you off. But we don't know of any reason for him to warn you off."

Yes, we do have a reason. I just didn't bother to tell you about it earlier, Piper mulled.

"This is where you are supposed to speak up and tell me what the hell's going on. I can get you a room here alongside Cranmoore's if you need time to think about it." Wylie said with a frown. Then he added, "I'm waiting."

There was no reason to be evasive. The embassy's security staff had been very helpful. Wylie was a smart man, and he'd played it straight. So he told him the rest of the story. All about Ross and the Bunker Operation with Gurney and his cameras. All about how upset the colonel had been. At the mention of Gurney's name, Wylie's head jerked up.

Piper saw the sudden move and took advantage of the opening. "What's Gurney all about?" he asked.

"He's a piece of work, that's what he is." Wylie replied quickly, repeating the story about the school bus attack. "Gurney was arrested on an anonymous telephone tip. O'Flynn just walked in off the street and turned himself in. Anyway, that's what one of my counterparts in MI5 confided to me over a bottle of claret one evening. Gurney was sitting in a hotel room in Carlisle, just on the English side of the Scottish border when he was arrested."

"Does the Parachute Brigade have a training area near Carlisle?" Piper asked. Wylie wanted to know why he asked, so he told him about the invitation that Gurney supposedly got from Two Para. Wylie had no idea whether there was a training area near the city, and didn't offer to find out.

"I read a newspaper story about O'Flynn, and it said he was captured in a raid on an apartment in Knightsbridge or somewhere," Piper ventured.

"That was just a cover story to explain how they came to have him in custody," Wylie volunteered. "I'm convinced this guy told me the truth, that O'Flynn just walked in off the street and turned himself in."

"You said something else about Gurney," Piper asked.

"I was saying that his story made no sense from the beginning." Wylie continued. "He was a young American naval officer on exchange duty with the British army. No suspicious things in his past. He carried a Top Secret (Special Intelligence) security clearance with compartmented clearances in Special Operations, Surface Warfare and Communications. They investigate your bathroom habits before you get one of those clearances. Then he goes nuts and blows up a school bus full of diplomat's kids. It's totally insane conduct. But what is even more curious is the way the crime was prosecuted. The trial was conducted by a British court under guidelines established by the Prevention of Terrorism Act and the Official Secrets Act. The normal procedure that should have been followed would be for the offender to be arrested and turned over to the American government for trial under American law. The Status of Forces Agreement between Britain and the United States should have taken precedence. But the British insisted on trying him themselves, and then insisted that he be moved to an American prison 'for his own safety'. And yet, O'Flynn, who supposedly executed the attack with Gurney is made a part of the general prison population somewhere with all the other IRA stoolies awaiting a new identity."

'There were no suspicious things at all Gurney's past?" Piper asked, remembering what Barker had told him.

"There were no suspicious things in our records," Wylie replied. "Why? Do you know something? By the way, are you the one that got the DOD interested in Gurney?"

"It's possible," Piper replied.

"That's what the secure phone calls to Dr. Barker were about?"

"Can I change the subject?" Piper asked. He didn't want to talk about Barker if it could be avoided. Wylie could make him tap-dance in a mine field if he wanted to, so he thought it best to be polite to the man.

To his relief, Wylie nodded an OK.

"What about the man O'Flynn? Where did they put him? Maybe the Brits would let us talk to him. He might know what all the fuss was about over Gurney," Piper said.

"I'll ask someone to check for us." Wylie said, and began to type on the computer's keyboard.

"Why did they want Gurney to be tried by a British court, but didn't want him to be imprisoned in Britain? Why would they do that?", he asked.

"The simplest answer to that lies in the concept of 'closed court'. We don't have that in American law. We can't try people in secrecy in the US, but they can do it in Britain under the auspices of the Prevention of Terrorism Act. However, in Britain, once the person is put in prison thing begin to reverse themselves. Under British law, no one can be locked away in solitary confinement unless they're insane; in the US we can do this in certain cases. So you use the best of both worlds and try him in secret, then ship him to Marion, Illinois, and keep him in solitary confinement. And it's all quite legal. We have no access to the records of the trial because of the Official Secrets Act and Gurney can't talk to anyone because he's in solitary confinement."

"I wonder what on Earth he would talk about if he could?" Piper asked. Then he straightened up and answered himself in a mock-serious tone as though he were the Pentagon's public relations officer. "He would talk about subjects likely to compromise highly-sensitive ongoing security efforts or make utterances which would the impugn the dignity and competence of Her Majesty's Government."

"Well done, Mr. Piper! Very well done, indeed. That's exactly what the British government would say if we were to inquire. However there might be another possibility." Wylie drummed his fingers on the table in thought.

Maybe Wylie's gonna go snooping, he thought with enthusiasm.

In response to his telephoned request, a rail-thin young man knocked once and entered Wylie's office.

"Yes, sir?" he asked timorously. He must have been in his late-twenties, but he looked much younger. He was wearing khaki cotton trousers and a yellow, wrinkled long-sleeved shirt buttoned all the way up to the neck. He had shoulder-length mouse-brown hair.

"That school bus bombing. . ." Wylie began.

"Thirteen months ago. Yes sir. What about it? I mean, what do you want me to. . ." the young man babbled nervously.

"Run me a chronology of the actions surrounding the bombing. I want. . ."

"It was actually a rocket attack, sir, as opposed to a bombing per se. The perpetrators used an anti-tank missile. If they had actually bombed the vehicle, then there would have been a large. . .""

"Yes, yes, I understand. Pay attention, Marcus. I want a time-list of all the events on paper so that I can visualize the things that went on and the sequence in which they occurred. I want it to include timelines on the movements of the American naval officer, Gurney, and the Irishman, O'Flynn, and all the police and security force goings-on that you can trace."

"What level of authorization do I have, sir?"

"The same level of authorization that you have for that program insert you've put in the Ladbrokes's betting shop computer. You have no authorization whatever. If you get caught where you're not supposed to be, I'll drop you in it up to your neck."

The young man looked downcast, but Piper couldn't tell whether it was because his extracurricular activities on the Ladbrokes's computer had been discovered or because he was being asked to something else that was semi-illegal.

"I'll sweeten the pot for you, Marcus. If you do this successfully without setting off any alarms, I will find the funds to buy you one of those multiple-CPU notebook computers you have been wanting."

"With two of the three hundred megahertz CPUs?" he asked expectantly.

"I'll get you one that has four of the CPUs if you succeed," Wylie responded.

Smiling broadly at the thought of the new computer, the young man blurted, "I'll start right this minute, sir! Oh, when do you need this, sir?"

"Within ten minutes would be fine, thank you, Marcus."

The smile disappeared first, then the young man vaporized after it, closing the door behind him.

"Everything with you is 'ten minutes', isn't it?" Piper smiled.

"You gotta give 'em goals, or they won't ever know what they can do. Let's go to the canteen and have a cup of tea, shall we?"

Piper was feeling quite comfortable with this middle-aged, divorced, harried black man, and he was obviously tolerable about his being there. They were barely seated when Marcus showed up and handed Wylie a thick manila folder. The young man was smiling broadly.

"He didn't do it," the young man said, still smiling. "Let me show you," he added, opening the folder and pointing to the top paper on the stack inside. Wylie moved it out of his reach.

"How about letting me be the judge of that, Marcus?"

"Eight minutes," Marcus replied.

"What?" Wylie responded.

"Eight minutes," Marcus answered, still grinning broadly. "You owe me a new four-banger three-hundred-megahertz computer, man!" he gushed.

"So go down to the supplies room and sign for it, and they'll hand it over."

"You mean you had it here all this time?"

"It's been here for two months, Marcus."

"And you didn't tell me? Why not?"

"Because you hadn't done anything to earn it. Now you have, so go get it and put it to good use, OK?"

"But. . ." the young man began, still wanting more of an explanation.

"You're wasting time, Marcus. You could be on-line right now if you had left earlier."

"Oh, right. That's true. OK. Gotta run. And, thanks again, sir." The young man turned, narrowly avoided a collision with a stunningly beautiful young woman, and never even glanced at her figure as he sped away toward the supply room.

Nodding first at the departing stick-figure named Marcus, then at the thick folder in Wylie's hand, Piper asked, "That guy did all this in eight minutes?" That's impossible. Nobody could do that in eight minutes.

"Nah, he probably had it already stripped out on the computer in an electronic folder of some kind. All he did was print it out and try to make us think he was a genius, that's all." Wylie was smiling at the thought, and sucking on his cup of tea.

Moving back to his office, Wylie sat down at the table rather than his desk. He opened the folder and began to read, passing each document over to Piper when he was finished. There was a color Xerox copy of the navy lieutenant's ID card. It was the first time he had seen the man's face. He was wearing the dark blue shirt and the black tie of what was called the Winter Working Uniform -- known in the navy as the SS uniform, because of the all-black look that it had. It was worn with a windbreaker jacket, not a suit coat. The collar showed the double silver bars of a full lieutenant. The face looked young and confident, nothing at all like a man who blew up school busses.

The ten pages of the timeline chart showed an hourly scale down the left margin. To the right of each time was a description of the event that had taken place at the designated hour and minute.

"Let's start with something that could not be faked or changed by anybody." Wylie had put his glasses on reluctantly and was flipping through the pages of the timeline rapidly. "Here is an event that can be confirmed by several unimpeachable sources. It's the time of the attack on the bus: 5:38 PM on the seventeenth."

The timeline showed it as 1738 hours, in the 24 hour military clock. Using military time, no one has to say AM or PM, because 1200 hours is noon, 1300 hours is 1:00 PM, and so forth.

"The largest variation we ever saw in the reported time of the attack was two minutes, and that can easily be explained by the fact that the witnesses' watches simply weren't set to the correct time," Wylie explained. Flipping forward more pages, he continued, "Now what did the genius Marcus see that caused him to say that he couldn't have done it?" He had gone forward too many pages, and had to flip backward through the list until he found it.

And there it was. Marcus, the computer genius, had even made a handwritten note alongside just to make sure everyone understood. It read "London to Carlisle: 301 miles". The notation was adjacent to the log entry that read, "1915 hours, Carlisle. Knocked on door of room 226 at Carlton House Hotel. Suspect Thomas E. Gurney opened the door and was taken into custody without a struggle by members of the Special Branch."

From 1738 to 1915 is one hour and thirty-seven minutes. Nobody could have left the scene of the explosion, traveled three hundred miles, checked into a hotel and been sitting there waiting to be arrested in one hour and thirty-seven minutes. Nobody. Not even Superman. OK, maybe Superman. Look for the blue tights with the big red S.

Gurney had been framed.

Then railroaded into jail.

Then hustled off to prison in the US.

But why? Just because some colonel didn't like him? It made no sense.

Piper began to look through a stack of the other papers when he found a document titled Room Inventory, Prince Henry Barracks. One item read: Contents of Trunk found in suspect Gurney's quarters. There was a picture of an open navy-type foot-locker. Gurney's name was clearly stenciled on the side, along with his service number. The attached list showed the contents: four twelve-volt motorcycle batteries, twenty-eight blocks of C4 explosive, three spools of electrical wire, four electronic timing devices, pliers, wire-cutters, a bullet-proof vest, a pair of boots, two dress shirts (white), a tie (color not noted), and a navy greatcoat. There was another list that showed the remaining items found in the room. Bed, chairs, table, sheets, towels, curtains; all the items were listed and described in detail.

"Strawberries," Piper said softly to himself.

"Strawberries?" Wylie queried.

Wylie looked at the papers again and exclaimed to Piper's amazement, "Of course, strawberries. Captain Queeg in The Caine

Mutiny using sand to represent the strawberries that he said the mess attendants had eaten. Where's the rest of Gurney's belongings that would have normally been here in the trunk? Where are the summer uniforms, the working khakis, the full-dress uniform? Where are his shoes and underwear? Where's his sword, for Christ's sake? Damn, Piper, you are really busting this thing wide open."

"And what happened to all his cameras?" he managed to insert. The only problem in working with really intelligent people is that you don't get to be a know-it-all very often. Sad, but true. Obviously, Wylie was also an old-movie fan. And smart as well.

"Maybe there's a more complete list somewhere else of the contents of the lieutenant's room. Perhaps they were found in a cabinet or something," Piper began. "But wait, it wouldn't make any difference, would it?"

"No, it wouldn't." Wylie affirmed. "Because if they were found in a cabinet in a corner of the room, it would only mean that someone had removed them from the foot locker to make room for the batteries and explosives and so forth. Batmen do the packing and unpacking, so it doesn't matter where the remainder of his uniforms are. What matters is the fact that someone removed them and put the contraband in its place."

"Perhaps Gurney removed the uniforms himself, and actually did hide the explosives in his own foot locker," Piper offered with a trace of sadness in his voice.

"Didn't happen." Wylie said firmly. "If he had gotten the stuff in Belfast before the trip back, he'd have put it in some other container so it couldn't be tied directly to him. If he'd gotten the stuff once he was back in barracks, there would have been a zillion places he could have hidden it other than his foot locker. No, somebody planted it on him. Remember, he wasn't back in London long enough to get settled in. He was off to Scotland almost immediately to that supposed meeting with the Parachute Brigade. And his batman, Delk, had been arrested and delayed so that he wouldn't be there to pack and unpack his belongings."

Suddenly, the computer terminal made a beeping sound and Wylie got up and moved over behind his desk. He picked up the phone while looking at the computer's screen.

Wylie came back to the table and sat down. "We've just gotten a nasty phone call from the British government's Home Office. They claim that we're holding a British citizen by the name of Cranmoore as a hostage here in the embassy, and they are highly pissed off about it. They say we better cough him up or there will be leaks to the newspapers. The ambassador has told them that he has no knowledge of such a person, which he doesn't, and that he will check into the matter. We have until tomorrow morning to let him go."

They looked at each other

"I'm going to have to turn Cranmoore loose tomorrow. You understand that, don't you?" Wylie asked.

"Unless you can convince him that it's in his best interests to assist us with our inquiries, as the British police always say," Piper responded.

"What more can we possibly hope to get out of him?" Wylie asked.

"Look, the guy is a retired low-level show-biz type that's got a good friend who's up to his neck in this business about Gurney. All these guys are connected together. What do you bet that the colonel sent someone to the restaurant to find out what happened? He finds out about the fight, and the waiter remembers that we took a taxi. Maybe he overheard me tell the driver to take us to the American embassy. Then he simply calls another old school chum in the Home Office and says, 'Why, these American blighters are being just beastly to old Arlowe over nothing at all. Can't you do something about it? His mother's just worried sick about him, and her heart's not been too good of late' and so on and so on."

"Whoops! I missed a clue. Hang on a second." Wylie went back to his desk and snatched up the phone, quickly dialing a five-digit extension. "Tell me what the first message from the Home Office said, and tell me why it wasn't in my PROFS folder," he barked into the mouthpiece. "Uh-huh. That's what I thought. No, not now. I'll get back to you later in the day."

95

"There was no first message. This is significant." he began. "Historically, the first message dealing with someone the Brits think that we may have snatched always says something very British-like, such as 'There's been a chap reported missing by his family. He's one of our free-lance lads, and we thought you might be able to shed some light on the subject.' This gives us a chance to speak obliquely about the fact that the only person currently of interest to us is a man we caught trying to sell dope to one of our security officers, for example. Then they go away and decide if they really want to make a fuss. If they do, then they send message number two, the one that says 'You've got him and we want him now. If you don't comply, we will drop you in the crap with the newspapers.' Then we make an ambassador-level decision as to whether we want to fight or not. The significance is that this time they started with message number two."

"What does that mean to us?" Piper asked.

"Again, simply put, I think it means that this man has sensitive information that they don't want us to sweat out of him, and that the longer we have him the better chance we have of finding out what he knows," Wylie replied.

Piper's mind was racing ahead, as it frequently did at times like this. "It's the pictures," he said softly. "Get Cranmoore in the Interview Room. I want to ask him a question, OK?"

"Why not just bust into his room?" Wylie asked. "I'll get Bob to open the door, you rush in and ask your question, then leave. That ought to shake him up a bit."

Bob appeared as if by magic, and the two of them went down a flight of stairs and through a locked metal door. It opened onto a corridor, green like all the others, vinyl tile floors, wax buildup in the corners, and several "Guest Rooms" on either side with metal doors. Two men in slacks and pullovers stood at opposite ends of the corridor. They nodded to Bob. "Here we are," he said, stopping at a door and snapping open the peep-hole. Inside, Cranmoore looked up expectantly.

Bob unlocked the door quickly and Piper rushed into the room, grabbed Cranmoore by the shirt front and pinned him against the wall. "You've got the PICTURES, you little weasel! Where are they? Tell me or I'll. . ."

Cranmoore struggled and held his hands over his face. "Please don't hit me again! I DON'T have the pictures. What do you think this is all about, for God's sake? If I had the pictures, I would have given them to Ginger Tom. How would I have gotten them anyway. I only. . ."

Piper dropped Cranmoore and zipped out of the room. Bob locked the door behind him. "Well, done, sir. You do have good instincts, just as Mr. Wylie says."

As they made their way back to Wylie's office, Piper asked, "Bob, what's Wylie's first name?"

"Mister," Bob answered seriously.

Wylie received the report of the interview with interest.

Piper began to lecture, a bad habit of his when he got excited. "The colonel must believe that Gurney, the amateur photographer who always went on movements with a camera, had taken some pictures on that last operation in Belfast that the colonel doesn't want made public. We know that Gurney didn't recognize the significance of what he had seen, because he would have immediately told someone about it. My opinion, Mr. Wylie, is that he had taken a picture of something without knowing its significance. What would Gurney have done with the film?" Then he answered his own question. "He would unload all the film from each of the cameras that he used, and send it out to be developed," he responded. "Exposed film is more sensitive to temperature and radiation that unexposed film, so you need to get it processed as soon as possible. You don't have to get it printed, mind you, just developed. This stabilizes the film. Developed film is much less likely to. . ." He stopped in mid-sentence as Wylie tapped firmly on the table with a pencil.

"I think I've got it now," he said with a smile.

Piper's eye's lit up as he figured out even more. "He would have sent the film out to be developed the minute he got back to London," he said. "He wouldn't have had time to get it developed in Belfast, because they left the following day or soon thereafter. He probably had the photo boys with the regiment developing and printing the stuff during the deployment, but he couldn't use them at that time because all their gear would have been packed away for shipment back to barracks!"

"So, you're saying that he would have turned it in at a commercial processing house here in London immediately after he arrived back, right? But wouldn't there be security implications attached to the pictures?" Wylie asked. "He wouldn't have just taken them to the local photo kiosk and dropped them in the slot, would he?"

"No, he would have taken them somewhere that would treat them very confidentially, like a place that specialized in processing for the professional photographer. These places would never make a copy or tell anybody anything, because professional photographs are always copyrighted material. These custom processors charge more for their work, but they are absolutely reliable in keeping a secret. Their whole business relies on confidentiality. They process stuff like the pictures of the new fall fashions and things like that. Things that are very sensitive to the industry. Holy smokes, that must be it! He dropped off the film, but never returned to pick it up!"

"Yes, but would they, whoever they are, still have the pictures after more than a year?" Wylie asked.

"Of course they would, because they are British and the Brits don't throw things away," Piper answered. "As an example, Gieves and Hawke, the men's tailor at Number One Saville Row still have the paper patterns of the uniforms that Captain Bligh of the H.M.S. Bounty ordered in the eighteenth century. The British actor, Charles Laughton, had them tailor a uniform from the original patterns for him when he played Bligh in 'Mutiny of the Bounty' in the thirties. So, this film would be the property of the photographer, and if he died, for example, it would be a part of his estate."

"I'll supply a cubicle for you to work from and get you a telephone and the London Yellow Pages. If you're going to work out of here, you'll need an ID badge." Wylie found a form in his desk and wrote Piper's name on it and some other indecipherable information. "Get down to the ID section for the badge. You don't have clearances, so you'll have to be escorted everywhere in the building, but that's the best I can do for now. Janet!"

A forty-ish blond woman popped her face in the door.

"Janet, this is Mr. Piper. You and he are going to call every photo processor in the London metropolitan area and ask whether they have any unclaimed photos that are under the name of Thomas Gurney. They would have been put in for processing about thirteen or fourteen months ago. Mr. Piper will join you as soon as I get him a badge."

"I'm on it Mr. Wylie," she said and disappeared.

"Must be nice to have a cooperative staff," Piper smiled.

"Yeah, well, this is good duty, Mr. Piper, and they know that I know all the bad duty stations where I can see to it they get sent. I know 'em because I've been there. Now go get the badge, then get busy and find the pictures while I come up with a way to keep Arlo the Great on ice for the time being." Wylie said.

Piper scurried off happily to the ID section and got his badge. Then he found Janet's cubicle, and sat down in the extra chair by the phone.

Nancy! He'd forgotten about Nancy. He couldn't keep trucking back and forth to Sidcup each day because it would waste too much time. He'd have to get a room near the embassy temporarily. And he'd have to find a way to explain what he was doing. And why he'd rather be here than with her.

He'd do it later.

CHAPTER NINE

MARION

First thing the next morning, after having made his excuses to Nancy the night before by phone, Piper continued wading through the London Yellow Pages, calling all the photo processors. Janet was through the D's, so he took E and F. For three straight hours, the conversations were the same:

"Good Morning, Very British Photo Processing"

"Hello, this is Mr. Gurney. I'm trying to find some film that I had processed over a year ago that I never picked up. The film was put in by one of my firm's associates who is no longer with us. I've been on an overseas assignment for a year and want to get my pictures. Could you check for me please?"

Short pause while phone-person checks the record. "I'm sorry, sir, but we have nothing under the name of Gurney on our records."

"Could you check as to whether you have any unclaimed processing under any name that was turned in about a year ago for processing?"

"I'm sorry sir, but all our processing accounts are current as of the moment. The oldest unclaimed processing we have is less than a month old. Sorry I couldn't help."

And so it went. All the people were very polite. None of them had ever heard of Thomas Gurney or seen his film. Janet, his cubicle-mate, was having the same results.

After lunch, he called Barker. "How you doing today, Jim?" he said as the phone was answered.

"Nice of you to get back to me before I retired, Lew," came the grouchy response.
"Hang on while I clear away some things." He was unceremoniously put on hold. After a pause, "I need to discuss some things with you.

Give me your extension there and sit tight. I'll call you back in less than ten minutes."

Yes, you'll call me back after you make sure that I'm really at the embassy in person, not giving out an embassy extension that's really routed to Vladivostok by way of AUTOVON and two cellular links. Always the careful one, is Jim.

"Yeah, OK. I'll be right here."

Perhaps five minutes passed before the phone rang. "This is Lewis Piper," he answered.

"Wonderful, just wonderful, Lew!" Jim's voice chided sarcastically. "You've forgotten that you're supposed to answer with only the five-digit extension! You should have picked up the receiver, announced the extension, then waited for the click that . . ."

". . .indicates that the call-monitor had kicked in, yes, I know, Jim. Sorry to have been so anxious to talk with you. What's got you on the rag today?"

"I am reminded that Murphy's Laws of Combat has an entry that goes like, 'There is nothing more dangerous than a brand-new second lieutenant with a compass and a map'. You are my new second lieutenant, Lew. You are ruining what little sleep I get. How you manage to get involved in these messes is beyond me. Ordinary people don't have these kinds of problems."

He took a deep breath and tried to relax. Jim was on a roll. It would be a long conversation, and he would get to do all the listening. "Get it off your chest, Jim," he said.

"Don't tell me what to do!" the voice snapped. "My plate was full already, and now it's overflowing, thanks to you," Jim continued. "Actually, it's not really your fault that I am so harried, but you are the only one I can chew on right now so you get to carry the can. First, it is now very apparent that Lt. Gurney was unlawfully convicted of whatever it was."

"Wait a minute, do you mean. . ?"

"Shut up and listen, Lew! Yes, it means that since we reviewed the events timeline surrounding the attack, it showed that Gurney could not have possibly been at the site of the school bus attack. That said, we've had to accept the fact that our British counterparts may have been a bit overzealous in their actions. But we still have to deal with the evidence that was found in his foot locker."

Wylie obviously put all the stuff we talked about on the computer, and now everybody in the world with the correct security clearance has access to the information.

"And now the foot-locker contents have been called into question because of what the CIA calls the 'strawberry theory'. Something to do with the fact that Gurney couldn't have put all that incriminating stuff in his locker without disposing of most of his uniforms, his dress sword, and a bunch of other stuff he would have needed at a later time. And nobody can find out what happened to the stuff, because the guy who did the packing and unpacking isn't around anymore. He's supposedly serving with a detachment of the regiment that's on duty in Belize right now, so we've sent one of our people from the Mexico City station to ask him a few questions. We should have answers in twenty-four hours at the most."

"Now the problem we face is how to get the record cleared and get Gurney released from prison. He's under a foreign conviction and sentencing which carries no provision for parole or sentence reduction. He can't be pardoned, except by the Queen, and nobody on the British side is about to go visit her and make that request , because she might ask any number of embarrassing questions. By the way, is next Monday a holiday or something in Britain? We can't find anybody that plans to be at work there until next Wednesday or Thursday. Anyhow, the only way that the lawyers here can see for him to get free is by retrial, and again, the British aren't too thrilled by that prospect either."

"Jim?"

"What?"

"Why don't you just get a tame federal judge to issue a release order, take it to the prison in Marion and make them turn him loose?"

"Jesus Christ, Lew! It must be nice to live in such a simple world! '. . .and the prince and the princess were married and lived happily ever after.' If we were to do something like that, the British would. . ." Then followed a list of all the bad things that would happen:

• The American F-111s at RAF Lakenheath would all have to find somewhere else to live.

• The navy's intercept station and submarine replenishment base at Holy Loch, Scotland would have to be vacated.

• No American rock stars would be given visas to perform in the UK (which means, under the Reciprocal Artist's Agreement between the two countries, that no British stars would be allowed to perform in the US).

• Masterpiece Theater would have to be canceled.

And on and on, ad nauseum.

This only served to remind Piper of one more reason why he hated bureaucrats and their ilk. And the ilk of their ilk.

"So why did you want to speak with me, Jim?"

"Two things. The first thing is about hospital visitors that may have spoken to my niece. The daily reports show nothing out of the ordinary. All the staff that were on duty were exactly who they were supposed to be. The only thing out of the ordinary was a tall British military type that just appeared in the ward and wandered about for a while. He never gave a name, but they asked him to leave after he spoke to several of the injured children and seemed to frighten them. Description is tall, as I said, regimental tie, mustache, dark reddish hair and. . ."

The colonel! The colonel went to the hospital to survey the results of his work and harass the victims. He truly is a monster!

"And the second thing?" Piper asked.

"Oh, yeah. You're just the kind of nosy guy that might be able to figure this out. There's interest in certain sectors here as to what Gurney might have seen on his exchange visit with the Army in Northern Ireland. I thought maybe you could find out if someone might be willing to cough up any of the pictures he took during his watch. I understand he was quite a camera-bug, and took photographs all the time."

"Gee, Jim, that's a great idea. Why didn't I think of that?"

"You sarcastic turd! OK, OK, you already thought of it. Any luck?"

"We just now started. We are in the process of calling all of the photo developers in London. We think that because Gurney was a bit of a professional, he would have put the film in for developing immediately upon returning here." He watched Janet methodically checking off the names in the Yellow Pages as she called.

"What are you rambling on about, Lew? I mean all the pictures he took, not just the last ones! What's so special about the last ones?"

"They are special because they're the ones that caused the problem, Jim. It's what he saw, and what he possibly took pictures of that are causing all the difficulties. I'm sure of it." He told him about how upset the colonel had been, and how he had chewed Major Ross out when he'd never even blinked before.

"So what did Gurney see?"

"I have to level with you, Jim, all I have is hearsay. Gurney told Ross that he had seen an IRA terrorist by the name of O'Flynn across the street, but that he didn't have a chance to get a shot off because a small group of people had gathered and his line of sight got blocked or something. Again, the easiest way to find out is to go see Gurney and ask him, Jim."

"Can't be done. He's serving the first part of his sentence as a sequestered prisoner. That means that no outside contact is allowed for the first two years of his incarceration. Nobody's allowed to speak with him except the prison staff and his attorney."

"So ask his attorney to speak with him."

"Can't be done. He doesn't have any further business before the court, so his attorney's been dismissed. He won't get another until it's time for his appeal to be filed."

"Then get one of the staff to ask him."

"They don't want to talk to him; they want to hang him for killing all those children."

"And since we know that he didn't kill them, that would be lynching, wouldn't it, Jim? It's real easy to see why all those Nazis on trial at Nuremberg were able to say 'I was only following orders' with a clear conscience, isn't it?"

"You smug, self-satisfied, son-of-a. . ."

"I'm sorry, Jim. I was out of order on that, and I apologize," he said quickly. "Correct me if I'm wrong, but isn't the purpose of sequestering a prisoner to keep him from transferring current highly sensitive security information to another prisoner who might then blab it to an outsider? I would bet that after more than a year of being locked up, first in Britain and then there in the US, he doesn't have a single thing that he could reveal that would threaten an ongoing operation. After all, the IRA and the British aren't fighting right now. They are in the middle of peace negotiations and are operating under a mutually agreed truce. Over half of the British troops have been withdrawn from Northern Ireland. So there aren't any ongoing operations there, right?

"Yeah, I guess you're right about that."

"So if you were to go to the British and ask for an end to sequestering, they would have to agree on the grounds of reasonableness, right?"

"Sounds good to me, so far."

"Now, suppose they won't agree. Wouldn't they have to tell you what ongoing operations stood a chance to be compromised?"

"In a perfect world, they would. But these are our faithful British allies we're talking about, Lew. They can just tell us that we have to abide by the terms of the transfer agreement or take the consequences of breaking the rules."

"How about sending them a UNODIR?" Piper queried. "Send the British a message that says UNless Otherwise DIRected, Gurney comes off sequestering immediately, and processing begins for his near-term release from custody. 'Current information shows clearly that he could not have been involved in the crime of which he was convicted; Freedom restricted is freedom denied; Unjust imprisonment is not to be tolerated because of inconvenience to the judicial system, etc., etc.,' things like that. They'll have a fit, but they will have to act on your schedule rather than theirs. And it might smoke out their contact over here in London as well."

"It stinks. It's a rotten idea. It will never work. I wish I had thought of it first," he replied. "I'll be in touch, Lew. Thanks. And say hello to what's-her-name for me, OK?" he added, sounding tired but grateful as he hung up.

"Yes, Carol?" The efficient looking administrative assistant had been standing quietly as he finished his call with Piper.

"Who's in prison?" she asked without thinking. She would regret it immediately.

"Are you having a good time eavesdropping on my official phone calls, Carol?" he asked. He was not smiling.

"I'm sorry. I couldn't help but hear you say. . ."

"No, of course you couldn't, you poor thing. When you open the door to my office without knocking, you have no way of knowing what I might be doing, do you? And then when you walk directly over to my desk and stand there in front of it like a god damned statue it's practically impossible to not overhear what I'm talking about, isn't it?"

The woman was looking at him and frowning.

"Open the door to my office," he said.

"And leave, is that it?" she responded coolly.

"No, just open the door to my office and then come back and have a seat. It's a new concept for you, I'm sure. It's called doing what you're told to do! Now open my office door, please."

Carol did as she was told. "I don't need to take a seat. I just need to leave these budget figures with you for review and modification."

He was having none of that from this little office viper. "Let's play a little game, Carol. Let's pretend that I'm a GS-23 and a Department Head and you are a newly-promoted GS-12 Administrative Assistant."

"Administrative Supervisor," she corrected, smirking at his error.

He continued, ignoring her attitude. "The following is a direct personal instruction to you, Carol Thomas, GS-12 Administrative Supervisor. Never enter my office again without knocking. When you get permission to enter, always leave the door open so that the people passing by in the hall may see and hear what is going on inside. I am making this an informal admonition, and if you so much as grit your teeth at me I will make it a formal one and haul you before the Disciplinary Committee. I know about your little games with the staff, Carol. You are carrying folders with the department budget figures that were rejected by the congressional liaison office yesterday. They have to be corrected and resubmitted by Friday. If anyone stops you as you wander about, you just show them the folders and tell them you are looking for whatever name pops into your mind. This way you can spend your whole day wandering about snooping and doing nothing useful."

"I'm leaving," she announced. "I don't have to put up with. . ." She had seen people looking in the office door. She knew they were lurking out of sight listening to every word being spoken by this horrible man.

"Don't even think about getting out of that chair, Carol Thomas, GS-12 Administrative Supervisor. You are to stay until I dismiss you."

"You can't talk to me like this. I'm a career employee. I'm not on probationary tenure, I have a career path," she countered with a slight tremor in her voice.

"Carol Thomas, GS-12 Administrative Supervisor, I know that these little tricks of yours are the reason that you were able to discover that Frank Chamblee in Accounting and Finance had a bookie and was making illegal calls from his office. You just popped in without knocking and caught him at it. And I realize that you got a letter of commendation and your picture in the newsletter for turning him in to the security office. You aren't a heroine in my book, you are a snoop, nothing more. Now get out of my sight and take the financial reports to where they actually belong."

As she rose, she could hear the scurry of feet as people fled out of earshot from hallway near the door.

"And don't slam the door on your way out."

She slammed the door anyway.

Why do I put up with this crap, day after day? he wondered. All this endless frustration. And I have a PhD and am a Department head. I can imagine what it's like down in the trenches. I hope the staff liked the show with Carol, it was the least I could do for them. All the talk about budget cuts and layoffs must be driving them crazy.

That stupid Lew Piper. Always whining about what it could have been like if he hadn't been cheated out of his career with the government. Yeah, it could have been like this, is what it could have been like. Instead of a secure future surrounded by vultures and snoops, managed by political appointees, constantly threatened and investigated because some weasel of a suspect got his front door kicked in by the cops and an investigative reporter found out that the warrant was flawed. Poor bastard Piper, he's forced to go to England and sleep with some British woman who is screwing his shorts off. My heart bleeds for him. Oh, Lord, what day is today?

He grabbed the small calendar off his desk and held it at arm's length trying to focus on the small numbers. Middle age sucks. Your belly gets bigger and your eyes go bad. Turning to the previous month, he surveyed the x'd days and calculated quickly. Yep, I was right. It's time for a business trip.

He had been happily married now for almost twenty-five years. His and his wife Karla had three daughters: Wendy, twenty and a junior in college, Margaret, called Maggie, seventeen and a senior in high school, and the youngest, his baby, Cathy, fifteen and a sophomore in high school. Five years earlier, he had finally figured out how to make his home life happier with the help of his family doctor. Visiting for a routine physical, he had commented that his oldest daughter was now officially a woman, having had her first case of menstrual cramps. He had asked him what his life was destined to be like when all four of the females under his roof were fully mature. What would it be like with four days of each week devoted to cosseting a different menstruating female? Fortunately, his doctor had the answer. When related females live together, such as a mother and her daughters, they all have their periods at the same time. So it had been only four days a month that Jim had learned to walk softly around the house. He viewed their monthly periods as the equivalent of a congressional hearing for him: They happened to him on a regular basis, and when they did, life was tough.

So, four days each month he arranged to be away on a business trip. It had worked like a charm for the past five years. Other men chose to try to change the nature of womanhood by standing around and getting in the way. He chose to evade, and his life at home was wonderful.

In fact, he needed to go to Los Angeles to follow up on the investigation of the second Falcon and Snowman case that had recently been uncovered. Just as before, two young men with security clearances had decided to sell classified information to the Russians in order to get money for their hobbies. But there was a difference this time. This time, the Russian consular official that they had contacted defected to the West and turned them in. Since the Russians and the US were now friends, the consular official decided that he liked the US retirement plan better than his homeland's. It was just business, not politics. The CIA didn't care, it was all brownie points as far as they were concerned.

The problem was, he hated Los Angeles. It was like Athens or Jakarta, only with better telephone service. Same foreign accents. Same surly attitudes of, "I've got mine, now you can try to get yours." Too much flash for him. And too many beautiful women. Starkly gorgeous women with suntanned long legs and firm, ample bosoms. His thoughts worried him.

Suddenly, he had a much better thought.

Section 17 of the current operational directives of the Department of Defense stressed the need for all department heads to, "conduct such cross-discipline liaison meetings as might be needed to assure the smooth and accurate inter-management of classified information". This was a meaningless paragraph, and a very dangerous one. This was the Poison Pen Paragraph. Division Twenty-Two had lost its department head to this paragraph after a spy was recently uncovered at the CIA. The DOD man's department had been sharing information with the CIA as a part of government policy. Thus, DOD information had gone to the CIA, and the spy had sold it to the Chinese. The CIA was in deep trouble over this, and to deflect some of the blame it invoked Section 17, saying that if the DOD had actually conducted "such cross-discipline liaison meetings, etc." as had been required by regulations, the spy might have been caught earlier.

It was a typical cover-your-ass move on the part of the CIA. Realistically though, all government agencies regularly used Section 17 throughout their own organizations to splash mud on others when they got caught doing something wrong. The effect was referred to as the

Five Ps: "Poison Pen Paragraphs Promote Paranoia", but nobody made an attempt to change anything.

He had not had a "cross-discipline liaison meeting" recently. These meetings kept his enemies at bay. Now was the perfect time.

And the calendar showed that tomorrow was the perfect day to start. The US Atlas told him how to get there. He dialed the Travel Section. "Get me an RT to St. Louis tomorrow, COD, rental car, no hotel, return open." Translation: One round-trip ticket to St. Louis, flight to leave at the Crack Of Dawn, get me a car, I'll find my own place to stay and I don't know when I'll return. He called his deputy, told him that he was leaving on a Section 17, and to make sure it was all there when he got back. Then he went home early to pack.

And none too soon. As he shared his plans, his wife said that he should try to stick around more often. One day, she said, his children would all be grown and he would have forgotten their names. He gave her a one-armed hug and a soft peck on the cheek. She scrunched up her shoulders and pretended to ignore him, but smiled at the back of his head as he walked away toward the den and his ever-present paperwork. One daughter could be heard on the telephone complaining to a friend that she was tired of the color of her hair. Another flung a magazine that had displeased her onto the living room floor. The third daughter could be heard surfing the cable channels, one second per station with the sound turned up too loud.

It was a perfect time for a business trip.

He was up first the next morning, and out of the house before it could catch up with him. Flying out of National Airport, plastic and cardboard faces lined the seats of the MD-88, each eating their plastic and cardboard breakfasts and reading their McNewspapers. A few thumps of turbulent air later, and they arrived at Lambert Field, St. Louis. He paid the girl at the counter in cash for a rental car upgrade to a luxury vehicle. She took the government supplied credit card, automated him a rental agreement that stated he was getting a Mercury Sable for the GSA rate of $28 per day. She neglected to put the $20 upgrade fee on the document. He signed the paper and watched as she separated his copies, folded them and placed them in an envelope. Switching the felt tipped pen to her other hand, she copied the license number and parking stall number from a plastic tag, then handed the folder and key to him with a pleasant smile. He walked to the courtesy bus that conveyed him to the nearly new Lincoln Town Car that matched the key she had supplied. He put his luggage in the trunk and drove out through the guarded exit. The uniformed man at the gate matched the car's license number and the sticker on the windshield with the number on the envelope. He removed the rental agreement and glanced at it, but said nothing.

He was driving a Lincoln, the government would be billed for a Mercury Sable, and the girl at the counter had money for lunch with her boy friend. The car rental company was getting screwed, of course, but nobody would ever notice as long as the stock price rose and the profits continued to come in on schedule.

He drove fifty miles East on Route 50, then turned South for fifty more miles on Route 57, and arrived at the gray concrete complex. Showing his credentials to the gate guard, he pulled into a visitor slot and walked into the main reception area.

Handing his credentials to the young Bureau of Prisons officer through the passage under the bulletproof glass, he asked to see the warden. The man didn't answer, only copying the name into a register and passing back the credentials.

"Is he expecting you, sir?" the officer asked politely.

Barker stared at the young man with his iciest stare. "What do you think officer?"

The man looked at him in confusion. His eyes began to turn toward the name in the register.

"Don't look at the register, son, look at me. What was the name on my credentials?"

"Dr. James L. Bartle, sir."

"Close, but no cigar. The name is Barker. Bartle makes the wine coolers; I run the Department of Defense's security section."

An older man in uniform came into the booth and stood beside the young officer. "What's going on here?" he demanded sharply.

"Shut -- your -- mouth," Barker said slowly and distinctly, switching his cold gaze to the new man. "I'm talking with Officer

Bennett here. When I have finished with him, then I will speak with you." The man did as he was told and stood silently. This was a specialty of his: projecting his will onto other people to make them better at their jobs. People never understood about the flaws in their capabilities until they were tested. He was a skilled taskmaster. His gaze worked even through bulletproof glass. He still had it. It made him happy. He needed to get out of Washington more often.

Returning to Officer Bennett, he became a kindly old college teacher. Pressing his credentials to the glass wall that separated them, he said, "The first thing you should have noticed was the gold rim around the ID. This indicates that the holder is a high-ranking member of the US government. The gold rim equates to a Major General in the army, for example." The man paled visibly and began to shift his feet in spite of his new, softer approach. "In the future, when the door to the outside opens, you should look up immediately. Don't try to impress people with how busy and important you are by continuing to look at something on the desk until they speak to you. While you are looking important, they could pop a small canister of nerve gas through this slot and knock you on your ass. Yes, I know, the guys in the back, if they're watching the monitor, would see it happen and cover the situation, but you'd still be dribbling on a bib for the rest of your life. And we wouldn't want that, would we?"

The young man shook his head solemnly.

Shifting his eyes to the sergeant that he had ordered to be quiet, he turned on the cold stare once more. "Snorting and puffing and saying 'What's all this, then?' only works if your an actor in a British movie. The proper response in the future to assist a subordinate who is having difficulties is to ask, 'May I help you, sir?' Is that clear?"

The sergeant nodded, completely cowed.

"Then, let's start over, shall we? Please tell the warden that I am here and would like to speak with him NOW! I'll have a seat over there and wait. Could someone get me a cup of coffee, please? Black, no sugar, and not decaffeinated."

He walked to the leatherette sofa and plopped down without waiting for a response. A moment later, the sergeant appeared from a side door and said, "Would you follow me, sir? The warden has your coffee waiting in his office."

Warden Robert Proxmire was a man in his early forties wearing a dark blue sweater vest over a plaid open-collared long sleeved shirt and khaki trousers. There was a color photograph of the President on the wall, along with some other pictures and certificates that chronicled the warden's career. It looked like his own office, only larger and less cluttered with trash.

"Sorry for the problem with the staff, Dr. Barker. They just aren't used to visitors down here in Southern Illinois."

"Forget the Doctor stuff. Just call me Jim. That's OK, people need all the training they can get before they get involved in something they aren't prepared for. Changing the subject, this must be a hell of a place to administer with all these high-profile prisoners. You have all the spies as well as all the so-called 'political prisoners', don't you?"

"We are the modern-day equivalent of Alcatraz," the warden replied carefully. "When a federal inmate requires secure handling such as is the case with convicted spies, they get sent here rather than being made a part of the general prison population. In addition, any inmate that acts as an unsettling influence in another federal prison, or shows violent or uncooperative behavior toward the prison staff can be transferred here on proper authority."

"You get a lot of publicity about being inhumane in your treatment of the prisoners, don't you?"

"Today's federal inmate, by-and-large, is much more savvy and sophisticated than in the old days. They tend to be better educated and able to justify their actions with the greatest of ease. Smugglers serving a life term for bringing in tons of narcotics will tell you that they were simple businessmen satisfying a pre-existing need. Terrorists will tell you that they are soldiers fighting a war, and deserve to be treated as POWs. Spies tell you that they were good employees of both sides and do not deserve to be punished, but that it is the leaders of the countries that deserve the punishment."

"So how do you deal with them?"

"When they come in the door, we strip them naked and take away all their personal property. Everything: rings, watches, religious medals. Everything. We x-ray them for contraband hidden in their body orifices. We dress them in our own carefully searched prison uniforms. At the start of their sentence here, they have no privileges - no TV, no books, no radio, no letters, no visitors, no talking to other inmates. Every time they are taken from their cell for a meal, a haircut, a visit from a lawyer, their cell is searched thoroughly. They each get a list of the good-time credits they must earn to get each privilege. It's up to them what they do with their time. Any violation of the rules and they lose it all and go back to square one."

"What if they just tell you to go to hell and refuse to cooperate?"

"Then they will never receive a visit, never see a TV program, never read a newspaper or talk to another inmate during their entire sentence. Every time they start a fight, the courts extend their sentences a few more months. Usually, they decide to play by the rules. Or they drive themselves crazy, as happens sometimes. When a person has spent all of his life doing exactly what he wanted to, including treason, murder, rape, narcotics, etc., it's sometimes impossible for him to realize that he's in a situation where he makes none of the rules, and he snaps."

"Then?"

"Then he goes into the prison's mental ward for treatment."

"He doesn't get sent to a separate institution?"

"Nope. He stays right here. The court sentenced him to serve his term here, and he serves his term here. Sane or insane, he stays here."

"What if a prisoner dies?"

"If I had my way, he'd be buried here as well until his sentence had lapsed. But we aren't allowed to do that as of now. Maybe in the future it will happen. I hope so. We succeed because we convince the inmates that they have no choice but to do it our way."

"And everybody comes around to your way of thinking eventually?"

"Yep, they all do. In the beginning, they deal with it different ways. We have a inmate now that is doing calisthenics six hours a day to keep his mind off the program. He's been at it almost a year now, but he'll come around eventually."

"Which inmate is that?"

"Nobody you ever heard of. He's an ex-navy officer that helped the IRA blow up a bus filled with school kids."

Barker listened, but his hands were starting to feel moist.

The warden continued to speak. "Look, you're an old hand at dealing with stuff like this, and I am willing to sit here and tell you about our facility as long as you want," he began. "But, rather than have me make an uneducated guess, why don't you just tell me why you are here?"

He was being serious, but not in an unfriendly way. For Barker, the official reason that he was here was to satisfy the needs of Section 17. It also gave his deputy an opportunity to run the department in his absence, and he got a chance to see if the man was an incompetent boob. It also got him out of the house and away from any tenseness at home. Unofficially, he was there because Gurney was there and because Piper needed information that only Gurney could supply. But nobody at the DOD knew that he had any new knowledge about Gurney's circumstances, so that would have to be played very carefully. He decided to do something extremely dangerous, and he had no idea why he would take such a chance. He decided that he would tell the truth.

But he would tell what Piper liked to call "The Japanese Truth", in case he was making an error in judgment. It would not completely save him if he were wrong, but it would muddy the waters.

Americans who have dealt with the Japanese know about their version of the truth. For them, "Japanese Truth" has come to mean a way of phrasing information such that if the question causes the person questioned to become hostile, the whole thing can be explained away as though it never existed.

For example, a Japanese would never say, "I want to have sex with your daughter." He would say, "How would you feel if I were to tell you that I wanted to have sex with your daughter?" Notice that he did not say that he wanted to have sex with your daughter, only that he wondered how you would feel if he were to ask. This is the essential element of Japanese Truth. Never say anything directly. Always speak obliquely.

"I have a question for you," Barker began. "What would your reaction be if I were to tell you that I had information that one of your inmates was about to be shown as innocent of all the crimes of which he had been convicted, and was about to be ordered released from custody?"

The warden didn't like playing the game. Either that, or he didn't understand the advantages. "Are you offering me advanced notice of the impending release of one of my inmates? Why are you doing this? Which inmate are you referring to?"

"Let me start again, if I may, and ask that you please listen carefully to how my question is phrased. I did not say that I knew anything about anyone being ordered released from custody. I simply asked what your reaction would be should I say such a thing."

"You talk like a Jap," the warden snapped.

"Bingo," Barker replied.

"I was stationed with the Marines on Okinawa for two years. All the Japs talked like that. It used to drive me nuts," the warden responded. "OK, OK, I know where you're headed with this. You have advanced knowledge that an inmate here is due to be early-released from custody because of a trial error. Since we've never met before, and you don't work for the Bureau of Prisons, you aren't offering me this information so I can make sure my skirts are clean and we haven't been mistreating the man. So it must mean that you want to interview the inmate and ask him some questions."

Barker never so much as fluttered an eyelash.

"From an official point of view, it is a non-event," Proxmire continued. "We are never involved in the aspects of investigating a inmate, apprehending a inmate, trying a inmate or sentencing a inmate. All we are involved in here is the incarceration of a inmate under the strictest of security considerations."

"When we get a duly authorized release order from the proper authorities, we start the standard Sentence Termination Procedures. They involve moving the inmate to a communal area where he is allowed to eat, read or watch TV on demand. The reading material and the TV programs are not reviewed or censored like they are for the general prison population. We assign unarmed guards in civilian clothes to the common area with the inmate to talk with him and begin to start his normal communications processes once more. Finally, we issue a suit of civilian clothes to the inmate, and return to him all the personal property that was taken from him when he arrived. The next day we hold a release hearing and the inmate is escorted out the gates of the facility and formally terminated from custody."

"What would you say if I were to tell you that I could name the inmate that is due for release, and I want an opportunity to speak with him?" Barker asked.

The warden thought for a moment about what he was being told. "Would you like some lunch, Jim? I'm feeling a little hungry, are you?" The warden had not wasted his time on Okinawa with the Marines, after all. It was a perfect Japanese response to a difficult question.

"Something light would be nice," Barker replied. "Perhaps a sandwich and a soft drink?"

The warden pressed a button on his intercom and asked, "Would you please bring sandwiches and colas for two to my office, please?" A voice on the other end replied, "Certainly, warden. Right away."

"Who is it you want to. . ." The warden held up his hand. "Let me start again. How would you feel if I were to say that whether or not you could speak with the inmate in question would depend on who the inmate was?" He was learning.

Barker pondered how to answer the question. If he gave Proxmire the name, and then was refused the right to speak with Gurney, then the warden would have the knowledge of who was about to be released, and he would have nothing. He solved the dilemma Japanese-style by saying, "You know, I am really getting hungry now that we have spoken about lunch. Do you know how long it will be before the sandwiches arrive?"

"Probably about another ten minutes or so," he replied with a grin.

"Would you mind telling me about those framed certificates on the wall over there in the meantime?"

And so the warden proceeded to explain each of the pieces of his career that adorned the walls of his office until the meal arrived. The sandwiches were roast beef with lettuce and nice, ripe beefsteak tomatoes, as well as ham and Swiss cheese with mustard and mayonnaise. The diet colas were cold and tasteless like all diet colas are. They ate in silence, only commenting on the food now and then and passing the salt back and forth. Later, a staff member came over from the kitchen and removed the dirty dishes and empty soda cans.

The warden began to ponder his next move. This man from the Department of Defense had traveled to the facility unannounced, supposedly to interview one of the inmates. He did not request permission to interview the inmate through normal channels, either because time was a factor or security was a factor. If time was a factor, then the inmate in question had information that was perishable and might be worthless by the time he was released. If security was a factor, this could involve a security leak. He needed to be very careful about this. He pondered what questions to ask.

"If such an interview were to be granted, how would you feel about submitting the questions in advance?" he asked.

"I would have no problem with that, provided I got to ask the questions directly of the inmate, and providing that I would have some freedom to respond to any follow-on questions that the answers to an original question might lead me to," Barker replied. It was working!

"Mrs. Dennison, would you come in here please and bring your steno pad?"

A plump lady of about forty came into the office, and they were introduced. She had tightly-curled red hair and looked like a middle-aged Little Orphan Annie. He thought up ten questions off the top of his head. She said that she would transcribe them and have the written copies within five minutes. When she returned with the typed questions, she handed the sheets of paper to the warden. He read each of the questions slowly, mouthing the words to himself.

"I don't understand this," he said. "These questions deal mainly with how the inmate traveled to some hotel, and the whereabouts of

118

some pictures. Doesn't seem like much of a thing to travel all the way down here for."

Barker looked at him blankly, trying not to give anything away.

"It's not the navy officer, Gurney, is it? He was supposed to be some kind of a cameraman as I recall. He's sequestered, anyway, so I couldn't let you talk to him. But if he's the one that's going to be released. . ."

Barker displayed more of the blankest stare that he could manage.

For a fleeting moment the warden recalled the little game that they had played each quarter on Gurney when they moved him into one of the two death cells and made him listen to the sounds of the test execution. He should never have gotten emotional about the man. If he let an interview with Gurney take place, there could be hell to pay. Half the guard staff had wanted to arrange an "accident" for him since his first day. The man had deserted his country and helped terrorists murder innocent children. Gurney was the only inmate who always had an armed guard outside his door, a man with orders to kill the inmate if a breakout was attempted. He had given those verbal orders himself. He had violated the simplest rule of his profession: Never Get Involved. And now it would surely come back to haunt him. Why did it have to be Gurney, for Christ's sake? Wait, maybe it wasn't Gurney after all. Maybe it was Walker or Ames or the Jew. Don't be ridiculous. It had to be Gurney, the questions pointed clearly to that. But if Gurney was innocent and came to any harm before he could be released, there would be even more hell to pay.

"Are you going to squeeze those papers to death, or have we got a deal?" Barker finally asked.

"I don't know why I'm doing this," he finally managed to say. "Give me the inmate's name and I'll have him brought to an interview room for questioning."

"Thank you, Warden. You are an honest man, and I like the way you handle yourself. I want to speak with Thomas Edison Gurney."

"Damn it! I knew it was him! I could tell by the questions!" *Oh, shit, the fat's in the fire now! He thought to himself. Why did I agree? I think I'll just tell this guy to go to hell and. . ."*

119

But, he'd given his word. Besides, the man was about to be released anyway. At least he'd have a few days to make amends. He pushed a button on the intercom. "Mrs. Dennison, ask the watch lieutenant to come into my office, please. And before you ask, no, there is no emergency involved." *Except the possible end of my career.*

A tall uniformed man in his mid-thirties came into the office. He wore the gold bars if his rank on the collar of his light blue shirt. He was of average height, very muscular, and had a shaved head. He looked mean as a snake.

"Jerry, bring inmate number," the warden consulted a folder on his desk for a moment, then continued, "one-one-five-oh-eight-three-nine to the large interview room."

"But Bob, that's. . ."

"Yes, Jerry, I know who it is. Now, go and arrange to have him brought to the interview room, please."

"But that inmate is still sequestered!" the lieutenant protested. "That would be violating the sentencing guidelines!" Then pointing at Barker with a scowl he barked, "And who the hell is this guy?"

"Jerry, this is a direct order. Bring the inmate to the large interview room now!" *Jesus, this is going to be even worse than I imagined! Jerry will have the whole guard force up in arms. I may end up with a mutiny on my hands!*

"I want the order in writing, warden," the lieutenant snapped. While the warden scribbled on a piece of paper, the lieutenant put his face in front of Barker and said with a scowl, "I said, mister, who the hell are you? I want an answer, and I want it now!"

Barker unfolded the credential case from his inside pocket and displayed the picture ID with the gold rim around it. "It has some really large multi-syllable words on it," he said softly. "Would you like me to read them to you so you don't have to wet your lips and strain your eyes?" He gave the lieutenant his best icy glare.

"DOD don't cut no ice around here, mister! You can stick you nice little ID. . ."

"Jerry, this isn't making it any better. It's only making it worse. Now, here is your written order to bring the inmate to the large interview room." The warden's voice sounded very old and tired.

The bald headed lieutenant looked at the piece of paper in obvious disgust, folded it and placed it in his breast pocket. "I'll get the damn inmate, Bob, but I'm telling you this is a bad mistake. You know these DOD types, and the inmate looks like. . ."

Suddenly, the warden came to life. "Lieutenant, if you ever call me by my first name again in front of strangers, or if you ever bridle over an order of mine again, I will personally cut your privates off and have them made into a bow-tie! Now, you haul your insubordinate ass out of my sight right now"

The lieutenant shot for the door, his face red with fury.

"And Jerry?" The lieutenant turned his beet-red face toward the warden. "If there's so much as a scrape on the inmate, so much as a red spot on his face or the slightest halt in his gait as he walks, I will send the entire guard watch to Guam for the rest of their lives. Is that clear?"

The lieutenant turned sharply to exit, but the warden was not finished with him. "Answer me, lieutenant! Is that clear?"

The bullet-headed man choked back what he wanted to say, and replied, "Yes, SIR, warden SIR! May I please be dismissed now to do my job, warden. SIR?"

"You're dismissed, lieutenant," the warden replied.

"What if the inmate resists?" Barker asked. "What if they mark him while trying to restrain him? What will you do then?"

"Not my problem. Any marks, and they all get transferred to the worst place I can think of. The damn guard force gets too emotional about the inmates anyway. It's bad for their objectivity. We're going to go over to the cell wing now. That's where the interview room is. I need you to remove all the items from your pockets and place them in this drawer here. They'll be safe, after all, this is a prison." He smiled at the thought.

"I want to keep my credentials if I may. It is the only way I have of introducing myself to the prisoner."

"Inmate," the warden corrected.

"Inmate," Barker echoed.

"Hand me your credentials, please, and let me look at them while you empty your pockets," the warden said evenly.

121

Barker watched as the man searched carefully through the leather folder, finding Karla's picture carefully tucked away. "Who's this?" he asked.

"My wife," he responded, continuing to empty his pockets into the drawer. Looking down at his pipe and tobacco pouch, he realized that he hadn't had a smoke all day. It made him very anxious.

"We'll leave your wife's picture here in the drawer as well," the warden said. "No offense. It's part of the rules."

"None taken," he replied.

They walked out the side door of the office and got into an electric golf car with the word WARDEN in big gold letters on the front. There was a flashing, rotating blue light on the metal top that pulsed as they silently motored along the deserted corridors. They passed through two checkpoints before they got to the interview room. A uniformed guard unlocked the door, and locked it from the outside after they entered.

If this is the large interview room, I'd hate to see the small ones Barker mused. The room was no more that twelve feet square, if that. Not wanting to sit with his back to a door, he moved to the single chair on the far side of the plain three-by-six-foot wooden table. Starting to pull it out, he discovered that it wouldn't move.

"Don't sit there. That's the inmate's seat. It's bolted to the floor. So is the table. We'll sit in these chairs," he said, motioning toward two plain metal chairs on the other side of the table. These were not bolted down. "Security reasons," he added. "Also, don't rise when the man is brought into the room. Getting out of your chair looks like a threat to an inmate, and it makes them defensive."

A side door opened, and a man in orange coveralls entered with guards on each side. He was in leg shackles, handcuffs and a belly chain. He sounded like Santa's sleigh as he shuffled to the waiting chair and sat down. He was slim, about six feet in height and looked to be about fifty years of age. He had a full beard and shoulder length black hair, and looked like Steve McQueen in the movie *Papillion*. Only the clear blue eyes were young, and they stared two holes straight through each of the two men in turn. He arranged himself in the chair as best he could and the guards stepped aside and moved to opposite corners of the room.

As he held up his credentials so the man could see his ID, the blue eyes snapped onto the gold-rimmed card like a fire-control radar.

"My name is Dr. James Barker of the Department of Defense, Mr. Gurney. I have a prepared list of questions that I'd like to ask you if you wouldn't mind."

CHAPTER TEN

LOGIC

Piper slept on a guest cot in an extra room near Wylie's office that night. The next morning, he found a disposable razor in the adjoining bathroom and shaved with the assistance of a bar of Lifebuoy soap. It was not the most comfortable of shaves. There was no toothbrush, so he scrubbed the surface of his teeth with what appeared to be a clean towel, and then took a shower, redressing in yesterday's clothes. Wylie found him in the canteen drinking coffee.

"How's the photography thing working out?"

"Not too good. We're down to the T's now, so we'll be done this morning. Janet's a fast worker, by the way, and very thorough."

"She used to be a field agent until some Polak jumped her on a surveillance assignment and tried to slit her throat."

"Did he cut her up pretty badly? She doesn't have any scars that I can see."

"The scars are all inside her. She was lucky that he used a knife instead of the silenced pistol that he was carrying. She let him get too close before she reacted, and ended up having to shove him under the wheels of a passing truck to escape. He was probably trying to get some kind of communist Merit Badge for killing with a knife, and instead a truckload of coal squashed him like a ripe grape. She just didn't want to play any more after that. I guess I can understand how she feels."

Piper changed the subject, because he never liked to dwell on frailties. "So you got any ideas for what we do when we get through the list?"

"I'm an administrator. I don't get ideas, I just follow procedures. You'll think of something."

And immediately, Piper got an idea. "Where's that computer guy that found the files for us? What's his name? Marcus?"

"What about him?"

"Somebody has got to have some software that uses Artificial Intelligence or something that can analyze unrelated pieces of data and draw educated conclusions. You know, something that you can feed a lot of data and let it manipulate it back and forth."

"Come on to my office and we'll ask him." Once there, Wylie dialed a number and said, "Marcus, come to my office right now. We have work to do."

Piper walked quickly over to Janet's cubicle and told her that he was going to be in Wylie's office. She was on the phone and had worked her way into the W's, so she just waved him away with a nod. When he returned, Marcus was there, twitching.

"Tell him what you want, Mr. Piper," Wylie said.

Piper explained.

"LOGICASE," Marcus said.

"What?" both men echoed.

"LOGICASE is what you want, sir. It's a National Security Agency program, and it's only a beta release, but I could give it a try if you like."

"We'd like," Wylie said.

Marcus headed for the door.

"Where the hell you going, Marcus?" Wylie snapped. "Just sit down here at my desk and sign on the terminal."

"No, sir, I need to be at my own terminal to do that." The young man looked very uncomfortable, and continued to edge toward the door.

"Nonsense, Marcus. You assured me that all the terminals in this section were the same type and that they all had all the same capabilities. Now sit down and get the job done!" Wylie was getting visibly angry.

"But I'm still signed onto my terminal in the computer center," Marcus explained. "I would have to go back there and sign off first, then come back here and sign on, then go back down there to retrieve the hardcopy anyway, so why don't I just do it in one trip?" His eyes pleaded for acceptance.

Wylie was about to agree when Piper said, "Marcus, stop screwing around and do a forced sign-on at the Station Chief's terminal and let's get started. We know what you've been up to." Instinct and years of experience had taught him to say things like this.

"Oh, crap. I thought you were just another civilian, but you're not, are you? Mr. Wylie, I swear that I have not compromised anything. It was the only way I could make sure that nobody could get into the system. If I hadn't. . "

"Stop babbling, Marcus, and sit your ass down at the terminal." Wylie snapped.

The young man's shoulders drooped. Caught, beaten, and whipped. Anybody in the world could have read his body language.

Sitting down in Wylie's battered chair, the bony fingers flew across the keyboard. First he executed a sign-off procedure for Wylie, then paused and peered at the darkened screen for a moment getting up his courage for what must happen next. The fingers moved over the keyboard entering the forced sign-on procedure.

Immediately, a psychedelic pattern in blazing colors flashed on the screen and the terminal's internal speaker began to play, "We All Live In A Yellow Submarine". When asked for a user ID, Marcus entered "SUPERTOOL" and supplied a series of encoded passwords The screen then displayed a video of a pretty blond woman doing something incredibly athletic to the sounds of "Jumping Jack Flash". As her performance reached its climax, the screen went bright red and displayed the motto "Sex, Drugs and Rock-and- Roll". The US national anthem played and the motto "God Save the United States of America" was displayed with the stars and stripes waving in the background.

"Let me switch over to the LOGICASE system and we can enter some data to see what happens. The system is out in the field in beta test as I said, and we need to give it as much of a workout as we can. Live data is always the best, I say." Marcus was beginning to brighten.

Once the system was initiated, it flashed its fancy logo on the screen.

LOGICASE is protected under US and international copyrights and is classified Codeword Top Secret

After getting past the numerous warnings about security and all the disclaimers about the fact that this was a "development copy" of the system for which no guarantees were made or implied, they began to enter pieces of information for the system to digest.

Gurney is a professional photographer.
Gurney has several expensive cameras.

"Tell it that he takes pictures, not just that he owns an expensive camera," Piper offered with an irritated shortness in his voice

Enter "Gurney took pictures in Northern Ireland," Piper commanded quickly.

"No, that's wrong," Marcus said.

"It is not wrong, Marcus. He did take pictures in North. . ." Piper was snapping, but Marcus still managed to interrupt him without causing offense.

"I mean the tense is wrong, sir. You have to always use the present tense with LOGICASE for some reason. If you mix up a series of statements, some in present tense and some in past tense, it sorts all the past tense statements to the head of the logic stream and then follows it with all the present tense activity. In this case, it would be as if Gurney used to take pictures in Northern Ireland, but then did something else. The problem with LOGICASE is that all of the development work is. . ."

"OK, OK, I've got the drift, Marcus. Just enter the sentence correctly and let's get on with it."

Gurney takes pictures in Northern Ireland.
He has the pictures developed by the regiment's photo technicians.

"Put something in about the fact that the pictures had military value. We're not talking about vacation snapshots here," Piper added.

His pictures are used acceptably in high-level briefings.
He has his cameras with him on the bunker operation.

"We don't know that," Wylie said. "That's an assumption."

"It's the key assumption, Wylie! If we don't assume that, then we have no business looking for pictures in the first place! The we'd have to go back to the beginning! Why was Gurney railroaded, if not for these pictures?"

"You are yelling at me, Piper," Wylie said evenly

His shoulders drooped. "Sorry," he said softly. "I get a little intense at times. Didn't mean to yell."

He sees O'Flynn speak to a man in a car.

His rifle shot is blocked by the car and the crowd.
He wants the film to be developed immediately.
The processing must be done in secure conditions.
The regiment's photo technicians are not available.
He is in Prince Henry Barracks, London.
He takes the film to <QUERY>

Marcus pushed the enter key and they all waited as blocks of words and symbols moved across the display. A response flashed on the screen.

WHAT MEANS <DEVELOPED> ?

SEE: MORE, GOOD, CAME, LABORED, AGED

"The word 'developed' is confusing to the system," Marcus said. He changed the word to "processed".

Immediately the screen changed.

WHAT MEANS <PROCESSED> ?

SEE: CHANGED, PREPARED, TREATED, MODIFIED.

Stupid computers! They don't understand anything! Piper gritted his teeth.

"What word describes the processing of film best?" Marcus asked.

"Treated," Wylie guessed.

They were having a conversation with an electronic device. Now, who were the idiots?

LOGICASE accepted the word "treated" without additional comments.

WHAT MEANS <SECURE> ? the computer asked.

SEE <GET, LAND, WIN, GAIN, OBTAIN>

Marcus looked at the screen for a moment, puzzling. "Let's see if it understands the principle parts of speech," he announced, then entered

USE <ADJECTIVE:SECURE>

"Adverb?" Wylie asked.

"Yes, can't you see?" Marcus answered. "Look at the question it asked about the word 'secure'. It asked if the word meant 'GET, LAND, WIN, GAIN, OBTAIN'. Those are all verbs. We want the word 'secure' to be used in the adjectival form as in 'The film is secure', so I told it that the word is an adjective. Let's see what happens now." He hit the ENTER key, and the system appeared to continue processing..

"Well, that's encouraging, isn't it?", Piper asked no one in particular.

"Maybe yes and maybe no," Marcus responded. "The system may be churning through a logic stream, or it may be hopelessly lost. We'll know in a few seconds."

HOW IMPORTANT <SECURE> ?, the system asked.

Success! They were still alive, and the system was actually trying to find them an answer.

Marcus typed in <VERY>.

The machine immediately responded

<FILM AT REGIMENT PHOTO TECHNICIANS>

Marcus typed in the word <NEGATIVE>. "That tells the system that it can't use this answer. It gets pissed off when you do that, in other words, when you tell it that it's made a mistake. Lots of time it refuses to continue processing. You can tell that this part of the system needs lots more development work. We could go back to the entry screen and include the fact that the film isn't with the regimental photo technician, but then we would have to start all over entering data."

"But we already told it that the regiment's photo technicians were not available," Wylie replied in an irritated voice. "It doesn't have a very good memory, does it?"

"I told you that it's in the field as a test system. It's bound to have a lot of bugs in it. That's why they send them to us, so we can find out what's wrong with them and let the developers know what needs to be fixed," Marcus added.

They were about to give up completely when the screen posted a new message.

<FILM AT SECURE PLACE PRINCE HENRY BARRACKS>

"Is there a secure place he could have left the film temporarily at Prince Henry Barracks? Maybe the security officer or somebody like that?" Marcus asked.

"No, Gurney would have wanted to get the film someplace where it could be developed as soon as possible after being exposed. It's not just a case of trying to keep it safe from theft or something like that."

With a shrug, Marcus entered <NEGATIVE>.

"That should finish it off. It hates being told 'no' even once, much less twice. So, let me call about the fingerprints. Maybe they've come. . ."

The terminal posted a new message:

<FILM AT NEAREST SECURE PLACE PRINCE HENRY BARRACKS>

"Stupid machine! Marcus cursed. "Just tell me the answer! What are you playing at? Don't make me ask over and over! NSA has to get this thing fixed!"

He typed QUERY <NEAREST SECURE PLACE PRINCE HENRY BARRACKS> and smashed down on the ENTER key with his fist.

The answer came back in a flash. "See how quick it responded?" Marcus said, calming down immediately. "I told you it knew the answer and just wasn't programmed to spit it out."

All three were staring at the computer's response.

<NEAREST SECURE PLACE PRINCE HENRY BARRACKS -- AMERICAN   EMBASSY>

"Oh, Lord!" Piper shouted. "He brought the film to the American embassy to be developed! Of course! Once you have the answer, it's all so obvious!"

"You mean the film's been here all along while you were making all those damn phone calls?" Wylie asked

"LOGICASE gives it only an 18% probability, Mr. Piper," Marcus said.

Wylie snatched up the phone, dialed a number and barked, "Who is this? There was a pause. "Well, Ms. Cumberland, this is Wylie, the Station Chief. I give you five minutes to find the film that was processed for a navy man named Lt. Gurney over a year ago. He never picked them up, so you still have them." Another pause. "No excuses, only results. The pictures are on my desk in five minutes or you are on your way to a small island in the Indian Ocean as a demoted photo technician." He slammed down the receiver.

A scant few minutes later, a woman entered with a large manila envelope in her hand.

They had found Gurney's pictures.

"Conference room," Wylie announced, leading the way. A few women, probably clerks, were sitting at the end of the big table drinking coffee and talking. Seeing Wylie enter with his normal daytime scowl, they hurriedly picked up their things and departed.

The pictures were in black and white, very clear and detailed. They had been printed in portrait size, approximately eleven inches by fourteen inches. Gurney's Leica camera had been fitted with an excellent telephoto lens and loaded with some very sensitive film. There were daylight views out the attic opening, and an artsy-fartsy view of Gurney with his face blackened by camouflage grease peering out the opening. He'd taken it with the self-timer obviously, and probably planned to put it in his scrapbook. There were only twenty-seven pictures, not a full roll of thirty-six. Piper checked the negatives to make sure the count was correct.

It was.

Toward the last of the stack, there was a picture of O'Flynn walking from left to right on the sidewalk across the street. Totally out of context with what he represented, he was wearing a dark baseball cap with the Gothic "D" of the Detroit Tigers on it.

"That would be the picture he took to identify O'Flynn before shooting him," Wylie said flatly.

Piper went through the sniper drill from memory. Now, set the camera aside and pick up the silenced rifle. Open the bolt slightly to confirm that there is a cartridge in the chamber, then close the bolt again securely. Rest the rifle on the bipod, bring the butt to the shoulder and sight down the scope. Take a standard breath of air, not too big and not too small, then exhale half of it. Hold your breath. Take up the slack in the trigger. Get a clear sight picture and squeeeeze. . .

The next picture was of the dark taxi and O'Flynn bent over speaking to the driver. The taxi was headed right-to-left in the picture, and like English taxis, the driver sat on the right side. Thus he was on the far side of the cab from Gurney, next to the far curb, and from the loft it was a high-angle view downward. O'Flynn had squatted down and was almost completely hidden from view. His left hand was resting atop the cab. That one small act, squatting down to speak to the driver, had saved his life that afternoon.

They looked at the last photos in the sequence and Piper continued to check them off against the negatives.

These would be the pictures Gurney took in frustration, knowing that the chance to get O'Flynn would never come again. Gurney had never realized the significance of the pictures, and that had been the cause of all his problems. Someday, perhaps, he would meet the man in person and try to explain it all.

The rest of the photos, down through the last one, were of the gathering of additional men around O'Flynn. The taxi left, and the men departed together in a group. The baseball cap and O'Flynn were hidden among their crowd, nowhere to be seen. In the final picture, a woman with her hair in curlers pushed a baby carriage down the sidewalk.

They stared at the pictures, spread out in a line over the long tabletop, in silence. None of them showed any kind of registration number for the vehicle. Gurney would have probably made a note of it in his operations logbook, but that would have long since been confiscated and destroyed by the colonel's people, whoever they were. Scooping up the pictures and replacing them reverently in the large envelope, they returned to Wylie's office in silence.

"Now that we have the pictures, what do we do next?" Wylie asked.

"Operational reports," Piper volunteered. "There might be a face in the crowd that the colonel didn't want seen. Maybe even the colonel himself."

"We don't have any of the operational reports in out computer, do we Marcus?" Wylie asked.

Before he could answer, Piper had another idea. "How many other computers have you broken into, Marcus?"

Marcus jumped like he'd been shot.

"I mean, you broke into the Ladbrooke's betting computer, so how many others have you gotten into?"

Look at this guy, Piper was thinking. I'll bet he can do a lot more than he's ever told anyone on the embassy staff. He was babbling about "only doing something to make sure the computers couldn't be compromised". I wonder. . .

"I want you to go into the database at MI6 and bring up all the data they have on the Army' posting to Belfast last year. Anything to do with a Colonel Reeves-Benedict, the commanding officer." He heard Wylie suck in a breath quickly, but not say anything.

Instinct and years of experience. . .

"You mean MI5, don't you, sir? Actually, the French have much better records. They keep lots more of the British stuff on line, as well as some of ours and a lot that the Poles and Hungarians have gathered. I go in on a regular basis and delete our stuff just to piss them off. One evening in a bar, I heard their systems guy bragging about how nobody could get into their system, so I went on their computer and deleted his sign-on just to show him what a jerk he was. The French transferred him to Martinique."

"And when you did it, you left a trail that the French can trace back to us," Wylie said sourly. "That's why we got that rocket last month from the French embassy."

"No, sir. They sent that identical message to all the embassies in London. I lifted their distribution list. And they'll never trace the spoof to us, because I used an electronic signature pattern and a sign-on that I stole from the Germans at the Bundesnachrichtendienst."

"You broke into the French embassy's secure computer system and deleted an operator's password just to get him in trouble, Marcus?" Wylie asked sternly.

"No, I deleted his password in the hopes that they would tightened up their security, not to get him in trouble. Think about it: he was bragging in a bar about how secure their system was. That's a ridiculous thing for someone with a security clearance to do. Anybody could have heard him"

"The French know everybody in our embassy, Marcus," Wylie continued, his face a dark mask. "They have all our pictures, and they know where we live. They knew that you were in that pub drinking and set the whole thing up to see if you would take the bait. And you did. So now they have one more little thing to throw in our faces if we ever irritate their government. American Embassy Spies Steal France's Secrets the headlines will read. And we'll owe it all to you. Congratulations, hot-shot!" He was not smiling. He looked as if he would never smile again.

"If you ever get your head out of the sand, Mr. Wylie, you may discover why everything around you is always so screwed up!" Marcus exploded.

Piper took a step backward to get out of the line of fire.

"What did you say to me, you little geek?"

"You heard me, Mr. Wylie!" Marcus yelled back, his eyes squinted in anger. "Who do you think gets all the information for your analysts so they can write their oversight reports that your superiors find so interesting? Me, that's who! And where does it all come from? The Company's input stream and the dailies? Not on your life. The feet-on-the-street guys you have working for the station here in the UK couldn't find their own rumps if they were sitting on them. They are all career-hounds that just go to the right parties, meet the right people, and write what they think Washington wants to see, yourself included. I crack the other embassy's computers to find out how their security system works, if it works at all. It has paid off by us having the best security system in the country. The information for your monthlies come from the French and the Germans mostly, because they have the best agents. Background information comes from the British, because they love gathering data, even though they're hopeless at analyzing it."

Marcus took a deep breath, offering Wylie a chance to interrupt. He didn't.

"Look at your department heads. Nancy Keller is so much in love with her lesbian landlady that we can only pray that the old boot doesn't turn out to be working for the Iraqis! Lopez in Commercial Branch is supposed to be recovering alcoholic. Yes, yes, I know. His family were murdered by a terrorist group in Egypt, and that's a terrible thing to endure. But he's not a recovering alcoholic, he's a hashish user, for God's sake! You urine test him quarterly, and it always comes out negative. Brilliant! What does Medical do to determine if the urine sample is really his and not someone else's that he's smuggled into the testing area? They take the sample's temperature, for God's sake! If it's close to 98.6° F, then everything must be OK, right? Where did they learn their testing procedures, in the Boy Scouts? Lopez lives with a French woman who gets him the hash, and gives him some of her urine in a baggie to carry in his jockey shorts all the time. Next time, do a DNA test on his urine and you'll find out I'm right."

"I snoop every big computer in the UK to find out if anybody is shopping our classified data around. Nobody from this embassy is selling, but our stuff does get around. Here, look at this." He made some keyboard entries, and a report entitled Operation Sultan Sweep displayed on the screen.

"Take that off the display immediately, Marcus. That's highly sensitive information!" Wylie said urgently.

Marcus left the display on the screen and turned to Wylie. "Who are you are afraid will see it? Is it this civilian who has a cleaner record than most of the station's staff?" he asked, gesturing at Piper. "This man is better than anyone we have on the payroll here. He's honest, he's resourceful, and he does good work. We've had all the gurus from DC in here and they haven't found out diddley. This man Piper found out what I was doing in less than two days. That's what you should be concerned about, not whether this guy finds out we're helping the Pakistani's build a weapons-grade nuclear reactor!"

Wylie let out a tired sigh. "Marcus, obviously we need to talk. But first, I'd like to get through with what we were working on, OK?"

"Outstanding, sir, and I apologize for what I said about your head in the sand. But before we leave this display, can I please show you something?"

Wylie nodded, and Marcus magnified the upper left-hand corner of the Operation Sultan Sweep cover page. He made some keyboard entries and just the faintest of lettering and numbers began to appear. "That's is the registry number of the copy in the Iraqi computer system. It's the same number as the copy in the French embassy's system. They both got it from the same source."

"Or one of them gave it to the other," Piper said.

135

"See?" Marcus said, gesturing at Piper and staring intently at Wylie. "This guy is good. You see what I mean about him being smart?"

"Can we please get back to the thing we started with, the Army regiment's last posting to Belfast?" Wylie asked tiredly.

Marcus nodded in agreement, and made some entries on the keyboard. Suddenly they were viewing British records from the French embassy's security database. Marcus did a computerized search on "Reeves-Benedict", but all they got were operational reports.

"Go to the French records and do the same search," Piper said without waiting for Wylie to give his OK.

Piper had not thought about it, but naturally, the French records were all written in French. His own comprehension of French was minimal at best. "Can you read this stuff, Marcus?" he asked.

"Certainement, mon Capitaine," Marcus replied with out missing a beat at the keys. "This is a biography on the colonel, this is the Table of Organization and Equipment for the regiment, the TO and E as it is called, this is. . ."

"What's this entry?" Piper asked, pointing to the screen. The Index description said,
"Transport privé du colonel dans Belfast".

"It says that the colonel has a civilian vehicle that he uses to drive around alone in Belfast. He always wears civilian clothes, and goes out on an irregular basis. Keeps it in a lock-up garage two blocks from the post." Even in French, both men could read the description: "un mini-taxi noir." A black mini-cab! That's what the colonel didn't want anybody to see! Everybody in the room was smiling except Wylie. He picked up the phone. Reciting the address directly from the computer screen, he barked, "Get our people to break into that lock-up garage in Belfast and go over everything in it with a fine toothed comb. I want an answer today, and I don't care how you get it!"

Three hours later, Wylie's terminal beeped. He tapped some keys and said, "The results are in on the taxi in the lock-up garage in Belfast. It had been wiped clean, and had all the marks of being driven by someone wearing gloves."

Piper's heart sank. An air-tight case against the colonel was slowly slipping away.

"But, apparently the colonel likes the occasional cigar, those H. Upmann's that come in the aluminum tubes. One of those empty tubes was found under the front seat, and it had a fine set of the colonel's prints on it."

Worthless. Anybody could have planted it there.

"That's totally worthless as evidence, of course, because anyone could have taken one of the colonel's discarded cigar tubes and simply put it under the seat," Wylie echoed. "However, the set of prints we found inside the trunk lid could not have been put there by anyone but the colonel. And there was also one smeared print inside the glove box that the lab thinks they can pin on the colonel."

Now things were beginning to look up a bit!

The phone rang. It was Barker. Wylie passed the phone to him across the desk.

"How's it going, Jim?" he asked.

"It's going fantastically, Lew! I haven't had this much fun since you and I were young pups back in the old days! Guess who I had a conversation with yesterday?"

"Jimmy Hoffa," Piper answered brightly. Wait till Barker heard his news!

"Close," Barker answered. "Lieutenant Thomas Gurney."

"How the hell did you manage that, Jim? Tell me about it!" He whispered to Marcus and Wylie what he had just been told. They both perked up immediately and began to ask questions, but he waved them silent.

"Lew, I hate to give you credit for anything, but that thing you told me about Japanese Truth sure came in handy at the prison. I worked it just like you said, and the warden just fell right into line. They had been jerking Gurney's chain and not letting him have a haircut or a shave, so he looked pretty hippie-like, but other than that he seemed OK."

"Jim, I have no idea what you are talking about. What the hell is that Japanese Truth, or whatever it was that you said?" he asked with irritation in his voice. Complements from Barker were few and far between, and he was about to step all over the only one he'd had in recent memory.

"You know, where you ask the question with the opening phrase, 'What would you say if I were to tell you that. . .'. You know, like that."

OK, now I understand," he replied dejectedly. That had nothing to do with anything called Japanese Truth. It was just the roundabout way that a Japanese businessman or politician tried to keep himself out of hot water when discussing something controversial. Other places in the world, it was called weasel-wording.

"Well, since you're not going to ask me, I'll just tell you that the pictures that Gurney took are. . ."

". . . here in the American embassy," Piper finished. "Yeah, we found them an hour ago, thanks to a computer program that can both think and scratch itself at the same time."

"What's the name of the program?" Barker asked.

"LOGI-something," Piper replied.

"Oh, yeah, LOGICASE. It's a piece of crap. Tell them to get NSA to send them QWIKWAY. It's a lot faster and it lets you tell it that it's wrong more than once without bursting into tears and crashing. Anyway, your boy is on his way to being free and I'm going to take the rest of the week off."

"Did you get anything else from Gurney, Jim? What other things did you talk to him about?"

"Well, it was pretty much as you had figured. Gurney said that he came back from Belfast with the rest of the officers. The plane was met at RAF Lakenheath by the colonel, who told him earlier by telephone that the Parachute Brigade had some kind of an exercise taking place in Scotland during the next few days and wanted him to participate if he could. The colonel had even gotten him a ticket on the night train to Carlisle for the following evening. But Gurney had a mind of his own and wanted to be able to photograph the scenery on the way there. So he changed the ticket to go during the day. He dropped off the film at the embassy first, then caught the train."

"And that got him to Carlisle too early to have taken place in the bombing in Surrey."

"Yep, that's a fact. He checked into the hotel where he had been booked by the colonel, so the cops knew right where to find him. He said that everybody was very nice to him, treated him politely, didn't rough him up or anything, so he figured that it was just some kind of a foul-up. He was put in a cell at the local police station, and was there about two hours. Suddenly, the door opens, and five or six men in civilian clothes come piling in and lock him in chains and put a hood over his head. He was driven away in a van for maybe an hour or an hour and a half, then taken onto some kind of secure installation. He said that it sounded as if the driver had to stop and present his identification papers to get them inside. He was put in a locked room, naked, then interrogated the next morning."

"No food or water?" Piper asked.

"He didn't say, but I think we can assume that's true from the way the rest of his story went."

"Are you telling me that it was a KGB Drill?" he asked.

"This line isn't that secure, Lew. Don't use phrases like that, OK?"

"You're talking to me in the office of the CIA station chief, Jim. The telephones don't get much more secure than that," he responded irritably. "What else? Anything of significance?"

"Well, you've said the codeword, so you know how it went."

"So, he wasn't present at his trial, he wasn't allowed to testify, he wasn't allowed to assist in his defense, and he never heard the evidence against him, is that it?"

"Yeah, that's about the size of it," his friend replied quietly. "Oh, one other thing. The report we got back from our guys in Mexico City contains a sworn statement by Trooper Delk as to exactly what he packed in Gurney's footlocker, down to the last pair of shoelaces."

"Did he pack any explosives or fuses or timers for the lieutenant?" The question had to be asked, just to be sure.

"Not a one. Just clothing. And he personally put the footlocker on the truck to be taken to the airfield for transport."

"Who are you going to fry for this, Jim? This is intolerable! The British government can't be allowed to get away with this. Who are they protecting?"

"We don't know, but it's somebody very sensitive and they're very serious about it." Barker's voice grew quieter. "We've got a high-level meeting with them tomorrow."

"A meeting about this?"

"No, about some other things."

"What other things?"

"The British have offered us a package. They offer Commonwealth support of the Cuban trade embargo, they will extend a some of our base leases in perpetuity, they will arrange for the French, Spanish and Italians to give us over-fly rights for the next twenty years, and they will give support troops and equipment for the drug war in Latin America."

"And, in return, we don't make them explain what happened to Gurney, is that right?"

"In return, we don't even mention Gurney's name to them."

"Jim, that is outrageous, even for the British! Why would we even talk to them on those terms?"

Barker sighed. "We have no choice, Lew. One of the royal family was possibly involved in this. If that got out, it could mean the end of their monarchy."

So that was it!

Piper hung his head in dejection. There would be no inquiry. Everything would be swept under the carpet "for the greater good of all concerned". Limply, he stared at the phone, then put it back up to his ear.

"What's he saying?" Wylie asked.

Piper looked at him with hollow eyes. "Listen to the tape, if you want to know. I don't want to think about it." He held onto the phone, eyes looking off into space, seeing nothing. All the colonel had to do was ask Gurney for the rolls of film when he got off the plane at RAF Lakenheath, and none of this would have happened. But the power-mad always have to be in charge. They always have to tell people what to do. They never ask. It's not their style. At least Gurney was going to be free, that was something. He was free until some paranoid bureaucrat felt that he knew too much anyway, and decided to arrange a convenient accident. Poor Gurney. And he hadn't done anything at all. Not anything. It was hopeless. It was all just hopeless.

Numbly tired now, Piper asked, "If you speak to Gurney again within the next twenty-four hours, Jim, tell him we appreciate his assistance. And thanks for all your help." Drained, he dropped the phone in the cradle, and went out of the Embassy in search of a Pub. He wanted a drink. He wanted lots of drinks.

CHAPTER ELEVEN

DREAMS

The dreary wetness of the early fall afternoon surrounded the two men as they waited in the shadows beside the country road.

Bejesus, this is no better weather than home, and that's a fact. We're damn pushed to set up this job so fast for the man, whoever he is. It's supposed to be a transport of some kind, he said, index number D585 JNY. Blow the front off with the PIAT, shoot anyone that tries to run and grenade the insides. Use the motorcycles to cross over the countryside. Stop on the bridge near to the pub. When it's clear in both directions, pitch the bikes in the river. Then, a quick beer with Sean and Freddie, and we're back off to home.

It's on toward five-twenty now, so it should be along any minute. Nice to be in the country, though. The roads are narrow and the hedges are high, just the place for an ambush. These royalist shits can never win just because they think they can't be beaten. They think it's bloody El Alamein in North Africa we're fightin' and they're not even close!

"Something's coming," Michael said quietly, peering through the binoculars. Michael was a good lad, tough as nails. The loyalist coppers had caught him and beat him with a metal pipe one time, and he'd never said a word. It was a comfort to have him along on this.

It was a medium-sized lorry that could be seen, square-fronted, painted a dingy gray or green, he couldn't tell for sure at this distance. It weaved its way down the slight hill, following a road whose path had been established in the middle ages by followers of Hadrian. As it dipped at the bottom, it disappeared from sight momentarily then suddenly reappeared as it climbed the next hillock. With the evening light at their back, it would be a simple operation to carry out successfully.

At the peak of the next hill, Michael confirmed the index number. It was the wrong one. A sign on the canvas cover over the back said "Furniture Removals" and a had a telephone number.

"Out of sight until they're past, Nick. Here's a place, just step through the hedge." But the satchel with the grenades became tangled in the sling of his 9MM Skorpion machine pistol and caused him to lose his grip on the PIAT. It fell in the tall weeds by the side of the road as the two of them slipped through the hedge to hide. He reached back through the opening in desperation to retrieve the weapon.

"It's deep in the grass. Don't worry, it's OK," Michael whispered.

And it would have been OK, except that at that exact moment a motorcycle came hurting toward the lorry. The driver of the lorry lunged quickly for the left side of the road and came within inches of running over the small pipe-like anti-tank weapon. But the collision was avoided and appropriate hand gestures were directed at the motorcycle by the lorry driver who then steered back onto the narrow paved surface. A light rain began to fall once more.

Nick and Michael heard someone immediately call out, "Wait! Wait! I saw something back there," and the lorry came to a stop at the side of the roadway. A figure wearing a white T-shirt and Levis popped out the cab's left door and ran directly toward where they were concealed. The young man searched the roadside and stopped by the PIAT, staring down wide-eyed. "Oi, Ronnie, come have a look! I think it's a bloody rocket!" Ronnie crawled out the driver's side and strolled over. They were looking at the object on the ground trying to decide whether to touch it when Nick shot them each through the head. Michael helped drag the bodies behind the hedge.

"See anything yet?" Nick asked, idly going through Ronnie's pockets to see if he had any money.

"Yes, it looks like a bus," Michael answered. He pronounced it "boose" in the Irish manner.

Nick pocketed the £25 that he found on Ronnie, and turned to the man in the white T-shirt. *You're a dumb fook with all your perfect eyesight, seeing the PIAT in the grass. If you'd played with yerself more and needed to wear glasses, you might still be alive right now.* He collected £14 from the man's pockets, looked at the gold-plated watch on the left wrist, and decided that he didn't want it. Grasping the man's chin, he moved the head so he could see where the bullet had entered.

Both men had been looking at the ground and he had shot each of them in the forehead. This bullet hole was a bit to the left of his aim point. He stared at the entry wound clinically, then straightened up and went to where Michael was peering through the binoculars.

"About four hundred yards away," he said flatly. "And the index number is correct."

"I hope it's the bloody Army, coming back from a cricket match. I'd love to butcher them bastards for what they did to Kelly," Nick said, stepping through the hedge and picking up the PIAT from the long, wet grass.

"Kill them for what they're doing to Ireland, Nick, not for what they did to Kelly. Their three hundred yards away now."

Nick gave the weapon a quick once-over. PIAT, or Projectile, Infantry, Anti-Tank. A warhead the size of a rugby ball, no, a bit smaller, more like an American football, and stuck point-forward on the end of a three-foot- long tube filled with propellant. Insert the tube in the launcher, fold out the blast shields, put it on your shoulder and fire. Resting the butt of the launcher tube on the ground, he idly peered at the dirty green paint on the projectile. From a distance he would look like a man looking at a shovel. There was some very faint stenciling in white letters. He brushed at it with his hand to clear away the rain droplets and dust. It read, "Deutsche Munitionsfabrik G.m.b.H. 11-11-43"

"Michael, me lad!" he called out, hefting the launcher to his shoulder with a smile. "We have to be getting some newer weapons. This was made for old Adolf on Remembrance Day in '43, before the two of us were born."

"They made the best, and we use nothin' but the best," Michael answered. "Get ready. One hundred fifty yards."

The bus was one of the modern ones with the large front window glass and the engine mounted back in the cabin alongside the driver. As it crested the hill at a distance of perhaps fifty yards, Nick fired at the chromium name above the radiator's grille. There was a reassuring crack as the fifty-year-old missile left the launcher and entered the vehicle just under the "L" in "VOLVO". Had it not been an old warhead, with its explosive charge oxidized by age, the projectile would have blown the bus to smithereens and killed Nick and Michael as well. After all, it had originally been designed to stop Russian and American tanks. A bus was not a tank. It had no armor.

The front of the bus turned into a ball of orange and black smoke which died down quickly as the vehicle careened to a stop in the ditch about thirty feet away. The blast had shattered the front end and disintegrated the wheels. Heads could be seen moving about in the smoke-filled interior. Michael idly shot the remaining windows out of the bus with a burst of fire from his machine pistol. All became silent except for a groan or two, oddly high-pitched, some muffled sobs, and the sounds of the crackling fire at the front of the bus. The familiar smells of cordite, rubber and burning flesh wafted about to tingle their nostrils.

Nick had dropped the launcher now, and approached the smoking ruin with his machine pistol at the ready. Michael smoothly replaced his empty magazine with a full one. They peered into the smoke filled cavern of death that was their latest creation. The driver, a man of perhaps fifty years, was burnt black and still sitting upright, strapped in the seat. The explosion had opened his chest and belly like an autopsy surgeon. From his old biology lessons, Nick easily identified the stomach, lungs, liver, small intestine, large intestine. . .

Back a bit from the wreck, Michael trained his weapon on the mass of twisted, burnt steel and broken glass. He was waiting for the Army to begin to fight back, and then he would machine-gun them all. Nick moved forward quickly but cautiously, and peered through a broken side window. The passengers were midgets or, at least small people of some kind. He attempted to brush away the smoke with his free hand. He was working the confusion out in his mind when a voice below the window ledge in front of him startled him. Startled, he flinched as the voice called, "Mommy! Please help me! I'm hurt!" It was an American accent. It was a child! They had attacked a busload of children!

Nick hung his head in tired disgust at what had just happened. "Ah, Jesus, Michael, come here. We're damned to hell now. We've just ambushed a bus filled with kids!" He turned away and retched. It was too much. It isn't right! They can't ask things like this of any man!

145

Something pulled at his arm. Michael was tugging at the satchel.

"Give me some of the grenades, Nick. Let's finish and be on our way. If you've not got the stomach for it, then stand by the motorcycles and I'll do the job by myself."

"Come here, Michael, and see what we've turned into!" Nick replied, and tugged at his sleeve. He and Nick looked in the nearest window. A small girl, perhaps seven years of age, her white blouse still tucked neatly into her dark gray pleated school uniform skirt, was flopping about in the throws of a painful death. Her arms flailed like white fish on the end of an unseen nylon line. On her back in the seat, she stopped moving suddenly and turned her face turned toward them. The eyes were wide with pain and terror. HELP ME, PLEASE! she mimed soundlessly. Then the open mouth froze and began to slowly fill with blood as the bright brown eyes glazed over in death.

Michael casually reached inside the bus and tossed the front of the little girl's skirt over her head. Pulling down the white panties, he observed, "Well, she's got no fur so she's too young to be screwing. Anyway, she's dead and that's the end of it, so give me some grenades and let's be done with all this."

Nick drew the Walther PPK pistol from his pocket, the pistol he had so recently killed the two lorry-men with, and shot Michael through the back of the head as he turned away.

Abruptly, one of the nearby black-clad referees blew his whistle and stopped play, the shrill noise echoing in the still air. He cautioned Nick for shooting a man who wasn't looking. Waving the yellow card above Nick's head, the referee then began the process of writing his name and number in the book. The small girl with the mouthful of blood sat up and smiled as the gore spilled down over her clean white shirtfront. She took Nick's hand and squeezed so hard that he felt a bone break. The referee kept yelling at him about something he could not understand, and kept poking him in the chest with his pen as he waved the yellow card around wildly. The man was probably one of those damn Yugoslavs they brought in for the international matches. He'd had enough of this foreigner's crap. Nick swung at the man with all his might, but only fell out of his bunk onto the concrete floor of his cell at Eastbourne.

Each time he tried to sleep, another version of the same scene played in his head. He had not been insane when they brought him here, but he would be insane before left. He was only here to be kept safe from the people he had informed upon, his old comrades in the IRA.

Confessing to the hospital's priest had been a waste of time. The man was used to dealing with the mentally deficient and barely listened to what he said. He had told him the whole thing in excruciating detail, but the priest only gave him two Hail Marys and two Our Fathers. Penance for murdering children. Deliberately murdering babies. It was not the same as bombing a pub where the Ulstermen drank and killing the children who had gone to the place with mum and dad. No, their dad was a sworn killer and the women and children always had to suffer for the sins of the fathers. But this had been different. He would have to speak with different people to make the nightmare go away. He would call the Americans. Perhaps they could help.

But how? Not through his solicitor, because the man would grass him to the British. After all, the British were paying the man. Perhaps one of the other lads would have an idea. He would speak to them during the exercise period in the yard.

At two in the afternoon, in the forty-five degree chill of the day, the prisoners were all led outside to exercise. The screws were all bundled up as though they were north of the arctic circle. The five Irishmen clustered in a group twenty yards away with their sleeves rolled up to show off to the guards.

"Who's got the fags today?" one asked, and reached for the proffered cigarette. It was Greene, the bomber who had stayed silent while the British had turned the rest of his team loose and then let out the word that he had informed on them all. At first, his old mates had refused to believe the British lie, but gradually their paranoia overcame them and they sent a man to the prison to kill him. But Greene had cut the man's throat instead and watched him gurgle blood bubbles as he died. A man he knew and trusted, sent to kill him by his friends. He told the grapevine that the man had been a turncoat. He must have been such to try and kill an honest soldier like himself. But the word came back that he was the turncoat, and that he would never live to see Christmas. He offered them a chance to back down, but they killed his brother instead as a warning. So he told the British everything he knew in return for relocation. Maybe the British were right. Maybe the Irish were all either stupid or crazy.

There was also Feeney, an assassin and a damn good one until he got shot in a botched ambush, hit by one of his own team and left to die.

And there were two others that Nick didn't know.

"The next man to get released," Nick said, "is to call the Americans and tell them to come see me." Four heads nodded in assent as the wind in the exercise yard blew their cigarette smoke high into the foggy air.

When he was returned to his cell, there was a parcel waiting on his bunk. It had been opened and pawed through by the screws.

"You bastards!' he screamed through the grate in the door. "I don't get a damn thing from you for a year, not a letter, not a phone call, not a whit. And then my Mother sends me a package and you can't wait to tear it up and throw it in my face!"

A guard came clumping down the corridor. No, not a guard, but the head man himself, silver braid on the cap and all.

The man looked seriously at him through the door's grill. "Whether you believe me or not, prisoner, this is the only package you have received since you have been here. And we did not tear it up, as you said. We x-rayed the parcel and saw that it contained items that we could not readily identify, so we opened it and examined them. The articles in question turned out to be some letters wrapped in a chain and a St. Christopher medal. We censored the letters the same as we do all the prisoner's, and then passed them along. If we were going to steal anything from you, prisoner, it would have been the cake, because it smelled delicious. So stop your ranting and enjoy what you have before I have it all taken away for inciting you to violence. Understood?"

O'Flynn spit at the man through the grill, but he only made a mess on the door as the cover was slammed shut. He returned to his bunk and held the letters lovingly in his hands. They were signed "love,

Mother", but they were written by his wife. He could tell by the script that had been paddled into the wee Killarney schoolgirl all those years ago by the nuns. She spoke of the children and how they missed him, and the pains came to his heart again. He steadied himself and looked at the cake. Only one-fourth of a cake, it was, by tradition. One fourth each for the Father, the Son, and the Holy Spirit, and the remaining fourth for the prisoner. God bless them all for thinking of him.

He would share the cake with Barney. A man alone can go crazy if he has no company, so Barney had become his companion. The name came from some American TV character that had been the last thing he had ever heard his daughter speak about. Speaking kindly, Barney was a largish mouse that lived in the hollow wall adjacent to his cell, a mouse that would come and share his meager fare when O'Flynn pulled the loose stone out near the baseboard and held out a bit of bread stolen from the canteen. Objectively, one would have too say that Barney was a rat, but a smallish one, however. He was as black as Satan's heart, but he was alive and always pleased to be with O'Flynn.

There was a wooden crucifix attached to the wall near where the stone came loose, so he had been able to pretend that he was communing with the Almighty while in fact he had been communing with Barney. He sat cross-legged on the stone floor below the cross and reached into the parcel that had been wrapped in brown paper by his wife. He placed the cake in its waxed paper wrapping on the floor in front, and pulled the stone from near the baseboard. Perhaps Barney was not in tonight. Perhaps Barney would not like cake with the hard, Irish sugar icing that his wife made.

"Barney?" he called softly.

The twitching, ever suspicious pink nose appeared in the two-inch opening. Slowly, Barney emerged from the opening into the cell, his head waving about to find the source of the wonderful smell teasing at his nostrils. O'Flynn watched his rodent friend search for a time, then lovingly broke off a piece of the icing - the best part of the cake - and held it out for him to take. Barney snatched the sugary treat and went to the near corner of the room, then sat up on his back feet like a squirrel and spun the piece around in his front paws looking for the appropriate place to begin eating. Then he devoured it like a starving man, almost in one bite.

O'Flynn broke off a piece of the cake for himself now, happy that his friend was satisfied. As he started to take a bite, he saw that Barney was rubbing his back on the floor in ecstasy like a cat. He never knew that mice did that. He paused and watched the show that his friend was putting on.

But it wasn't ecstasy. They were convulsions. There was foam coming out of Barney's mouth now. Two more twitches and he was still.

O'Flynn threw the piece of cake against the wall and screamed at the top of his lungs against the murderers who would give him poisoned cake to feed his only friend in the world. He heard the boots clomping down the hallway toward his cell, and had an idea. He would find out who had tried to kill him. Quickly, he stuffed Barney's lifeless body under his cot, and as the cell door opened, he lay on the floor screaming in imagined pain.

"What the hell do you think you're up to prisoner? You can't be making this kind of din in the afternoon, son. People are trying to sleep," the warder chided.

"Oh, Christ, Will, look at this!" another voice could be heard to say. "It's the damn cake! Somebody's poisoned the man. Call the doctor and help me get him to the infirmary. Jesus, does nobody check on this stuff? Oh, Lord, there's going to be hell to pay for this, Will. What will they do to us? It happened on our rounds!"

"Shut up, you whinger, and help me get him to the doctor. At least he's still alive, that's something."

The two men struggled with O'Flynn and dragged him down the corridor, terrified all the time at what would happen to them.

The doctor on duty looked surprised as the two men burst in dragging a third one by the arms.

"What's all this, then?", he asked.

They told him. He sent them immediately back to the cell to retrieve the cake, and they scurried away. They returned with the parcel and held it out tenuously for the doctor to examine.

"Never mind," he said. "Put it over there on the table. I can smell the strychnine from here. It's an advantage that comes from not smoking, as a matter of fact. You might consider that if you are having troubles with your cook. Unfortunately, there's nothing we can do for the prisoner. The minute that he bit down on the first mouthful, he absorbed a lethal dose through the mucous membranes in his mouth."

O'Flynn frightened the wits out of all of them by sitting up from the bed and saying, "Then it's damn lucky that I didn't eat any of it, isn't it?"

But at least now he knew that the staff hadn't been the ones that had tried to kill him. And he knew that his wife hadn't been the one, so that just left his friends in Eire with the Irish Republican Army. He could only pray that the Americans would come before they tried again.

At noon the following day the call arrived at the American embassy. "Tell whoever might be interested that Nick O'Flynn would be liking to have a chin-wag with the CIA, if that were possible. He's in Eastbourne as Case Number 77-1033 under the name John O'Halloran, a convicted wife-murderer," the husky voice on the telephone said. The desk officer waved his hands wildly at the people in the room and made sure the monitor and trace circuits were active. Then he asked for a repeat of the message saying that he was having trouble hearing because of some background noise at the caller's end. The voice responded that it was "that bloody Airbus taxiing away from the gate and making noise like all the banshees from hell", and repeated the message word for word again. The desk officer asked who Nick O'Flynn was. The caller hung up.

Analysis of the monitor tape confirmed that the noise was the compressor scream of an Airbus' engines, first in start mode, then in taxi mode. The sounds were moving away and getting fainter, so the airplane was taxiing away from the phone's location. That indicated that the call had been made from an airport where an Airbus was about to depart. A schedule check with the airlines database confirmed an Airbus flight leaving Charles de Gaulle airport near Paris at the time of the call.

Sitting behind his desk and drinking a cup of cold coffee, Wylie stared at the report from the previous evening. He keyed in some changes to the security criteria so that fewer people would have access to the document.

It was ten in the morning and Piper was sitting in front of Wylie's desk. He saw him suck on the cup's contents and wince. He winced back in sympathy.

"Where did you sleep last night?" Wylie asked idly as he stared at his computer terminal.

"On the cot next door, just like the night before."

"How's your lady-friend feel about your being off on your own?"

"She understands. She'll be there when we're done." Yeah, right, sure she would. He was a dead man on the far side of a burnt-out bridge.

Wylie's chocolate face seemed more creased than usual, his hands tapped nervously on the desk. His eyes were bloodshot. With a sudden, smooth move of his right hand he swiveled the computer's screen around.

"Read this while I go get another cup of coffee and drain off some of the earlier ones," he said as he got up from the gray swivel chair and lumbered away.

The Brits hid O'Flynn in a prison to keep him out of the clutches of the IRA Those Irishmen would make him die a painful death for informing on them if they could, because it serves as a warning to others. He pressed the key marked "Page Down" and read some more.

Voice Technology section said that their was a 97% probability that the caller was Irish.

Additional statements had been added to the report. One said that two former IRA members had been released from Eastbourne the day before and had were being relocated to New Zealand with new identities. Another entry said that Air New Zealand had a one-stop flight to Auckland that departed Charles de Gaulle forty-five minutes after the Airbus they had heard in the background left for New York.

Conclusion: a high probability that Nicholas O'Flynn has passed a message to one of the men who was leaving on relocation and asked him to call the American embassy. The man had chosen to call just before he boarded the plane, thinking that he would avoid the possibility of being traced to his new home in New Zealand. He had no chance of concealing this information from the CIA and its technology.

As Wylie came back in the office, Piper quickly hit the "Page Up" key twice and leaned back in his chair.

"I don't care about you reading the entire document, Mr. Piper. No need to be coy."

"Sorry for trying to pretend," he responded. "I forgot that I was dealing with a professional. By the way, Eastbourne is a prison for the criminally insane, isn't it?"

Wylie sat down and gave him his patented tired look, shrugged his shoulders and turned the screen back around so that only he could see it. "What to do, what to do," he mused out loud.

Piper sat quietly, watching the dust motes rise in the morning sunbeams.

"OK, here it is: we're not going to touch this. Officially, that is," Wylie began. "I don't need the heat from MI5 and MI6. Even though there's no reason that we couldn't have found out through other means that O'Flynn is being detained at Eastbourne. But I don't want to get involved in a Q and A session with the British Home Office. In addition, the call may have been a trap just to see what we would do."

"Why not simply call your British contacts and tell them you want to speak with O'Flynn. Tell them that you know he's going to be relocated, and that you want to ask him what he knows about, as an example, IRA money-raising among the Irish families in New York City," Piper offered. "This is too good an opportunity to miss. O'Flynn is one of the players in that scene that occurred in front of Gurney's eyes that night in Belfast. He may be able to tell us who the other people around the taxi were."

"Intelligence work is just a simple little pastime to you, isn't it, Mr. Piper?" Wylie looked seriously exhausted now. He sounded worn out as well from the day-to-day hassles of trying to guess where the next memo-missile was going to come from. Suddenly, his creased face lit up in a smile. "Yeah, why not? I'll call them and say that I know O'Flynn is scheduled for relocation and that we want a chance to interview him before he leaves. If they say they want to monitor the interview, I'll tell them we have heard that he may want to speak about some British citizens that collaborated with the IRA. If the British want to officially monitor the interview, they will have no way of using the famous 'plausible denial' if they are questioned. However if they aren't present at the interview, we could promise to share the information with them if it was appropriate. If it was bad news, they could always look at it off line. Yeah, I like that idea a bunch! You want to go talk to O'Flynn, Mr. Piper? I'd rather use you than one of my people because. . ."

"Plausible deniability, in other words?"

Wylie frowned and said, "Well? Yes or no?"

"Of course I'll do it," Piper answered. "I'll go first thing tomorrow morning."

"Horse crap! Go now, it isn't that far. It's down in Sussex somewhere. Get the job done for Christ's sake, and let's get this monkey put to bed!".

"Mixed metaphor," Piper said. "Get the monkey off our backs or put the matter to bed. Not both."

"Get out of my office," Wylie said, pointing toward the door.

Checking out a nondescript Vauxhall four-door hatchback and getting directions from the motor pool, he paused for some take-away sandwiches and ate them as he drove. Wylie was right: in an hour, he was there. It was a large gray stone expanse in the middle of a large green meadow. It looked just like all the prisons he's seen in the British movies.

"Lewis Piper to see John O'Halloran, number 77-1033," he said to the graying man in the blue uniform at the front desk.

"Yes, we know Mr. O'Halloran's number, thank you Mr. Piper. And we also received a call about your visit. We're actually quite well-informed here, thank you."

Snotty old coot, he thought.

Looking down officiously at some papers on the desk while reaching out his hand to Piper, the man said, "Some identification, please, preferably with a picture that actually looks like you."

What an officious butt-head. He handed over his Texas drivers license.

"Texas?" the man said with raised eyebrows. "How incredibly droll. The very essence of the American cowboy comes to mind. The very same essence that we attempt to scrape off our boots and leave on the doorstep. However. . ."

Even though he had not expected this kind of treatment, Piper knew from years of practice how to deal with this particular type of self-important British twit.

"Do shut up and get Mr. O'Halloran to an interview room quickly before I call your superior. And your superior would, I assume, be anyone in the South of England with at least one O-Level in something like Dressing Oneself Without Assistance. Find some Armenian immigrants to try your music hall act on. I'm sure they would find it irresistible."

The man's head snapped upright instantly. He scowled, but did as he had been instructed. A younger man in a blue uniform led Piper to the interview room after patting him down for prohibited objects like cigarettes and firearms. Unlike the snot at the front desk, the man at least apologized for the inconvenience.

In the interview room together, Piper introduced himself to O'Flynn without offering to shake hands. It was in the rules. No touching of any sort.

The man looked exactly like his pictures, except older. He was dressed in prison gray with no laces in his shoes. They sat opposite each other at a table in the middle of the large room. "Show me some identification, please," O'Flynn asked.

"Got none. They took it away at the front desk," Piper bluffed for no reason.

"Show me your wallet, Yank. They didn't take that at the front desk did they? And, congratulations for saying 'front desk' instead of 'reception', which a Brit would have said. So? Are you going to get out your wallet?"

He removed it and put it on the table between them.

"Why does your left hand have a quiver about it, but not your right, Yank?" O'Flynn asked with a smile.

Questions about his tremor irritated Piper and he had a tendency to snap back at the questioner. Needing O'Flynn's information however, he managed to be civil. "I got a compression fracture of the skull and some shrapnel in my back in Viet Nam. It came from a bullet or a mortar round, nobody knew which. It caused some neurological damage that gives me that tremor you see."

"Did they get all the metal out, or are you still carrying some about with you?" O'Flynn asked with a genuine look of curiosity on his face. Piper noticed for the first time that the man across the table from him actually had a quite youthful face. His skin was clear and unblemished, but the creases at the corners of the eyes and mouth were deep and dark and looked as though they had been drawn on with a black pencil.

"They got it all out, I think. Nothing ever shows up on x-rays," he responded.

"I got cracked in the side once and got a couple of ribs broke," O'Flynn said softly. "Then I took another in the upper arm here," he said patting his left shoulder. "They never got all the bits and bobs out, and it hurts like the devil when it's cold and damp. I'm hoping they'll relocate me to Tahiti where I'll never be cold again as long as I live. Ever been there?"

"Tahiti? Yeah, but only on a stop-over to Australia. Just sat around the airport Nauru, that was all," Piper replied. He was enjoying the small talk.

"Do the women really walk about with their tits in the breeze like ye hear?" O'Flynn asked with a smile. "Jesus, I'd love to see that sight!"

"Not any more," Piper told him, sharing his sadness at the news. "There's always the nude beaches at Bondai in Australia, if you get the chance. Acres and acres of. . ."

"I'm married, ye know," O'Flynn interrupted. "Got a wife and two daughters that I'll never see again. She knows it, too, does Bernadette, my wife. I told her, when I go into hiding and they try to give you a chance to join me, don't ever do it. It'll just be the Micks tryin' to smoke me out. If we're to be together, then I'll be coming to get you in person. We've got a code, her and me, particular words that I have to say if I call, just to let her know that I'm not under threat and all that. But it's all for nothing. I'll never be free. I'll never see her or Megan or Janine again, and it breaks my heart."

The old eyes with the dark creases at the sides stared unfocused at the table as one finger traced an invisible pattern on the wooden plank top. Suddenly, he was back to reality. "So, are ye goin' to show me what's inside yer wallet, Yank?

Piper pushed it an inch closer to O'Flynn with his steady hand.

"I'll not be touching it, me lad. I only want to see what's inside."

He unfolded the plain and worn leather thing and placed a Visa card and an American Express card between them.

"Very nice! You have credit, I see. Look in my eyes and tell me the number of your Visa card."

Piper recited it from memory

"If this is your wallet," O'Flynn continued quickly,"
then you'll be able to tell me what the embossing says down in the corner without looking, won't you?"

"It says Genuine Buffalo Calf," Piper answered easily.

"And what's in the place where the money's supposed to be?" O'Flynn asked with a smile.

Piper put the English bank notes on the table and about seventy US dollars as well.

"Tell me who won the FA Cup last year, or I'm not saying another word to you, Yank."

Piper had no idea. He knew nothing about British soccer, the game they called football over here. He was finished before he even got started. "I'm sorry. I don't know anything about the FA Cup. I guess we're through . . ."

"No, we're just beginning. Any Brit, or anyone even living in Britain would know the answer to that. So you must be genuine, then. How do you come to remember your Visa number then?"

"I have a good memory for numbers and facts, that's all."

"Damn good thing you didn't memorize the FA Cup scores, isn't it?"

Piper chuckled and shrugged his shoulders. O'Flynn was a man who had spent his adult life in the shadows, and it showed.

"Where do ye want me to begin?" O'Flynn asked.

"Start with why you had your friend call the American embassy and say that you wanted to talk with us."

"Simple. One of my bloody mates is tryin' to kill me, is why. I never trusted the bastard, not after what he had me do to get free. He's got no morals and he's got no soul, so he tried to poison me with a bloody cake from my wife," O'Flynn answered.

"I'm not trying to start an argument here, buy how do you know it wasn't sent by your wife?"

O'Flynn told Piper about the parcel from home and the death of his pal Barney. "I never thought about it until later, but I'm sure my wife never baked that cake. All about the parcel seemed correct. There was a letter in my wife's handwriting, pretending to be my mother and saying how upset Bernadette was and how she couldn't bear to write me in prison and how much the girls missed me. That part was letter-perfect, just as we had always arranged: If I was in prison and my wife wanted to write to me, she would always write as though she was my Mother. And my mother would write pretending to be Bernadette. That way, if the Ulstermen or the Brits were forcing either of them to write, I'd know the letter was bollocks immediately. So, kind old man that I am, I give Barney some of the cake and he snuffs it on the spot. I hide Barney and pretend that it's me that's et the cake. I listen to the guards talking as they drag me off to the infirmary, and they're all, 'Oh Christ, we're for the chop, because he's died on our round' and 'Jesus, doesn't anyone check these parcels?', so they had nothing to do with it."

"Maybe it was the prison administration that did it," Piper ventured.

"No, ye see, if they'd been the ones, they'd have had to let the guards in on it, or pull them off for an emergency meeting or something. That way, no matter how loud I screamed, I'd be left in the cell to die. They couldn't have taken the chance that a fast-reacting guard could have rushed me to the infirmary and gotten my stomach pumped. No, it has to be the Brits. It has to be Harry and his friends."

"You said something about the cake earlier."

"Yes, if I had been noticing, I'd have known that Bernadette never laid eyes on that cake. Ye see, it was traditional Irish - right down to the sultanas baked inside, ye know, them dried white grapes. I hate sultanas, and Bernadette knew that. She never put them into our celebration cakes. But they were in this one. I could see them. So it weren't hers, and it weren't any she had ever seen."

"That's a very persuasive analysis, Mr. O'Flynn. I have to agree with you," Piper said.

"In my business, Yank, you either learn to think or you make plans to die young."

When he walked out of the prison two hours later, he had the complete story. O'Flynn had let it be know in the loyalist part of Belfast that he wanted out of the IRA conflict. He had seen plenty of the violence and had been a front-line part of much of it. He eventually got put in contact with a man he knew only as Harry. Harry was definitely British and well-educated. O'Flynn could tell that by the man's accent and the cut of his clothes. He met Harry several times and passed him information about some of the ongoing operations to prove his good faith. Harry acted on the information and agreed to keep him out of it. No one ever suspected him of being a turncoat.

Even though he had a phone number for contacting Harry, and even though he met with him on a half-dozen occasions, he never saw the man's face. Harry always wore a cap or hat of some kind, and always stayed in the shadows with a muffler or coat collar hiding his face. He remembered that Harry's eyes were blue.

Harry had been the man in the taxi who pulled up and spoke to O'Flynn in Belfast the night that Gurney was up in the attic on watch. They had arranged a street-meeting and O'Flynn had chosen the place. Harry told him of his efforts to find him a home for him, and said he was working on getting him amnesty so that he could turn himself in. O'Flynn was desperate to get out, and was terrified that he would be discovered. He begged Harry to save him. He reminded him that he had supplied information, and would supply more once he was safe. Harry told him to be patient, and at the meeting on the street he was given a cellular phone. Harry said that he would be contacting O'Flynn from then on for information, not the other way around. He was told to expect a call within the next two weeks. O'Flynn was unhappy, but he had no choice but to do as Harry told him.

The call had come very quickly, perhaps two days later. Harry wanted O'Flynn to arrange an ambush within two days on a particular stretch of road in Surrey. It was described as an attack on a commercial vehicle and he was given the vehicle's index number. Everyone in the vehicle was to be killed, no exceptions. If he did the job correctly, Harry would bring him in and he would never be linked to the murders.

O'Flynn jumped at the chance to finally get done with the IRA. It was one more ambush of the hated English, no more, no less, and he accepted without qualms. He and a close friend named Michael, whose last name he would not say, came to London on a commercial flight. They had forged papers. The drew pistols, automatic weapons, grenades, and a rocket launcher from an IRA storehouse there and set about to make the attack.

Two truckers stumbled onto them at the site and stopped. He killed them both and drug their bodied off the road. They left the truck parked by the side of the road, and the ambush went off as planned. They hit the vehicle with a rocket and fired on it with automatic weapons. When they moved forward to finish off the occupants with grenades, O'Flynn discovered that they had attacked a busload of children. He was mortified at what they had done. He refused to throw grenades into the bus to kill the survivors, and killed the man named Michael when he said he would do the job anyway, children or not.

That was his description of the school bus attack. No American was involved, just him and Michael doing what Harry had told them to do. He called and confronted Harry with what he had been ordered to do, but Harry just passed it off as the fortunes of war. As agreed, Harry gave him the address of a safe house where he could turn himself in to the police and receive amnesty for his deeds in return for telling on his friends.

If his story is to be believed, then the police should have found three additional bodies at the scene not connected to the school bus, each of whom had been shot through the head with a small-caliber pistol.

Piper decided against calling Wylie immediately, and chose instead to drive to Nancy's house and surprise her. He'd been gone two days now, and he could turn the car in at the embassy tomorrow just as well as tonight. If he'd been paying attention to his surroundings instead of thinking about Nancy, he might have noticed the blue Jaguar sedan that followed him as he left the prison.

CHAPTER TWELVE

ROADBLOCK

Everywhere he turned, the traffic was terrible. There were giant diesel trucks and huge busses and zillions of cars, all apparently going the same direction as he. Everybody had decided to go see Nancy Carpenter at exactly the same time. Finally, he decided that he'd try the M25, the main freeway circling London, and see if that was any better. It took him a full half-hour to go the seven miles to the on-ramp. It was dark now, and he was getting tired. And feeling his age. Maybe he was too old for this anymore.

As soon as he got onto the M25, the traffic began to slow down as if by magic. Apparently, God knew that he was in a hurry, and had decided to screw around with him. The traffic in all three lanes gradually slowed to a stop and stayed there as the evening's rain began to fall over the assembled multitudes.

He was in the outside lane, the one next to the grass verge separating the eastbound and westbound traffic. He was headed east, so naturally, the westbound lanes looked like a speedway, all the cars were moving so rapidly. All he could see in front was about a mile of traffic, all three lanes stopped dead, leading up and over the top of a slight incline. He let the engine idle and turned down the volume on the radio he had tuned to classical music on some offshore station. The interval timer cycled the wipers back and forth across the windshield every twenty seconds.

A tap on his window nearly startled him out of his skin. It was a woman police constable, about mid-twenties, blond, asking him to shut off the engine and leave the headlights on, saying there would be somewhat of a delay. No kidding, Sherlock What was your first clue? But she looked fetching in her uniform with the "Traffic Warden " badge over her ample left breast, wearing her neat black rain slicker. The top buttons of her blouse were undone, and he could see that she had a nice-looking set of boobs. He watched her in the rearview mirror as she walked past the car behind him into the darkness beyond. She looked like she had a nice body under all that frumpy clothing. She had a cute accent, too, but it wasn't British. It was a kind of Nordic something, maybe German. Must be an immigrant from the Common Market. The man behind him hadn't obeyed her instructions to leave his headlights on. Maybe he was just slow. Everything else was slow this evening, so why not him?

Ahead, flashing lights could be seen through the drizzle as the wreckers tried to untangle the mess. Two men in the same type of dark blue rain suits went walking past the passenger side of the car. Between them they carried a pair of eight-foot aluminum poles wrapped in an orange cloth that looked like an oversized stretcher. He saw them pass the car behind him and then stop and move the poles down from their shoulders. Then he saw two more men carrying the same type of long orange-cloth poles coming at a fast pace following their comrades. As he watched, each man took a pole and began to unwind the cloth that stretched between them. The young woman appeared by his window again, just as someone yelled a single word that sounded like "Sofa!".

Sweet Jesus! It was a trap!

Cold sweat shot out of his pores like ice rockets. He absorbed them and began to stabilize his breathing. The poles and orange cloth had been a screen to shield his car from the view of the other motorists in the traffic line. In the rearview mirror he saw that the screen in back was almost in place; the men in front were having a problem with theirs because of the sharp gusts of wind. A large dark-uniformed man was running toward his car with a determined look on his face and a large sledgehammer clutched in his left fist.

As he fired up the engine, he leaned on the horn to throw off their rhythm and swung the front of the Vauxhall directly at the blond with the big wahoos who was trying to get something out of her jacket pocket. He bounced her shapely body off the hood and then on to the ground. She made a grunting sound as she hit off to the right somewhere. The sledgehammer man swung and missed, then threw the thing at him and missed again. Zero for two, and tough luck for the bad guys. The rear window of the hatchback exploded and disappeared as a bullet struck it. Scrunching low in the seat, he covered his left eye against flying glass fragments as two more bullets hit the left side of the windshield. Europeans, he thought casually, amazed once more at how violence had a calming effect on him, then amazed again that he was spending precious brain power analyzing the situation. They put two shots into the left side of the windshield. They had been under stress and had been aiming for the driver. Only the driver wasn't on the left side as he is in wherever they came from; the driver was on the right because this was England. If an Irishman like O'Flynn had been doing the shooting, most likely he would be dead by now. He tore directly across the verge toward the westbound traffic and swerved at the last minute, managing to avoid crashing into the concrete drainage ditch hidden in the grass. So now the only way was to drive parallel to the traffic jam, and hope that there were no ditches or fences in the way. Near the front of the jumble of lights, the Vauxhall's engine and shock absorbers were complaining loudly about being used as an off-road vehicle when another concrete ditch appeared. He steered left, directly for the blockage in the roadway, and began blowing the horn continuously. People were scurrying for their lives to get out of his headlight beams as he turned onto the paved shoulder, skidded briefly, then shot onto the clear road ahead of the commotion. It wasn't a wreck, either, it was just a huge truck stalled crossways the freeway. A roadblock. A setup. He saw a blue Jaguar sedan trying to follow his path from the grass verge onto the freeway, but a policeman in a yellow slicker stepped out swinging a shovel and broke one of the car's headlights. The driver apparently didn't want any trouble with the police, and the car skidded to a stop.

Yellow slicker. Of course! The police wear yellow rain-suits, not blue ones. They wear yellow for visibility. They want to be seen. And Traffic Wardens give tickets to people whose parking meters have expired. They don't patrol the freeways. And they don't fumble in their pockets when challenged, because they don't carry guns like the blond with the accent did.

There was only him and the open road now, so he took the first turnoff and headed North. The main goal now was getting out of London alive until things cooled down. They knew how his mind worked, so that meant they had access to his government records. So the right thing under these circumstances would be to do things the wrong way. That would be dangerous, but it would not be expected.

There was obviously a transmitter attached to his car, and it was broadcasting his location. It was pouring rain, and he had no time to stop, crawl under the car and remove the device. So, he needed to immediately abandon the car and find another means of transport. He found himself driving through a sleazy London suburb now and looked to be the only white man in sight. He parked the car on the street in front of a billiard hall fronted by a group of black youths standing in the entry to keep out of the rain. Hoping beyond hope that someone would take the car and lead the bad guys away from him, he left the keys in the ignition and slammed the door loudly to attract attention. Feigning a limp to appear slow and non-threatening, he hobbled off down the sidewalk to look for a train station, a bus stop, anything to get him out of here. The black youths watched him, but did not follow.

Suddenly he was overcome by fatigue. He was not used to this level of exertion, mental or physical, and his adrenaline rush was abruptly wearing off. Then his salvation appeared in the form of a brightly-lit Jamaican bar.

Back at the Embassy, Wylie yelled at Janet to check with the garage to see if Piper was back from Eastbourne. He had already called Nancy at the number that he had been given, and she said that she hadn't heard from him for two days, and asked if there was a problem. She was told that they were making a routine inquiry, that was all. The Administrator at Eastbourne said that Piper had checked out at a little after five that afternoon. It was now eight-thirty. Could be the traffic, Wylie thought, and decided he'd stay another hour and wait.

Answering the phone, he expected it to be Piper telling him that he'd be in tomorrow, the traffic was too terrible for him to drive back tonight, he had a splitting headache, he was hungry and needed to stop for a bite to eat, but all he got was the Desk Officer telling him that the Vauxhall had been seen driving recklessly around a stoppage on the M25. Surrey Constabulary were also checking out a report from a witness that said a pedestrian had been struck by the Vauxhall as it fled the scene, although the injured pedestrian had not been found anywhere. Another witness had said that shots had been fired at the car as it sped away.

"What the hell is going on?" Wylie mumbled under his breath. "Janet! Call Marcus and tell him to get his skinny ass in my office right now!" Wylie yelled as loud as he could, hoping that she was there to hear him. *Gotta get some help. This thing is rolling out of control.*

Marcus peered around the edge of Wylie's door. "Yes, Chief?"

"Get in here and shut the door behind you. No, tell Janet to get us all some food and some beer right now, before she goes home. Tell her to get the money from petty cash. Go away, Marcus! Do it, and then come back and shut the door. I need to talk with you."

Marcus went mumble, mumble, to Janet who wasn't pleased with the idea at all and said so. "I didn't ask for your opinion, Janet. I asked you to do it and to do it now," Wylie barked "Yes, but what kind of food Mr. Wylie? Is your stomach still giving you trouble? Would some Indian take-away be OK? Or should I get pizza? Italian sandwiches? Give me a hint, Chief."

"Janet. Food, hot. Beer, cold. Fuel for the furnace. Something to keep me functioning while I find out why Piper isn't back and what all this crap is about a Vauxhall with a registration number that says it's one of the embassy's cars is doing running over people that aren't there when they go and look for them. GO, Janet. NOW."

"You sure that you need me, Chief?" Marcus asked, showing just the minimum amount of his body in the doorway.

"Yes, I'm sure, Marcus. Get in here and close the door behind you."

Marcus shut the door.

"You ever been shot at, Marcus?" Wylie asked.

"Yes, once in the Sudan by some tribesmen that thought I was. . ."

"Shut up, Marcus. It was a rhetorical question. The point is, we are being shot at now, and we have to find out who is doing it. We have a civilian who is asking perfectly innocent questions about a US Navy officer convicted of helping the IRA, and :

    a. He's rousted by some damned retired magician in a restaurant, and now

    b. He's disappeared off the face of the Earth after going to speak with a turncoat IRA man in Eastbourne prison.

Now, I'm asking you, Marcus, just what the hell do you think is going on here? Have you got a single decent idea in that brainy head of yours?"

"First of all, Chief, I wouldn't classify Mr. Piper as Missing in Action just because he hasn't returned from Eastbourne yet. There may be all sorts of logical explanations to rationalize the delay."

"Marcus, that's bogus and you know it. Don't start blowing sunshine up my butt, sonny. I ain't the ambassador, I'm the head spook here. The Surrey Constabulary reports seeing the Vauxhall signed out by Piper driving recklessly around a stoppage on the M25. Somebody reports seeing a pedestrian hit at the scene, a pedestrian who can't be found by anybody. Another report says that shots were fired at the car. Gee, Marcus, does any of this sound even remotely like a clandestine operation mounted by person or persons unknown? How many phone calls do we get on a yearly basis about one of our vehicles thundering around the scene of a accident? Marcus, I need your brain. You ain't much to look at, but you're all I have. Now, tell me. Use your logical, unemotional, anorexic, computer-dweeb brain and tell me what happened when Piper went to see O'Flynn at Eastbourne Prison."

While Marcus composed his thoughts, Wylie took a bottle of Jack Daniels from his desk drawer, unscrewed the cap, and took a mighty pull at the contents. "You want a taste?" he asked Marcus.

"No thank you, sir," Marcus replied politely.

"You don't like drinking from the same bottle as a black man, is that it, Marcus?"

"You promote me to the same GS-level as you, and I'll drink your butt under the table, Chief," Marcus snapped.

"You got a deal, you narrow-assed white boy. For tonight, and for tonight only, you and I are equals. Now take a pull on the Jack and let's hear some smarts pop from your thin-lipped white mouth."

Marcus tilted his head back and poured the amber liquid directly into his open mouth until it was full, then swallowed without so much as a blink.

Wylie was impressed, but he didn't let it show. "OK, hot shot, you can drink from a bottle. Babies can do that. Tell me about Piper."

"It's O'Flynn," Marcus said. "He's the key. The bad guys know that he knows something, and they think that he told it to Piper. Whatever it is, it must be devastating, that's all I can say. Piper probably doesn't even recognize the significance, the poor bastard. The bad guys just got fixated on the target and began to tell themselves that if they can just get this one more guy to shut up, then life will be safe once more for the intellectual few."

"So you believe that the bad guys are the Brits, right?"

"Easy to check on, Oh Dark-Complected One," Marcus answered as the sour mash hit his circulatory system. "Call the facility at H. M. Prison Eastbourne and ask after the welfare of the prisoner known to the staff as John O'Halloran. I'll bet dollars to doughnuts that the minute that Piper left, some British gentlemen walked in the front door and asked to speak to the same person that Piper had spoken to. They'd have to ask exactly that way, because they wouldn't have known how O'Flynn was registered."

"What the hell are you talking about, Marcus? MI5 knew where O'Flynn was. They knew he was in Eastbourne prison. Sure they did."

"They absolutely did <u>not</u> know where he was. If they had known, they would have killed him in a heartbeat and never had to worry about the matter again."

"Oh, God," Wylie moaned out loud. "I told Parnell in MI5 where Piper was going, and I told him that he was going to interview O'Flynn. I'm the one that got him in trouble. It never occurred to me that they didn't know where he was. After all, I thought they would be in charge of protecting him!"

"No they're not his protectors at all. That the Home Office's job" Marcus responded. "One of us better call the prison and see if O'Flynn is still alive, or if he accidentally hanged himself in his cell just after Piper left."

Wylie pushed a piece of paper with a phone number on it to Marcus, saying, "You do it. I might get somebody else killed if I did it. What a bonehead thing to do!"

Marcus dialed and asked after the well-being of the prisoner registered as O'Halloran, then nodded his head and said 'uh-huh' then nodded his head some more. More nods, more 'uh-huhs' and then he said thanks and hung up the phone.

"Well?" Wylie asked.

"Just as we figured. Five minutes after Piper left, a man with MI5 credentials that said his name was Anton Reeves, walked in the front door and asked to speak with the same prisoner as the recently-departed American. He was told that he was required to identify the prisoner by name and Case Number, and to have the proper paperwork, but the man replied that he and the American were together and there was just one more question that he had to ask to complete their investigation. They told him, no paperwork, no visit. They also said that people from the Home Office, with the proper paperwork, came in later last night and moved the prisoner in question."

"So O'Flynn's gone?"

"Or he's dead."

Both men stared at the floor in silence.

"I hope he made it," Marcus said quietly. "I hope that he's on his way to be a gardener in the Royal Botanical Gardens in Adelaide, South West Australia."

Still no word from Piper. Nothing left to do but have another pull on the Jack, which they both did.

Janet returned about a half-hour later with Domino's Pizza and British-made Budweiser to find two drunks arm-wrestling at the Chief's desk. She deposited the food next to their straining elbows and left for home immediately, snorting about how little boys never grow up, they just get older.

The Desk Officer called with an update as they were eating pizza and drinking beer. Surrey Constabulary's follow-up included the fact that the origins of the traffic tie-up that the embassy's Vauxhall had been associated with were very confusing, if not suspicious. A lorry driver, one Dieter Mossbacher from Hamburg, German National ID Number 77Z552127866, Eurocom Commercial Drivers License 788D55177, employed by HannoLloyd GmbH of Bremen, had been seen with his twin-tandem 15-meter trailers stopped on the verge of the M25. Proper reflective warnings and blinking signals had been deployed, and police reported seeing him using a two-way radio, so they assumed that he was arranging for assistance and left him alone. Witnesses stated that at about six-thirty PM, the tractor and it's two trailers began to move onto the M25 at slow speed and gradually continued at an acute angle across the road until all three lanes were blocked, whereupon the vehicle stalled and would not restart. When the driver was questioned, he did not speak English. A German-speaking constable was dispatched to the scene, but could not make himself understood. He stated that the driver's accent was very guttural and didn't sound anything like German to him. A tow-truck operator called to the scene could not find anything wrong with the vehicle, and when he attempted to start it, the engine ran smoothly. After a copying of documents, the driver was allowed to continue his journey to Dover and thence back to Bremen. The suspicious part was that later checks by the constables revealed there was no company name HannoLloyd registered in Germany, and the identity card number and the drivers license number given by Dieter Mossbacher were false. An immediate search along the M25 turned up the truck and trailer parked at a roadside petrol station and restaurant establishment near Leatherhead. The driver was nowhere to be found. Investigators were going over the truck now for fingerprints and whatever else they could turn up. An additional follow-up bulletin would be issued, they said.

As the traffic jam eased after the truck was moved off to the roadside, several witnesses had stated that a number of people dressed in dark rain suits had gotten into two station wagons parked by the side of the roadway and forced their way into traffic in a reckless manner, causing at least one minor collision. The station wagons had sped away without leaving the required information behind. Both cars had Belgian number plates. Additionally, a Jaguar sedan had been momentarily stopped by the police when it attempted to circumvent the traffic jam in the same manner as the Vauxhall, but it had been released when the number plate proved to be restricted.

"What do they mean, 'restricted'?", Wylie asked.

"That's the British way of saying that it's assigned to one of the intelligence services and the local cops are instructed to offer the occupants what we call in America 'professional courtesy'. Those guys were probably Piper from the prison," Marcus replied hoarsely.

The two men sat through the night waiting for more information. At seven AM, they got it. The Desk Officer read a message that had just come over the direct link with the local law enforcement establishments.

The message read, "Hampshire Constabulary reports that a Vauxhall, index number H299JVX , matching Piper's car from the embassy motor-pool, was involved in an accident at about 0530 hours this morning. A passing motorist reported seeing a blue Jaguar sedan, registration unknown, appear to sideswipe the Vauxhall, sending it off the road. Both cars were traveling at a high rate of speed, estimated to be in excess of one hundred miles per hour at the time of the collision. The Vauxhall left the roadway and traveled no more that twenty meters before striking a tree and bursting into flames. Hampshire Fire Brigade, called to the scene to bring the blaze under control, report that the single occupant was burned beyond recognition. They are in the process of recovering the body, which will be transported to the Hampshire Pathology Laboratory for identification. Follow-up messages will be issued as appropriate."

Wylie slumped in his chair as he handed the message to Marcus. "I got him killed. Me and my stupid mouth got him killed."

Now he had no more choices. Now there was only one thing that he could do. Wylie was thinking out loud.

"I understand, sir. Someone will have to break the news to his lady friend in Surrey. What was her name? Nancy. . ."

"Carpenter," Wylie finished. "No, Marcus that's not what has to be done. I've got. . ."

"Of course, sir, the paperwork and the reports. My suggestion would be that none of this be mentioned. There is no reason to. . ."

"Shut up, Marcus! Just shut your damn mouth about women and paperwork! No, what happens now, Marcus, is that I go kill Reg Parnell. I haven't killed anyone in almost five years. Four years and seven months, to be exact. I'm going to enjoy this, that rotten bastard."

"Well, sir, you will have to go through the formalities. You will have to put the plan and the rationale in front of the Action Committee, and the Ambassador will have to be notified."

"There will be no presentation to any committee of any kind, and no one is going to tell the Ambassador anything. I am simply going to kill Reg Parnell, that is all. All I have to do now is decide how and when and where."

Marcus stared at his boss with a worried look.

"Marcus, there is a code in this business. You wouldn't understand, because you're not a field agent. In the field, there are no shades of gray, just black and white. Enemy or Friend. No sometimes-friends or semi-enemies. The British are our friends. Parnell took the information that I gave him and used it to kill Lewis Piper. To make sure that the British understand the seriousness of what he did, I will now kill him."

"But that makes no sense; you'll just start a war."

"It makes perfect sense, and there will be no war. Marcus, policemen are really just ordinary people. They have things they love and things they hate, just like everybody else. They have wives and husbands and children and mortgages just like the rest of the world. Didn't you ever wonder why, even in this era of narco-terrorism and escalating violence, more policemen's families, their wives and kids, don't become a target of the bad guys?"

"That's a disgusting thought," Marcus replied, "to get at someone through harming their family."

"And selling Crack to grammar-school kids, and using twelve-year-old girls for sex, that's not disgusting to you? It happens every day, and nothing we have done so far seems to be able to stop it. And yet, these same amoral, violent people don't attack a policeman's family. Why is that? Didn't you ever wonder?"

Marcus shrugged his shoulders, worried about the placid look on his boss' face.

"The answer is, Marcus, that to attack a policeman's family is the same as putting the muzzle of a pistol in your mouth and pulling the trigger. It's suicide. The policeman and his friends will hunt the perpetrator down. There will be no arrest, no trial, just death. It will be sure and certain, and it will be painful. Welcome to the real world," Wylie said without emotion.

The Ginger Tom

Of course, Lewis Piper was not dead because he was not the one driving the car when it crashed and burned. That person was a of the joy-riding teenager from the place he had parked the car, but Wylie had no way of knowing that at the time

At ten o'clock in the morning, Anton Reeves knocked once on the door of his Section Head's office at MI5, then entered the high-ceilinged sanctum.

"Good morning, Sir," he said in a cheery voice.

"So you believe it to be a good morning, do you Anton?"

"Yes, sir, I do. I can report that our problem with the loose ends of the Irish matter have been taken care of permanently. Home Office has apparently moved the man O'Flynn to his relocation as of last evening. And the American, who was quite a handful if I may be allowed to say, met with an unfortunate accident in Hampshire early this morning. A fatal automobile accident in a Vauxhall with a broken rear window."

The young man had done a splendid job on this matter. With less than an hour's notice he had driven to Eastbourne with another staff member, attached a transmitter to the man's car, put a tail on him as he left the prison at Eastbourne, organized and equipped a group of contract Europeans to trap the man in his car and kidnap him. When that failed, he managed to trace the car to a deserted road in Hampshire and have it and its occupant eliminated. However, the Section Head never liked for his staff to be too pleased with themselves, particularly when it involved independent thinking. Anton Reeves came from the proper background for the service, a double-first at Oxford and all that, but he was still too full of himself to really be trusted. His father was a multi-millionaire, something to do with real estate, but that could not be helped. One can't expect all the money to be in proper hands nowadays. A gentle upbraiding was called for in this case, just to remind the lad as to exactly where the power lay.

"Before you start passing champagne all around, Anton, perhaps you might give this report from the Hampshire Police chaps an overview." The Section Head passed over the document without looking at him.

The form was headed "Preliminary Pathology Report". It listed that the report was on a deceased person, male, incinerated in an automobile accident. The first classification was to check-mark either "Male", "Female" or "Not Determinable". "Male" was checked. No other notations were made on the body of the report. At the bottom, under "Comments", was a notation that because of the charring of the body in a fire, no further information could be made available on the deceased until a routine autopsy was performed.

"Just as a personal favor to me, Anton, would you be so kind as to check out a car and drive over to Hampshire? I know it's an inconvenience, but just in case you had the wrong man killed, it would be good to have this information as soon as possible, don't you agree?" Ice was caked on each of the Section Head's words.

"But it was the correct car, sir, there can be no doubt. . ." he said, visibly pale as he handed back the paper.

"Anton?"

"Sir?"

"I hope you realize the position that you have placed us in if this incinerated person does not happen to be the man, Lewis Piper. It will mean that he is on the loose somewhere with all the sensitive information that O'Flynn passed to him. And worse than that, Anton, he knows that you tried to kidnap him. If he happens to see the news coverage of the accident, he will then know that you tried to kill him. I hope that it is clear that you were the one who decided on that particular course of action, and that its disclosure will reflect on you personally and not on the service. Do you understand?"

The young man nodded soberly, saying, "Yes, Mr. Parnell," and left the room thinking about the long drive to Hampshire

CHAPTER THIRTEEN

SCRUFFY

A white man in the place meant that he was about to have a problem. He was either the police, Inland Revenue, or some other kind of trouble-maker. Prescott had run this bar for many years now, and had made a decent living catering to the whims of his Jamaican customers. It was difficult work at times balancing the competing desires. Some of his patrons liked to smoke a little Ganja while drinking his dark rum. It reminded them of the warmth of their home island. But the Narcotics Squad frowned officiously on their habits. Then there were the dangerous young neighborhood entrepreneurs who worked to leverage a man's taste for marijuana into the more powerful and expensive cocaine and heroin. Many of these could either be smoked or inhaled directly. But the powder was greatly addictive, and the people who used it were unstable and made more trouble than they were worth. As the white man approached the bar, he was carefully picking his way around the random tables with their various occupants, careful not to jostle anybody. A few turned to Prescott for a sign of some sort, and seeing none on his expressionless face, returned to their drinking, card playing and conversation.

Prescott motioned to Monster and Koko, then nodded toward the man as he continued his journey from the front door to the bar at the rear of Club Kingston. The two black men detached themselves from the wall they had been holding up and prepared to earn their retainer. Monster was from Haiti and could not read or write. But he weighed 350 pounds and could bite the neck off an unopened beer bottle, chew up the glass and bottle cap and swallow them with no noticeable side-effects. Koko was from Jamaica like himself, and had hoped to be a professional boxer until he took too many punches to the head. Now he hummed wordless songs and whispered secrets to people that only he could see. Both men lived nearby in dingy rooms and kept order in Prescott's bar for their keep. There was not much work for them to do in reality, because most people never wanted to argue with 600 pounds of anything that looked like Monster and Koko.

"I'd like a Red Stripe if you please, sir," the white man said politely. He had an American accent. Prescott held up his hand to stop the big men. They hesitated, then went back to their places. He got the man a cold beer from the fridge under the bar and removed the cap. Placing it in front of him, he asked, "Anything else?"

The American drained the beer without taking the bottle down from his lips. The man must have been thirsty. He was dirty, too. Not dirty for a Jamaican, mind you, but dirty for a white man. His hair was short and badly cut, and his leather jacket was torn at the elbow and too big for him. He needed a shave as well.

The man unfolded a crumpled £5 banknote in his left hand and asked, "Is this enough for two more beers, one for me and one for you?"

"That would be exactly correct change, thank you sir. And thank you for the beer as well," Prescott replied with as close as he ever got to a smile, putting the bill in the cash drawer. He opened both bottles and gave one to the American. Holding his bottle up, he said, "Cheers."

"Cheers," the man replied, and this time only drank half the bottle before he put it down.

Prescott eyed the man thoroughly. The man looked weary, and has dark circles under his eyes. If he was trouble, he was very good about it. But then, if he was trouble, there was always Monster and Koko.

"As I said before, is there anything else I can do for you?" Prescott asked.

"I need to use a telephone," he said, and before Prescott could point toward the pay phone on the wall, added, "I need a cellular phone."

"Cell phones are very expensive, sir. Are we talking Domestic or International calling?"

"International."

"It would be at least £50 for such a cellular telephone. For that I could guarantee that it would work for at least six hours."

The American reached in his shirt pocket and removed several bits of paper, one of which was a £10 note. "This is all I can afford. I need to make two calls, one now and one later. I'll make them sitting right here at the bar, and you can listen if you want."

Prescott pondered a moment. Here was this white man, sitting in a bar in the blackest section of southern England. If he was working for British Telecom trying to find out about stolen cell phones, then what he had just said was called entrapment. Besides, there was a cricket bat behind the bar. And, again, there was always Monster and Koko if things didn't work out with the bat.

Prescott was about to answer when the man spoke again. "Is there any chance that the telephone fee might include two more beers?"

"You mean one for you and one for me?" Prescott asked. The man nodded. "I think that would be exact change, thank you sir," as he straightened the £10 note and put it in the till. A cardboard box was lifted from under the bar. It was filled with clean, folded bar towels. Prescott pulled first one, then another, then another cellular telephone from under the towels. He handed the white man a Toshiba flip-phone, saying, "Here, give this one a try."

The man punched in a number and pressed SEND. Prescott heard the other end buzz and a voice say something as he pretended to wipe off the linoleum bar top. "I'm in deep trouble, Jim. Somebody just tried to kill me," the white man said. "I wasn't sure you'd even be in today. You said something about taking the day off when we spoke last. Yes. I went to interview the Irishman and got jumped on the way back. Only Wylie knew where I was going, so he has to be the guy who gave me to the other side."

"I heard from Wylie this morning, Lew."

Piper gave a start. "What did the rat want?"

"He called to say that he'd gotten you killed by not realizing that MI5 didn't know where the Irishman was being held until he told them. The only thing he didn't tell them was the name that the Irishman was jailed under, so they couldn't get to him. Apparently, they tried, but it didn't work, and in the wee hours of the next morning the Home Office moved him to his new location purely by chance. He told me that he knew that you and I were friends and that he wanted me to know that he was going to take care of the problem personally."

"You're saying that he's going to kill the guy, whoever he is? Wow, Jim, that's no good! They guy will get a state funeral and his apparatus will still be in place. Plus, Wylie will probably kill himself as well out of shame. The guy's had a lot on his plate lately."

"Yeah, your right, but didn't you just call Wylie a rat not ten seconds ago?"

"OK, OK, I was wrong. I admit it. There's another guy on the embassy staff, a guy named Marcus. He could have informed on me just as well, and I never even thought of him. Why do I always think of the black man first off, Jim? What's wrong with me?"

"Sounds to me like you're a racist and you're just trying to make excuses for it," Barker replied. Then he chuckled and Piper knew that he was joking. "What's the Brit's name, Jim? I mean the guy he told."

"Not on this line, if you please. We'll play your favorite game, and see how well you can do. Just listen to the statements. Don't give me any answers, just think about it, then call Wylie and see how well you did. I'll tell him to expect a call. That will give you credence, and he won't think that you're going to try to kill him, OK? Ready?"

"Yeah, Jim, but it's still not a clear line."

"We're dealing with the Brits, so they won't know what we're talking about, Lew."

"Go ahead, Jim."

"The first weekly television series specifically made for broadcast in color."

Bonanza, in the early 60's.

"An actor on the show from your neck of the woods."

The middle brother, Parnell Roberts, from Waycross, Georgia.

"Pull on your earlobe, then use the first name.

Sounds like Parnell.

"Got it?"

"Got it."

"Now give me thirty minutes while I find our friend and tell him to expect a call. Think up a plan while I talk him into putting his vendetta on hold."

"I've already got the plan. Make sure Wylie is a straight-arrow, Jim, or he won't miss the second time."

"Call me back before you make your call, and I'll confirm one way or another."

"Done." It would be a long half-hour. He pressed END and began to punch other buttons on the phone.

"What you doing, man?" Prescott asked curiously.

"I'm getting the Last Number Dialed out of the telephone. I wouldn't want the wrong person to know who I called. No offense intended."

"None taken," Prescott answered. "What's the problem? Did you kill somebody? Who is after you? And, hey, you know that anyone with the right equipment can listen to cell phone calls. Ask the Royal Family"

"I don't particularly care if anyone hears what I say, just as long as they don't know where I am calling from."

"If you have a security problem, I could ask Monster to look into it if you would like."

"Which one is Monster? Is he the one in the Hawaiian shirt or the one that talks to himself?"

"He is the one in the Jamaican copy of a Hawaiian shirt, although, in fact, he is from Haiti originally. If you point them out to him, Monster will make them go away permanently for £50. For £100 he will kill them and eat them in front of you."

"I'll keep that in mind," the white man said seriously.

Prescott almost smiled for the second time in the same day.

He held out the phone to Prescott, saying, "Thank you," and started to get down from the bar stool, but he stumbled and almost fell.

Prescott let him keep the phone and said, "Keep it for your later call. I'll include it in the price because you bought me beer. "If you want to lie down, there's a cot in the back." The man almost said no before he could add, "I'll ask Monster to make sure you are not disturbed." He motioned and the tent-sized Hawaiian shirt ambled forward.

"M'sieur will sleep in back on the cot for a while. Make sure he is not disturbed, please."

"D'accord," the tent said. Prescott led them through a curtained doorway to a small room. There was a day-bed, remarkably clean for such surroundings. It looked beautiful to him.   "Give me an hour and no more, please. I have to make that call."

"No fuss. I'll call you in an hour." As Prescott slipped out, Monster did an about-face in the doorway and leaned back, blocking it completely with his bulk. An organic door. Piper was asleep the minute his head hit the pillow.

It was closer to two hours later when Prescott finally shook him awake and handed him a cup of boiling hot coffee. "The real Jamaican stuff," he said proudly. "My family steals it direct from the groves and send it to me."

The fog was lifting, but the tension had made him hurt all over. He was slow, but he was alive. One more time, he has been reluctant to accept that someone would want to harm him. Him, of all people. Harmless little him. Him, the security consultant who never hurt a soul. Except for going to a prison and interviewing an IRA terrorist who told him that an educated man with a British accent had gotten him to kill a busload of children. Gee, why would anyone not want the people of this star-crossed isle to know all about that little detail? And who would have the resources to set a bunch of Germans on him in a faked traffic jam on the M25? Who would be able to read his old records and see the notes on his weakness for women, thus to send a blond with a nice smile and a big chest to speak with him in the queue of stopped traffic?

They had been right on the money. If a man with a German accent had spoken to him, he would have been on his guard in an instant. When the blond in the uniform had moved in front of the Vauxhall to block his exit, he had almost stopped as a reflex. Open the doors for the fragile little things, Lewis, or they will get their white gloves dirty. Hold their chairs for them so they can balance their purses and arrange their skirts before sitting down. Someone had read his record. Someone in the government, his government, had given it to them. The blond hadn't been raised in the deep South, however, because she let her pretty smile twist into a mask of hate as she tried to draw her pistol. Ah! If only she had gone to Agnes Scott Girl's School in Atlanta, they would have taught her to smile even while preparing to shoot someone.

And he would have been dead.

The coffee was helping, definitely helping.

He tapped lightly on Monster's back, hoping that he would step aside and let him out of the room. He did. Piper looked at him, and said, "Je m'appelle Lewis. Et vous?"

"Monstre, M'sieur."

"Merci, M'sieur Monstre. Merci pour tout", Piper managed in his best high-school French.

"No sweat, M'sieur," Monster replied with what passed for a grin.

Piper turned right and stumbled down the hall toward the barroom. Monster reached around him and snapped open the curtain. As they stepped inside the bar, the patrons at nearby tables dropped their drinks and got out of their chairs, moving toward the front door.. It was exactly as though he had come through the curtain firing a shotgun into the crowd. Chairs, glasses and beer bottles had crashed to the cluttered floor and broke into foam-covered splinters of brown and clear glass.

"EASY, EASY!" Prescott shouted over the commotion. "He's a friend. He's OK."

A light-complected woman with wide, staring eyes pointed a shaking finger in Piper's direction. She was unable to speak. She could only stare and point. Self-consciously, Piper looked behind him and for the first time realized that he only came up to the middle of Monster's chest. The man's chin was a good four to eight inches higher than the top of Piper's head. And Monster had on his Bad Look, the one that would cause a hungry lion to consider becoming a vegetarian.

"That is only Monster, he is part of the Security system here," Prescott was saying. "He is the reason that all our gatherings here at Club Kingston are so peaceful and friendly. Please, please, everyone sit down and continue your festivities. The management will replace all the drinks that were accidentally spilled in the commotion, free of charge." Warily, everyone returned to their seats like cats after a scolding. It would take a while for the jollity to return; it had been one hell of a fright.

As Piper moved to a stool at the bar, Monster moved to rejoin Koko in the shadows.

"You are a nice man," Prescott said softly. "And I don't know many white men I say dis about. What are you called?"

Before Piper could respond, a deep voice came from the edges of the room's darkness, saying, "Lewis," like the French, pronouncing it Lou-ee. Monster had good ears to be able to hear above the din of the room.

"Well, Lou-ee, what do you need now?"

"I haven't made my call yet, so I don't know," Piper replied.

"If you have a problem with security, then it is always better if you choose the place. Don't you agree?"

A Jamaican bar-owner was instructing Piper about security procedures. And he was right.

"Are you suggesting that I should have my friend come here?", Piper asked, fingering the cold bottle of beer Prescott placed in front of him.

"You are safer here than where you have been lately. Is that not right?"

Right as Rain. The man was a natural. "Why are you doing this for me?" Piper asked.

"It is a sad truth, my friend, that black men do not trust white men. But it is only their own white men that they do not like. My people do not like the British white man. Africans do not like the Afrikaner. But take the Afrikaner and put him in Harlem, and the black man sees only a white foreigner. Take a black man with a British accent and put him in Mississippi, and the Governor will ask him to stay to dinner."

Amazing.

And absolutely correct.

More than sufficient time had passed by now for him to call Barker back, so he did. He picked up on the first ring. "Dr. Barker!" the phone snapped in his ear.

"Hey, Jim, it's me. What's the . . . "

"Where the Hell have you been, Lew? I said half an hour, and it's been three or four. Wylie and I are almost engaged to each other, we've talked so much in the meantime."

"It's been maybe two hours. Don't exaggerate."

"Yeah, well, we were worried. Like maybe they had traced your location and. . ."

"Well, they didn't, so tell me how Wylie took the news. And tell me why the CALLBACK system didn't tell you my telephone number."

"CALLBACK? You mean the Codeword Classified telephone call tracing system that we spent 20 Million dollars on, the one that we just found out can't ID a British Telecom cellular phone transmission? THAT system? Is THAT the one you're asking me about?" he yelled down the line.

"Glad I could help the DOD find a hole in their system. So, what did Wylie say?"

"He was so happy that you were alive, I think he may have had tears in his eyes."

"What a pussy."

"No, just a human being who made a mistake."

"Thanks for your help, Jim. I'll call him now." He dialed the number from memory.

"What!" Wylie barked into the phone.

"Tell me about Parnell," Piper asked softly. It was the first time he'd ever been dead. He was enjoying the feeling.

"Jesus," Wylie croaked, "I'm damn glad to hear your voice. I thought for sure I'd gotten you killed." Then a sniffing sound came down the line. "It was more than I could take. I'm getting too old for this crap."

"How'd you hear about the traffic jam?"

"We got a report from the Surrey Constabulary that an embassy car had stormed around a road accident on the M25."

"Yeah, but then you knew that I'd made it out of the mess. Why'd you think you'd gotten me killed?"

"Because the same car was run off the road in Hampshire early this morning and crashed into a tree. It burned with the occupant trapped inside. I thought it was you, that's why. Your file said you weren't a stay-put kind of guy when you were threatened, so it made sense you'd be on your way out of London."

Piper thought, Jesus, those guys were really intent on making me disappear off the face of the Earth. A shiver ran down his spine, but he shook it off and said, "Time to play hardball, Wylie. Are you game?"

"Pick the time and place, I'll bring the armament. I owe you big-time."

The entire operation was already planned inside Piper's head. He created field operations in the same way Mozart wrote symphonies: In ink, perfect and correct the first time.

"Wait a minute, is there an ID who died in the car crash yet?" he asked suddenly.

"Not yet. They're performing the normal autopsy on the victim, so I sent Marcus down to Hampshire to oversee and confirm. He needed to be out from underfoot for a while. Our friends have a man there as well."

"Find a way to either stall the autopsy or, at the very least hold up publishing the results. Don't let them know the victim's ID. This is very important. They must not find out the victim's identity right now."

"Any ideas as to how I can make the Hampshire authorities do that?" Wylie asked.

"A call from the Ambassador ought to do it. Tell them you need to notify the next of kin first, and that you will have the British government chop off their interagency funds if they screw up. Tell them that the report is to be given to Marcus, and Marcus only, to be brought back to the American Embassy. And have the wrecked car trucked back as well. And have it covered with a tarpaulin so no more evidence gets washed off by the rain."

"Assuming that it's raining, you mean."

"It's always raining in this wretched country. Make sure only embassy people handle the car. Our friends will be concentrating on the body in the morgue, and won't have thought about the car yet."

"What's so important about the car?"

"Probably nothing, but it's a way to mess with their minds."

"Got you. Anything else?"

"Call me back on this number when it's all arranged. Then we can meet and I'll tell you the next step."

"Done," Wylie answered and hung up.

Wylie would use the Voice Assist system, the one that changed a voice as it was transmitted down a telephone line. He would make the call himself, telling the Hampshire people that he was the Ambassador, and that they had better do as he said. He'd make it work. He had to. It was the keystone of the plan. Wylie had also not asked for his telephone number. The CIA's trace system obviously worked better than the one at the Department of Defense.

Within half an hour, Wylie had called back to say that they had just made it in time. The autopsy was complete, and they were about to release the results when the "Ambassador" had called them. Marcus was on his way to the embassy with the only copy of the report. The pathologists had been told that they would be working in Bosnia with shovels as part of the UN Graves Commission there if they so much as talked about the report in their sleep. A wrecker from the embassy with three strong backs aboard was on its way to get the car. Now they could continue.

"When Marcus gets back, call me. He needs to bring his notebook computer and a cellular link so we can go shopping around the computer systems like we did the other day. I'll tell you where we'll meet when you call, OK?"

"You got it. Want me to call your lady-friend and tell her anything?"

"Don't call anybody and don't use any more names. We've got the advantage now, and we have to keep it."

Wylie hung up, giving only a short grunt of agreement.

CHAPTER FOURTEEN

THE PLAN

"Marcus is back now and brought the autopsy report," Wylie spoke into the phone. "You'll be interested to know. . ."

"Not on the phone," Piper hissed. "We'll have plenty of time when we meet. You and Marcus take a taxi to Trafalger Square. A large black man in a Hawaiian shirt will be standing near Lord Nelson's column. Walk up to him and say that you are there to be taken to see Lewis. Pronounce it Lou-ee, like the French. He'll understand. He's from Haiti."

"Where are we going?" Wylie asked. "You know, just in case we end up talking to the wrong black man and get taken for a ride by some pimp."

"Take a phone with you. If there is more than one six-foot-five, four-hundred-pound black men wearing a Hawaiian shirt standing near Nelson's column, give me a call and we'll make a new plan," Piper chuckled.

"What's this guy's name?" Wylie asked.

"He's called Monster, that's all I know him by."

"Oh, wonderful, just wonderful," Wylie sighed.

"And make sure you're not followed, just in case we're not as smart as we think we are, OK?"

Two hours later, Monster, Wylie and Marcus twitched into Club Kingston. Marcus was carrying a briefcase in each hand. Both men were rumpled as though they had been played with by a large cat, and then tossed aside. Monster looked like Monster always looked unless something had provoked him: large, black and unbothered by the surrounding world. He ambled over and stood near Koko and to resume his ordinary job of holding up the wall. Marcus and Wylie joined Piper at a table in the rear corner of the club.

Wylie held out his hand, saying, "I'm sorry I almost got you killed, Piper. I would have fired any of my people if they made a stupid mistake like that. I hope that you let me make it up to you."

"You're fired," Marcus said softly.

"What?" Wylie asked.

"Nothing," Marcus responded softly while grinning, "I just wanted to hear how it would sound."

Before Wylie could get further distracted, Piper said, "Forget it. It's done and over. Let's move on."

Prescott crossed over to them from behind the bar and asked, "May I bring you gentlemen a beverage?"

Wylie spoke up immediately. "A bottle of bourbon whiskey and a glass. And four cold beers." Looking at Piper and Marcus, he asked, "You guys want something? I'm gonna drink everything I just ordered all by myself."

"I'll have a glass and four cold beers," Marcus replied. "We have work to do, and you'll never drink a bottle of whiskey by yourself, so we can share that."

"I'll have a cup of coffee," Piper said, completely puzzled. Somebody had to stay sober in the group. "You guys want to tell me what happened?"

Wylie began. "Marcus, show our recently dead friend here what you have in your new briefcase."

Marcus put a large satchel on the table. It was black leather and stood on its bottom with a leather flap that folded over the top to close it. It was big, like the kind that accountants carry in the US. He laid it on its side, unsnapped the flap and began to remove items and place them on the table.

"I sat on the jump seat so I could look out the back window and see if we were being followed," Wylie rambled. "Man Mountain and Marcus shared the taxi's back seat, but only barely. I spotted a taxi following us with two guys in the back seat. Next time I looked, the same taxi was still behind us. They weren't pros at the job; they followed us too closely to have had much experience. They should have dropped back a bit in the traffic now and then. I asked the driver to make a left turn and then a right to see if they'd stay with us. They did. I could see one of the guys in back pointing the driver at us with his index finger. The giant asked if there was a problem. I said, yes, I think we are being followed. He said something in French to our driver, and the guy stopped right in the middle of traffic. The giant gets out, walks behind our taxi and cold-cocks the taxi driver and the two guys in the back. Then he emptied their pockets, put all the stuff in that briefcase, brought it back, handed it to us and we drove away. Ain't nobody followed us after that. I kept checking, half expecting the police to take an interest, but we drove straight here without being stopped."

Marcus was sorting through the various items in each of the wallets. "This guy must have been the driver. He has in £ 215 his wallet along with his ID and a taxi permit. These other two are government types, about £150 in each wallet, one has identification saying that he is an Assistant to a Deputy Undersecretary, and the other has a Whitehall ID. There's a pistol in here, too. They're both spooks, I'll bet. I can look them up on the computer if you like."

"There's no need," Piper responded confidently. "They followed you from the embassy to see what you were up to. Probably been following you for months and you just never noticed. It's not important."

Wylie downed a quarter of a glass of whiskey in one swallow. Marcus took a bite of whiskey and followed it by drinking an entire bottle of beer without stopping.

Wylie continued to blither. "That big guy is a sight when he gets pissed off, man. He was out of the taxi and had whomped those three guys before they had a chance to figure what was happening. He is one scary black man. I mean, he's so fast! He looks like a big tub of lard, but he doesn't jiggle when he walks. He's solid muscle. I need to get a quieter job, maybe something in a war zone." He poured out another quarter-glass of whiskey and drank it in one gulp.

Marcus started to put the items back in the briefcase, but

Piper reached out and picked up a small notebook. Thumbing through it, he saw the notation Hampshire County Medical Examiner, followed by a telephone number. "Who was the government type at the morgue when you went to get the autopsy report, Marcus?" Years of training had taught him what to ask.

"He said his name was Roger-something. No, wait it was something-Rogers, Anthony, no, it was Anton. Anton Rogers. He was from the Home Office, he said."

"Naturally," Piper continued. "Of course the Home Office would send a minion out to Hampshire to check on a traffic fatality. Makes perfect sense, doesn't it" He waited for Marcus to take the hint.

"Wait a minute," Marcus exclaimed, digging through the wallets again. "Of course! This is the guy, the one who's an Assistant to a Deputy Undersecretary, his name is Anton Rogers! He didn't look much like this picture, however."

"And he looks even less like this picture after being pounded on by Monster, I'll bet," Piper concluded with a smile. "I was wrong, it was important. They followed you hoping to steal the Autopsy Report, most likely."

"Why would they think I'd have it on me?" Wylie asked. "And why did you want it kept from them?"

"They would have had no idea whether you had it or not. But if you did have it and they could get a look at it, that would have closed the loop for them. That is, if they had been able to confirm that I had been killed in the crash. I was the final loose end that they had to worry about. Conversely, if they found out that I hadn't been the one they murdered by running the embassy car off the road in the dead of night, then they'd have known that I was still out there with everything I learned from O'Flynn. Since they are capable of ordering the murder of children and the conviction of an American naval officer to cover their rear ends, then God only knows what they might have done if they'd found out I wasn't really dead. They probably thought you might take the report home to study. Everybody likes a good Autopsy Report as a nighttime read. I know I do," Piper replied His attempt at humor was wasted, however.

"So what do we do now?" Wylie asked.

Piper laid out the plan for them, detail by detail. Marcus listened wide-eyed. Wylie listened and didn't like what he was hearing.

"OK, OK, I know I said that I owed you, and that we would follow your plan because of it. But I never thought it would be anything like this. You don't even kill anybody! You sound like you plan to talk them to death -- like they'll do what you want if you will just go away and leave them alone. It will never work, Piper. These guys have to be taught a lesson, and the only way they are going to learn is if someone puts a bullet through their heads."

Piper let him rant until he ran down. He was a brave man with a strong code of honor. He wasn't saying to let someone else do the killing. He was offering to do the killing himself, to put his own life on the line to atone for having put Piper at risk and almost getting him killed. He would walk directly up to them, look them in the face and blow their brains out onto the ground.

He thought about the choices, then made his decision. "I want you to kill Parnell and the colonel, Wylie."

"All right! Now you're talking, Piper," Wylie exclaimed enthusiastically. "Now, the way I figure it, they'll. . ."

"But not right now," Piper added.

"I'm confused," Marcus added. "First, you say. . ."

"Yeah, what do you mean not right now? If not now, then when?" Wylie asked.

"First we kill their souls, then you can have what's left," Piper said solemnly.

"Oh crap! It's more of your Oriental philosophy shit, isn't it Piper? A billion drops of water falling on a rock, wearing it away. That take a thousand years, Piper! We aren't going to live that long."

"Their souls are what we want first, Wylie. These are evil men, and they are supported by their evil organizations. And their organizations support them either because they do not know that they are evil or, worse than that, because they believe that their evil deeds cannot be proven. If they are both found dead in their beds tomorrow morning, they will receive respectful funerals and memorial services. Their comrades will eulogize them in formal speeches and for years to come in many informal ways, and the evil will continue. We have to stop the evil from continuing and spreading."

"That's a big order, Piper. We'll have bad guys as long as we have people on Earth. I think you're dreaming, man. Give me an example of what you are talking about."

"Commandante Paulo."

"Oh, the child molester," Wylie responded. "What about him?"

"Who's Commandante Paulo?" Marcus asked.

"Tell him, Wylie," Piper said with just the hint of a smile.

"He was a guerrilla leader in Central America in the Seventies, sort of a Che Guevara type. He always wore a black stocking mask, long sleeves and gloves, no matter what the weather was like. He worked on his own, as well as with the Cubans and the Sandinistas, and he was damn good. He drove us nuts with his hit-and-run tactics, burning down factories and plantations. Most of the big landowners just paid him bribes to stay away"

"He spoke Spanish, English, Russian, German and something else."

"Korean," Piper interjected.

"Oh, yeah, Korean. He gave interviews on American news shows and told how he was trying to give the peasants a voice in their governments. Of course, what he was really doing was running a highly successful narcotics trafficking operation. He was pumping billions of dollars of heroin and cocaine into the US through Mexico and the Caribbean. His men loved him because he treated them well and paid them in cash. He had sort of blue-gray eyes and all the women wanted to have his baby."

"Then one day it turns out that he likes children, boys and girls under ten years old mainly, much better than women. Some kids were hurt pretty badly by his sexual appetite, internal injuries and all that, and the parents brought them to local doctors for treatment. The whole story came out then, and when it did, he disappeared and all his support evaporated. Nobody would admit that they had ever worked with the guy or even known him. His whole operation collapsed like a house of cards. It was though he had never existed."

"Jesus, what an animal," Marcus whispered softly.

"And it was all a set-up. I know, because I ran the operation that built the plan and planted the evidence," Piper said.

They both looked at him in astonishment.

"You had kids molested just to get this guy in trouble?" Marcus said with a look of disgust. "Jesus, you're no better than he was."

"No, Mr. Holier-Than-Thou, I did not have any children molested just to get this guy in trouble. What I did do, however, was spend the time to find out what would be guaranteed to turn people

191

against him and then arrange for molested children to identify him as the culprit. And while you are up there on you pulpit of self-righteousness, don't forget that this operation accomplished what thousands of troops and millions of dollars had never been able to do before. Unlike Che Guevara, who was such a psychotic cold-blooded murderer that Castro had him shipped out of Cuba, Commandante Paulo is not a hero to our college kids. His memory is not revered by any of the current guerrilla movements in the world, or by any other movement. And he was the most successful terrorist leader in Central America. If the IRA had recruited him and listened to him, the British would have been driven out of Northern Ireland fifteen years ago. And, more importantly, nobody wears a Paulo T-shirt or has a Paulo poster on his bedroom wall. And it's all because we killed his soul first."

"And his body, what happened to that?" Wylie asked.

"Nobody knows for sure. There were several corpses that fit his general description that were later found hacked to death by machetes, but nobody ever made a positive identification. And again, more importantly, nobody cares."

"Wait. Wait. If this 'Kill The Soul First' thing is so successful, why isn't it used more often?" Marcus asked. "Why do we still get involved in assassinations?"

"I know the answer to that," Wylie offered. "Because it's damn hard work, isn't it Piper? Not just anybody can do it, can they? There's no way to write a manual on Killing The Soul, is there?"

"That's part of it, of course. The other part is the natural male instinct to show that he's better than the other guy, that he can hunt him down and blow him away. The problem is that it doesn't work over the long run. The body goes on display, and everyone says how handsome the guy was, how he was always good to his family and a pillar of the church. The world forgets what a maniac he was immediately after his death. But if you kill the soul first. . ."

"Then the body dies of its own accord," Marcus finished.

"Now you've got it," Piper answered.

"But I have another problem," Marcus said softly. "I almost hate to bring it up, but . . ."

"God Almighty, Marcus. What now?" asked Wylie.

"I have no problem with destroying the Colonel. His involvement in this is so evil and so obvious as to be undeniable. But the evidence against Pernell is circumstantial, persuasive, but circumstantial. I hate to say it, but somebody in his office other than him could have made the call and set the plan in motion to silence Piper without him even knowing about it."

"This is not a democracy. We are not going to take a vote on this. If you don't want to play, Marcus, get your ass out of my sight; if you do, then get to work," Wylie snapped.

"But it never hurts to be sure, does it?" Piper smiled at Wylie.

"Ah, Christ! We're never going to get anything <u>done</u>! We are just going to talk it to death and play 'What if?' games until we all die of old age. You are acting like my bosses back at Langley, Piper! Shall I prepare a Position Paper and schedule some cross-disciplinary meetings? Is that what you want?" Wylie was yelling and waving his arms around, swatting at his bureaucratic demons.

"Ten minutes," Piper said softly. "I can make Marcus a believer in ten minutes, Wylie. You got ten minutes to spare?"

"Whatever," Wylie replied in obvious exasperation.

"Marcus, find the crime scene photographs of the bus attack and put them up on the computer, please."

Marcus tapped at his keyboard, then said, "Here they are," starting to turn the screen so Piper and Wylie could see them.

"I don't need to see them, Marcus. Just tell me what <u>you</u> see there." Marcus described the bus with the front blown open, the driver covered with a sheet, various views of official-looking people standing around, and a fire hose on the ground.

"Any pictures of policemen in uniform?" Piper was staring at the tabletop as he spoke.

"No. Just people in civilian clothes."

"When there is a wreck on a public road, who gets the call?"

"The police."

"The <u>Uniform Branch</u>, to be more specific," Piper lectured. "There are no uniforms in these pictures, so who took the pictures such that not one single uniform showed up in them? It damn sure wasn't the

Metropolitan Police, was it? So the regular cops had been on the scene and then they were replaced by these guys, whoever they are, right?"

"OK."

"Moving on to a second point: Do you think O'Flynn lied to me or not?"

"There's no way to know for sure, but we assume that he told the truth because what he told you darn near got you killed."

"Sometimes you can be so dense, Marcus. Of course we can know for sure. Find the original crime scene photographs, Marcus." After a few keyboard entries, Marcus said, "Here they are."

Still concentrating on the tabletop, Piper said, "Now you see uniformed police, right? And where did you get these particular photos, by the way? From the Germans, I assume?"

'I see uniformed police in the pictures, and I got them from the French Intelligence Service because they steal more thoroughly than the Germans, if you can believe it. And Jesus, I sure missed looking for the body on the ground next to the bus."

"That would be Michael, dead with O'Flynn's bullet in his brain. What else did you miss from the original photos?"

"Everything, apparently: the moving van parked on the side of the road, the two dead bodies of the van's occupants behind the hedge, and Michael's abandoned motorbike."

"And who has the power to make all these inconvenient items disappear from the "official" photographs, then get "Official Secrets Act" and "Prevention of Terrorism Act" stamped all over everything and swear everybody to secrecy? Nobody but the MI-5 Section headed by Reg Parnell, the Colonel's best buddy? Case proven."

"But why did the Colonel have to order such a brutal killing?" Marcus continued. "Why not just get one or two Americans killed in a bar-fight? Why attack a busload of children?"

"If you want people to blindly follow your leadership without question, you have to hit them in the guts, not in the brain. If you make an intelligent argument based on logic, everyone will ignore you except the Editorial Board of the New York Times. But if you kill children, particularly white children, you are instantly detested and condemned without question. If you hope to succeed as a terrorist, don't hurt a woman's kids or mess with a man's beer supply. It's simple fact of life. The Colonel had to order an act of barbarism so vicious that the British would act without question and the Americans would keep the whole thing quiet for fear of a national backlash against God-knows-what."

"Now can we move along with our work?"

"Yeah, but what do we do first?" Wylie asked.

"Wylie, you and I get to rest for a while, and Marcus gets to start the investigative part. Marcus, your job is to research the entire British psyche and find two things so repugnant to them, one each for the colonel and Parnell, that it will kill both of their souls. No blowing up school busses; that's already been done."

"Piece of Cake," Marcus replied with a smile. Using his notebook computer and a cellular phone, he began to tap out instructions on the keyboard. Prescott pulled up a chair after locking the front entrance after the last departing customer. He and Wylie began to exchange What-It's-Like-To-Grow-Up-Black stories. Piper scrootched down in the wood chair, put his chin on his chest and began to nap fitfully. Snakes and blond women with pistols chased him in his sleep. A soft voice kept calling him "Martian" or "Martin", or maybe "Marlon".

"Piper?" the voice said, finally loud enough to awaken him from his neck-stiffened nap. True to form, he had drooled on his shirt front. Mr. Class sets the standard for after-work behavior yet another time.

"Fmmnnhh?" he answered intelligently to Marcus.

"Can we go over what I have found now?"

"Certafullysh," Piper answered as he levered himself to his feet. "But first I have to splash some water on my face." He hobbled behind the bar and turned on the cold water. Cupping his hands, he filled them with water and deposited half of it skillfully on the lower part of his face, including the insertion of a quarter-cup up his left nostril. The rest he spilled on the drool-mark on his shirt where no one could notice. My reflexes are as good as ever, he thought. What a shame. I thought I was improving. Mr. Class then dried his face on a beer-soaked bar towel and joined Wylie and Marcus at the table.

"You look like hell," Wylie offered.

"Stick it in your ear," Piper rejoined happily.

Marcus cleared his throat ceremonially. "I've looked at the local news reporting for the last fifty years," he said. "The only things that seem to really get the British public riled up are the mistreatment of animals and anything that has to do with crooked policemen. Wife-beating or assaulting women in general has been gaining over the past five years. But purposely injuring animals really sets them off. They went really berserk over the IRA explosion a few years ago that killed four of the Guards horses on parade, and they didn't seem even remotely as concerned about the two guardsmen that were killed or the ten others that were wounded in the same attack. On the other subject, the single largest news story in the past twenty years in terms of Letters to the Editor and column-inches of stories was concerning the policemen that were found to have fabricated evidence in the Guilford pub bombing. The five Irishmen that were convicted. . ."

"I understand, Marcus. Let me think for a moment," Piper said. They sat in the musty silence of the Club Kingston listening to the hum of the electric fan in the corner as it struggled to stir the fug in the large room. Piper drew patterns on the sweaty green oilcloth table with his finger.

Wylie saw that Piper's eyes were far away as he thought. He had heard about the way this man planned an operation. He did it the way Mozart composed music, he had been told: Perfect from beginning to end. Perfect the first time, with no holes, no mistakes. It was like watching Rembrandt paint or Michaelangelo sculpt. The lids would squint, then open wide as an idea blossomed, then blink as the idea was discarded. The stubby fingers with all the scar tissue from his former life in the field pointed at things on the tabletop, drew lines to other things, then drummed a mournful pattern as reality overcame desire. The pattern changed as the squint returned for a long time. There was a closing of the eyes for a moment while the plan was replayed from beginning to end. The palms went flat on the table as a final gesture.

"Greyhounds."

"Greyhounds?" Marcus repeated.

"The colonel has a stable of racing greyhounds. I read about that somewhere in his record," Piper said matter-of-factly. "There was a picture of a greyhound in one of the papers a few days ago. It had a broken leg and had been starved. We show that he was one of the colonel's dogs, a former winner who lost an important race. In a fury at the dog losing, the colonel beat him with a chain leash, locked him up for a week without food, then took him out in a forest somewhere and threw him out of a vehicle at high speed, causing the dog's leg to be broken as it struck the ground. Find that dog. I want him. I want him tied to the colonel."

"I don't understand," Marcus ventured. "Where did this come from? Are you saying that this story is the truth? How did you know?"

"Marcus." The hazel eyes bored a hole straight through the skinny young man's corrective lenses. "Make it happen. Make it true. Make it perfect. Do it. You are a smart man. Act like a field agent and get the job done."

Marcus blinked. He had never created the truth to fit a situation before.

"You gonna think about Parnell now?" Wylie asked.

"I've thought about him already."

"And?"

"We need a Gas Man, some BZ and some C7."

Wylie blanched and gulped. Nerve gas. Piper wanted a specialist and two types of nerve gas. That was all his career needed at this juncture. Didn't this guy ever forget anything?

"To answer your question before you ask it, no, I never forget anything that interests me. Never. To illustrate: BZ is a colorless, odorless neuro-reagent that when dispersed in air causes the mind to lose its ability to concentrate. Squirt it in someone's face and they can walk, they can talk, and they can remember their name. But ask them to count out loud from one to ten, and they'll make it no further than the number three before they forget what they were supposed to do. Then they will stop, look around, and be generally confused."

"C7, on the other hand, is a colorless psycho-reagent that is rumored to have a slightly sweet odor like glycol-based antifreeze. It is a hallucinogenic compound that causes the subject to believe that the most terrifying things are attacking him, even to the point of creating the impression that their own body is about to explode. Small doses are enough to render someone psychotic and suicidal for the rest of their lives. Any questions?"

"Yeah. Assuming that I can get this stuff, what does this have to do with Parnell?"

"I will want you to telephone Parnell this morning, then hand the phone to me. He doesn't know my voice, and I will say something like: "The man has escaped. He untied himself and has escaped from the house. Help us find him. He can ruin us all." I will then hang up. This will imprint into his brain, but it will have only the slightest overtones of threat. He will be confused, but not afraid. When can you get the Gas Man here?"

"He's here. I'll have to do it," Wylie replied. "I'm the only one in the embassy that's had the training."

"Where does Parnell live?" Piper asked no one in particular.

"One moment," Marcus answered, pounding away at the computer's keyboard. He scribbled something on a piece of paper from his notebook and passed it to Wylie. It read, "22C Firkin Terrace, Knightsbridge. No housekeeper. Wife and children scheduled to return in three days from a visit to family relatives in Toronto, Canada."

"How's the greyhound project going, Marcus?"

"I've found the dog's location, the starved one in the paper, and checked on his condition. He's not in the best of shape, and may not last out the week. We may have to find another subject."

"How do you connect the dog to the colonel, Marcus?" Wylie asked.

"A veterinarian surgeon from our on-call list that I sent to examine the dog is about to find a microchip planted under the animal's skin which will show that it's one of the colonel's dogs."

"A microchip! How in the hell . . ?"

"That's how valuable animals all over the world are protected," Marcus answered. "It's actually more like a microdot, a small microfilm document that is about the size of half a grain of rice. Racehorses, ostriches, dogs, cats, everybody's doing it."

"How are you going to. . ?"

"Boss, I can either tell you how I'm going to do it, or I can get it done. I can't do both. Mr. Piper said for me to act like a field agent and

Make It Happen. I'm in the process of making it happen. I don't have time to talk."

Dismissed, Wylie turned his attention to Piper as Marcus went back to whispering into a second cellular phone and tapping on the keyboard. "What's next?"

"You wide awake? It's almost daylight."

"I'm awake. I asked what's next. I want to get this done so I can kill both of these guys."

"We need an Ops Team to get inside Parnell's house and. . ."

"It's a row-house," Marcus interjected. "It's built right up against the houses on either side, common exterior walls and all, so any loud noises will definitely be heard by the neighbors." Then he went back to his cell phone and his computer.

". . . and set the gas canisters and plumbing so that we can surround him with a BZ atmosphere when he goes in the front door. That will disorient him. We need small speakers and transmitters so we can watch him and talk to him while he's under the influence. While the Ops Team is in there, they have to set up a special scene in a back room, maybe the laundry room or something. Whatever it is, it has to be a small room, even a closet will do, and it has to be near the rear door. We'll guide him toward the room, telling him he's in danger and that he needs to pick up a pistol that we'll supply for him. The only problem I have is that. . ."

And then the problem solved itself.

"Cranmoore," Piper said softly. "That's the answer. It's perfect. Wylie, how large a blood sample was taken from Cranmoore when he was examined? And do you still have it?"

Overhearing, Marcus switched to another line in mid-sentence and dialed a number. A few mumbled sentences, and he had the answer. One hundred cubic centimeters, about a half-cupful. And it was stored in the fridge in the Dispensary at the embassy. It would have to do.

He outlined the rest of the plan for Parnell in detail to Wylie, who nodded in agreement.

"Now that you know it all, what do you think? Will it work?"

"Only one way to find out, Piper, and that's to get out of here and make it happen."

CHAPTER FIFTEEN

MAKING IT HAPPEN

Wylie pulled some strings and got them access to an embassy property in Knightsbridge. Prescott was asleep behind the bar when they got ready to leave, and waved them off with a grumble as Piper tried to shake him awake to say good-bye. He put a Twenty-Pound note on the bar top after writing Thanks for everything across the face with a ball-point pen. The front door of the bar had two locked deadbolts and livebolts in the top and bottom. The back door had only a spring latch, so the three of them went out that way into the dank, urine-infested alley behind.

Piper and Marcus were the only white people on the Underground platform at that time of the morning. Wylie smiled because he blended in perfectly. It was early, sometime after Six AM and the trains were only half-full. They agreed on their timeline for action and got off at their respective stops.

Piper went to the British Museum. He was dead-tired, and desperately needed some sleep. He had asked Wylie to bring him some keep-awake pills from the embassy, but that would take some time. In the meanwhile, there is no better place to sleep than in the reading room at the British Museum. Get a reference book on Invertebrate Paleontology, find a cubicle, put your head down on the book and sleep. Piper set the alarm on his quartz watch to wake him in two hours, then laid his head on the chosen volume taking care to position his left ear directly on his watch. It was an old Navy trick, and it always worked perfectly. If the watch was covered by your ear, when the alarm went off the sound would drill directly into your brain and wake the crap out of you. There would be little noise that would escape into the surroundings. All the neighbors would hear were the scrabbling of a jerked-awake person trying to shut off the wrist alarm and shake the thunderbolt of sound out of his head. And always in Piper's case, they would also hear the sounds of him griping about his overactive salivary habits as he mopped up the drool-pool.

Two hours later, he was blasted awake according to plan. He made a quick visit to the rest room, pausing only to place his reference volume on a wooden cart marked with a sign saying that you weren't allowed to replace the volumes yourself, even if you knew where they went. Let the professionals do it for you. You'll put it back in the wrong place and no one will ever be able to find it again. Good plan.

Ten-thirty, and he was standing out front in the drizzle as agreed. Well, standing out front was what he had agreed to do. The rain was optional, courtesy of the British climate. Then Wylie appeared, driving a Ford Commer van that said "British Telecom" on the side. There was nothing less conspicuous in a residential neighborhood than a telephone company van. It was a perfect choice.

"There's a pair of coveralls in the back for you," Wylie said as he pulled away into traffic. "You can put them on in while I drive. The pills you asked for are in the top pocket. Don't take more than one every two hours or you'll fly back to Dallas ahead of the airplane."

Struggling into the blue coveralls as Wylie swooped through the traffic, Piper realized what he must look like by now: unshaven, dirty, unkempt hair, body odor, sloppy clothes, cushion-soled black leather shoes. Perfect. Just like a British Telecom installer. Welcome to reality.

22C Firkin Court was third from the end of a row of four look-alike two-story adjoining houses, all cut from the same cookie-cutter 1920's mold. "What's the plan for entry?" Piper asked. "Park down the street and come in the back way, or. . ?"

"Park in front, open the van's side door, and I'll tell you what to carry. We are going to walk up the front steps, I'm going to stick the key in the door, and we'll go inside. Then we set the trap and get the hell out to the observation room."

"What? Just walk in the front door? Where did you get the key? What if the neighbors call the cops? What then? What if he has a burglar alarm?" The pill that he had swallowed dry as he put on the coveralls was beginning to kick in.

"Yes, I have a key to the front door. Where I got it is none of your business. There is a burglar alarm, but it's been disarmed at the central site. The neighbors will not call the cops to report a BT van and two BT employees. Parnell's a spook, same as me. He probably hasn't even met his neighbors. If they haven't been properly introduced, they can't pal around together, can they? Remember, this is England, not America. No introduction, no buddy-buddy."

Wylie pulled up in front and set the hand brake. They both piled out and began to load down with canvas tool bags and spools of wire. There were also two small telephone-sized Cardboard boxes marked with the BT logo.

"Careful with that one. It has the blood in it," Wylie said. "And once we're inside, no talking. I don't know if there are any passive listening devices installed, and we don't have time to sweep for them. Here's a notepad. Any questions, just write them down and show it to me, OK?"

Piper nodded in agreement. He watched as Wylie hefted a brown canvas toolbag and then gingerly tucked another BT cardboard box under his arm. That would have the nerve gas canisters in it.

As planned, they went up the stairs and straight into the house. Before shutting the door behind them, Wylie put a special wire clip in the lock's outside keyway. Anyone trying the lock would find the key impossible to insert, and the noise would alert them. What they would do about it then was anybody's guess. Wylie pulled him to a room at the rear of the house adjacent to the back door. It was a storage and pantry combination room, about six by eight feet in size. There were cans of vegetables and jars of fruit and jam in neat rows on the wall shelves. This would be the room that Cranmoore was supposedly locked away in by Parnell. Wylie made a "let's get busy" sort of motion with his hand and went back toward the front of the house.

Opening the large canvas satchel, Piper found a series of large clear plastic zip-lock bags. One contained clothing, so that seemed a good place to start. Instantly, the wafting smell of feces told him that this was probably the stuff that Cranmoore was wearing when he lost bowel control during his interrogation. He tossed the clothes in a lump to a corner of the room and put a cardboard box on top of them with gloved hands. The next bag contained a towel with dried blood on it. This he placed in an opposite corner on top of a small bag of sugar as though it had been used as a pillow. Then came a bag with notes written in pencil, saying things like, "I am alone now - trapped in my own private Colditz, deserted by every friend, and persecuted by a government that I never meant to offend. The beatings have stopped for now, at least." Sentimental crud, Piper thought. But it's good stuff. Nobody will realize that Cranmoore wrote it about the Americans instead of the British.

There was a very small bag of whitish things that were probably skin flakes or dandruff. He sprinkled them about liberally. Everything was too orderly, though. The scene was sterile, as though someone were planting evidence. He set about to disorganize things by kicking the papers about the small space. He pulled cans of vegetables and tins of condensed milk off the shelves and scattered them about on the floor. Then he found the trowel. This would be how Cranmoore escaped, by prying the door open with this trowel. I hope the darn thing doesn't snap in two in the process. Closing the door from the inside, he found that there was no place to lever against the lock. Shrugging, he squatted slightly to approximate Cranmoore's height and hit the door with his shoulder. It popped open easily, splintering the door facing and sending the striker plate flying into the hallway with a clatter. Instantly, Wylie's worried face popped into view, holding a finger in front of his lips for silence. Piper shrugged an apology and went back to work.

Opening the small BT cardboard box, he unwrapped the stubby plastic syringe of blood from the bubble-wrap that surrounded it. Pressing the plunger, he managed to put a nice spray pattern on the canned goods on the shelves, then added a few drops on the bare floor in several locations. Hopefully, it would dry quickly and nobody would analyze the drops for the chemical stabilizers that had been added to prevented the blood from clotting.

Stepping out of the pantry, Piper pulled the door almost closed, then surveyed the outside scene. The striker plate had landed on the floor about ten feet away from the back door. There were small splinters from the door frame scattered around in a random pattern. Perfect. Now, how did Cranmoore get out of the house? It was obvious. He had simply unlatched the nearby back door and gone around the side of the house to the street.

Wylie motioned for him to come to the front room, scribbled the word "Finished?" on his pad then held it up to Piper, who nodded vigorously. Wylie pulled a piece of waxed paper from the side of a black cylinder and put the discard in his coverall pocket. Once the paper was removed, it showed a sticky adhesive pattern along the side of the one-inch diameter cylinder. Placing it against the door jamb about five-and-a-half feet from the floor, he pressed hard to secure it in position. A label on the side of the cylinder read, Majestic Insect Repellent. Guaranteed to Work Under All Conditions. British Chemical Co. PLC, London. Wylie arranged a fine wire so that it hung loosely down underneath the cylinder. That would be the antenna for triggering the device, Piper mused. A sinister blue-steel nozzle pointed directly into the face of anyone opening the front door. Wylie turned and pressed something that looked like a six-inch piece of tape to the opposite wall.

A quick check of the premises, and they were done. Wylie opened the front door and removed the wire from the lock's keyway. Then he shut the door and motioned for Piper to follow him out the back door and around to the front of the house to the waiting blue van. They were following Cranmoore's route of escape, tracking bits of evidence as they went. Wylie was a professional, but Piper couldn't resist testing him once they were driving away down the street.

"Why wouldn't Cranmoore just go out the front door? Wouldn't that have been quicker? He would have been in a hurry to get out of there."

"Don't jerk me around, Piper," Wylie responded with just the barest hint of a smile. "You know he couldn't get out the front door because it had a keyed deadbolt on both sides and he didn't have the key. That's why he went out the back. It only had a snap latch." Yes, Wylie was good, he had to admit it.

They threw the toolbags and the small cardboard boxes in the blue van and sped off down the quiet street without speaking. Wylie navigated the traffic in Knightsbridge like the professional he was. He seemed to be enjoying being out in the field once more. He was humming a tune softly under his breath. It was Camptown Races, of all things. As they moved slowly down a side street, a garage door facing the street began to rise open. The opening startled a shabbily-dressed man as he was passing on the sidewalk, and he stopped and peered inside into the darkness. Piper made a move toward the door handle to get out and push the man out of the way, but Wylie slapped him on the knee, then pushed the remote control for the door to close it again and continued to drive slowly down the street. He was right, of course, Piper thought. Getting out and pushing the man aside would have just called attention to the van and themselves. Wylie had good instincts, and Piper was rusty. Piper watched in the van's side mirror as the shabby man watched the door close, then threw up his hands in confusion and wandered off talking to himself. He would never remember the blue British Telecom van or its occupants, only the strange door magically opening and closing. That night, the man would sit in a Pub with a pint of beer and comment about the door to a friend, who would agree that the World was going to Hell. After a leisurely trip around the block, the shabby man was nowhere in sight, the door opened again and they drove inside, closing it behind them.

A short young man with a crew cut appeared from the darkness, asking, "What was all that about the door?"

"I'll tell you at the debriefing session. Just wipe the van down, get rid of all the stuff, and return it to BT, OK?" Chastened, the young man stood patiently as they struggled out of the coveralls and handed them over. Wylie motioned to a white Ford Escort two-door and told Piper to get behind the wheel. The door opened once more and the Escort moved smoothly out on to the narrow street.

"Left," Wylie said. Piper drove as he was directed for about ten minutes, the Wylie said, "Park in front of that newsagent's shop over there." He pointed out the direction. Once the car was parked as directed, Wylie said, "Lock the car, put the keys in your pocket, and let's go this way." They started walking back in the direction from which they had come from. Abruptly, a faint noise indicated that the Escort's engine had just been started. As they turned at the first corner, Piper looked back to see the white car being driven away. All this was done very smoothly. Once around the corner, they immediately went down some steps to the Underground, bought two tickets, boarded a train, changed twice, and finally ended up back in Knightsbridge at an apartment house called The Green Gables. Taking the lift to the fifth floor, Wylie walked directly to Apartment 523, took a key from his pocket, opened the door and walked inside. There were three people in the apartment, two men and a rather pretty young girl of perhaps twenty-two.

"How's it going, Jenny?" Wylie asked, not waiting for an answer. "Come have a look," he said to Piper, motioning to a window at the back of an adjoining room. Looking down, he saw that they were not only back in Knightsbridge, but looking out a window no more than a hundred feet from Parnell's front door at 22C Firkin Court. Wylie had not looked behind once during their car or subway trip, simply trusting in the route's complexity and good organization to make sure that they weren't followed. The man was really good.

"Time to make your call," Wylie said, looking at Piper and handing him a telephone already ringing at the other end.

"Two Six Five Double-Seven," said the woman who answered.

"This is Commander Fife," Piper said in his passable British accent. "Admiral Sir John Washburn would like a word with Mr. Parnell, if you would be so kind."

"Certainly, Commander. I'll put you through directly."

After only a moment's pause, Parnell came on the line. Never having heard the man's voice before, Piper could only assume that it was actually Parnell speaking.

"Sir John, how nice to hear from you," he said pleasantly. "How may I be of assistance to the Royal Navy?"

Lowering the register of his voice, but retaining the British accent, Piper spoke slowly and distinctly. "He's escaped, you imbecile. He's gotten clean away, and he knows everything. You have to find him. He will destroy us all." Quickly, he hung up. It had been difficult for him. Wylie had forced him to think on his feet, had pushed him into the line of fire with no warning. He had only mentioned the call once, back at the Club Kingston, and they had never done any detailed planning to flesh out how the call should be played. He glanced up at Wylie, half expecting a smile that indicated that he had enjoyed watching him under the gun or perhaps a complement on a job well done. He got neither.

"Who's Admiral Sir John Washburn?"

"He's the Senior Fleet Officer at HMS Victory, the Portsmouth Navy Base," Piper replied. "Commander B. J. Fife is his aide-de-camp. I read the names. . ."

"In the newspaper," Wylie finished. "Yeah, it figures you'd be smart enough to use real names, not some made-up junk."

Not much of a compliment, he thought, pouting a little. "What's next?"

"We wait for Parnell to decide that it's time to go home, then wake Cranmoore from his chemically-induced sleep and turn him loose near a police station. We've been programming him hypnotically under sedation. He'll tell the right story, you can count on it."

"Marcus on Channel 6," one of the men said. Wylie grabbed a handset and barked, "Speak to me." Then he stood quietly and listened, never saying a word, never even changing expressions. Finally, he said, "Nice job, dweeb. You might just make a field agent yet."

A compliment? Marcus gets a compliment and I get nothing? What's going on here? I just did the greatest stand-up, think-on-your-feet threatening phone call that has ever happened, and Marcus gets. . . "

"Man, Marcus has really eaten the Colonel's lunch with that greyhound thing," Wylie began. "He got into the local police computer and entered the fact that there have been five other recent complaints of animal cruelty out at the colonel's farm, and they have all been quashed very mysteriously. He made it point to involvement by Whitehall. He started last night while we were still in the bar by getting SAS to lay on a raid at the farm and kidnap the real dog. They also planted some interesting evidence in an outbuilding that ought to finish the colonel for good."

"Sweeper on Channel 23," the young woman said, handing the handset to Wylie. Again Wylie just listened, this time for only about ten seconds. "Parnell's left the office in a chauffeured Daimler," he announced. "Sweeper will follow to make sure it's not just a late luncheon appointment and let us know. Tell Plasma to get ready to spring Cranmoore." Hand-held radios were spoken into, sometime two at one time.

"Postman," one of the men said, pointing out the window toward the house. "Let's do a sound check." A large computer terminal came to life, and a picture began to emerge slowly and come into focus. Bits of the picture were in focus, and bits were blurry. Then all the bits came together in focus and they were looking at the front room in Parnell's house. The picture moved around as one of the men worked on a computer keyboard until they were looking directly toward the inside of the front door. Standing in the shadows of the room, they watched as the postman walked up the front steps and inserted a quantity of letters and magazines through the slot in the front door. The computer monitor showed the mail dropping to the floor and a two small speakers played the sounds that accompanied the action.

"Visual and sound checks OK," the man said. But there was a problem. The postman was standing in front of the door, looking down at a piece of mail in his hand. He wasn't moving; he seemed to be staring at an envelope.

Oh, Lord! The BZ gas cannister must have sprung a leak, and the postman is losing his concentration. It must have seeped through the letter box slot in the door. When he bent down. . .

"Is it possible. . ?" Piper began.

Wylie's eyes bored a hole straight through him and he moved his head almost imperceptibly from side-to-side. Piper stopped in mid-question. Wylie and I must be the only ones in the room that know about the BZ. That was close!

The postman finished reading whatever it was, skipped down Parnell's front steps and continued on his rounds.

"Sweeper on 23," the girl said.

Wylie listened, then spoke. "Parnell is 95% sure to be headed here. Give the signal to cut Cranmoore loose. Let's move it, people!"

All three of the people began speaking into hand-held radios again. The computer operator was giving the signal about releasing Cranmoore. "Our friend needs to get some air," he said. "Negative control."

That meant to do it as planned unless they got a call telling them to stop.

"Dweeb on Channel 16," said the girl. Marcus.

Wylie listened, but this time he made comments. "It's too early. Stonewall them for now. It makes them hungrier and it will help to convince them that they are on the right track."

Newspaper people sniffing around the greyhound story. Wylie's right. Give 'em the stall and watch 'em start drooling.

"Daimler turning onto home stretch. Arrival in thirty seconds."

"Have Sweeper confirm the number plate. I don't want any mistakes," Wylie said to no one in particular.

The young woman spoke, "Sweeper confirms number plate as H285SCL. I spell: Hotel Two Eight Fiver Sierra. . ."

"Thank you," Wylie interrupted. The woman fell silent and immediately turned her attention to the computer display, completely unperturbed at being cut off in mid-sentence.

They watched as the dark blue Daimler with the H285SCL number plate pulled up in front of Parnell's house. A uniformed driver got out and opened the rear passenger door. Parnell stepped out onto the sidewalk and went immediately up the front steps without so much as a nod to the man. Used to the treatment, the driver closed the rear door firmly, walked around the front of the car, slipped behind the wheel and drove off down the street.

"Sweeper is to stay with the Daimler and report its position every two minutes until it's back in the Home Office motor pool," Wylie announced quietly.

Parnell was on the small landing at the top of the front stairs now, trying to get his door key into the lock and having a problem of some sort. The keys fell from his hand to the gray stone surface of the landing with a clinking sound that echoed softly in the room monitor played through the computer.

"Everybody freeze," Wylie snapped. "He may be suspicious or just nervous, but he'll have look around as he picks up the keys. No movement of any sort." Everyone at the window viewpoints stood completely still. Parnell bent over, retrieved the keys quickly and stared at the door lock for a moment. Then he straightened up, inserted the key quickly and went inside.

He was looking for scratches on the lock to see if anyone had been fooling with it. That's why the keeper wires were always made of copper. Copper is too soft to scratch the steel face of a lock.

Wylie turned his attention to the computer monitor. Parnell threw his overcoat on a nearby chair. Wylie's index finger moved to a small transmitter in his hand. Before he could press the button, a buzzing sound erupted over the speakers. Parnell put his briefcase atop a small table, snapped it open and fished out a cellular telephone.

"Yes, what is it?" He listened intently. "Don't use my name, sir, if you please. These devices are not even remotely secure, as you well know. Now what's all this about a dog?"

Parnell fidgeted in his living room with the cell phone pressed to his ear.

"I can't wait any longer on this," Wylie said softly. "Cranmoore is being put back into circulation and the Colonel is calling Parnell to bitch about his greyhounds. It's time." Then he pressed one of the buttons on the small transmitter.

"What the devil was that sound?" Parnell exclaimed. "No, no, not on your end. It was here. A popping of some kind. Like a tiny champagne cork. The central heating? Oh, yes possibly. Now where were we? Something about a greyhound that has gone missing? So you want me to alert Special Branch, is that it?" Then he giggled. It was a stupid-sounding high-school-girl kind of giggle.

The room was filling with BZ as planned.

"Drinking? Of course not! Well , yes, I had a drink of water at the office. It was that new Lemon Evian water from France. Have you tried it? It's quite tasty, actually. Really! Such language! And you a man of means and rank and all. You sound quite silly, old man."

Parnell recoiled from the cell phone and looked at it in surprise. "You have no right to speak to me like that, Ginger. I'm going to ring off now." He set the phone down heavily on the table next to his open briefcase.

"You're on, Mimi," Wylie said to the girl. "Make him shut off that damn phone, and then get him to do what we planned earlier."

Mimi spoke into a hand-held microphone as they watched the monitor over her shoulder. "Turn off the telephone, please, Reginald," she said in a perfect public-school English accent.

Parnell looked about the room. "What phone?" he asked, never even blinking at the voice.

"The cellular telephone on the desk in front of you, Reginald," she answered evenly.

Parnell picked up the cell phone and stared at it dumbly for a moment. "Press the OFF button, Reginald," Mimi intoned. Parnell punched a button, then continued to stare at the phone as if hypnotized.

Wylie motioned to Mimi, and she took her finger off the TRANSMIT key. "Make sure that damn thing is off, Mimi. I don't want him getting any calls and either not answering or answering and giggling to the colonel again. If it's off, the caller. . ."

"Will just get a message saying, The number you dialed is not available at present, Mimi interrupted. "Yes, I know why you want it turned off, Mr. Wylie. May I continue, please?"

Wylie waved a hand in agreement.

Piper smiled at seeing Wylie upstaged by such a youthful face.

"Damn Psychology PhD s anyway," Wylie grumped softly out loud.

Mimi was back on the microphone. "What lights can you see on the cell phone,   Reginald?" she asked pleasantly.

Parnell was staring at the object in his hand. He did not answer.

"What lights are winking on the cell phone, Reginald?" she asked again.

Parnell continued to look at the phone in his hand, then said, "What am I doing here? What is going on?"

"Jesus, that house must have a massive draft of air through it," Mimi said, in her own peculiar mumble. "The gas is wearing off. We have to speed up the sequences or he's not going to cooperate much longer."

"Maybe he's just. . ." Wylie tried to begin, but Mimi cut him short.

"Listen, you may be the Station Chief and all that crap, but I got my Doctorate working with this universally illegal substance, and I'm telling you that the gas is dissipating and that we have about a microsecond to change our plan. When the subjects start saying "What" at any time as a reference to anything but not being able to hear what you asked, THEY ARE COMING OUT OF THEIR COMA! Have you got that? Now, do we move on or watch the whole operation go down the toilet?"

"Move on," Wylie answered, holding up both hands in surrender.

"Get out the back door, Reginald," Mimi commanded. "And do it this instant. You are in danger. Only you can save yourself."

"Make him look in the pantry," Wylie interjected. He would regret it.

Mimi spun on him, her green eyes flashing. Piper had not even noticed that they were green before. "Damn you, Wylie! Keep your mouth shut, I'm working a sensitive situation here, and I don't need you grandstanding. I know what I have to do! I've memorized the operation plan down to the last comma, and I don't need your constant intervention to. . ."

"Parnell has stopped walking," Piper said, looking at the monitor.

Mimi's green eyes flashed at him for a second, then turned to the computer screen. Parnell was half way to the back door, and was coughing. "Look in the pantry, Reginald," she instructed. Parnell continued to cough and stand rooted to the spot. "Look in the pantry. It's the only way that you can be safe, Reginald," Mimi said softly.

Quickly, staggering now, Parnell made his way to the pantry door and pulled it open.

"Call the police now, Jack," Wylie said to the taller of the two men in the room. Jack could be heard explaining to the telephone that he was a neighbor of a Mr. Parnell at 22C Firkin Court and that there was a massive row going on inside, with much yelling and the sounds of a struggle.

Parnell opened the pantry door.

Wylie pushed a button on a small transmitter. There was a hissing sound.

Parnell crashed backwards, hitting the wall and tumbling to the floor.

"You have let him escape, Reginald," Mimi said evenly. "You had Cranmoore here and you let him escape. He knows about the American naval officer and the colonel and he will tell the police everything. You will be ruined. You will never get your knighthood. You are a stupid, stupid man, and deserve to lose everything that you have worked for and be sent to jail for the rest of your life."

Parnell was rolling on the floor, trying to thrash the demons away from his soul with flailing hands. Mimi continued to hound him with the same words, over and over. "You let Cranmoore escape, you stupid man," and "You will lose everything." Over and over, she repeated the phrases.

Finally, Parnell stopped rolling on the floor and became still.

"Go outside and find Cranmoore, Reginald," she said. She repeated the phrase until Parnell righted himself on unsteady feet and charged out the back door of the house. As his image disappeared from the monitor, everyone went to the windows to watch the proceedings.

"Where is he?" Piper asked without thinking.

"He's gone out the back of the house, obviously, and presumably down the rear stairs into the back yard, or garden," the tall man named Jack answered. "He may be thrashing around in the weeds searching for Cranmoore, or he may have fallen down the back steps and broken his neck. Mr. Wylie, do you want me to go have a look?"

Wylie shook his head slowly, staring fixedly at Parnell's house. "Never mind. The police will be here soon, and they'll find Cranmoore for us. In the meantime, he won't get far. He's going to be pretty disoriented, isn't he Mimi?"

"He's going to be absolutely psychotic after that whiff of gas that he took full in the face. He'll be lucky to be able to speak in complete sentences for the next hour or two."

A peripheral flicker on the monitor screen caught Piper's attention. "It's Parnell! He's going back inside the house." Everyone crowded around the monitor. Parnell could be seen coming up the back stairs at a trot, taking then two at a time. He raced into the living room and immediately turned right through a door into an adjacent room.

"What's in there?" Mimi asked.

"Master bedroom," Wylie answered flatly. "Maybe he's going to take a nap. Where's the damn police? I swear, I thought at least we'd be able to get a cop when we needed one. We may have to. . ."

Parnell came out the bedroom door, turned sharp left and disappeared out the back of the house. He was carrying a small automatic pistol in his right hand.

"Oh Christ!" Mimi exclaimed. "Now he's got a gun and a faceful of psycho-gas, and he's beyond the control area, so we can't contact him to get him calmed down. He'll probably. . ."

At that moment, several things happened within what seemed like microseconds of each other. Parnell came bursting from around the side of his house, pistol in hand, running into the street directly in front of a police car. His Old School Tie was waving in the breeze. His suit coat was unbuttoned, and the tail of his shirt hung out loosely. The police car screeched to a halt, stopping only inches from his legs. The driver and passenger both got out of the car, slowly putting their caps on their heads as though it was the most normal thing in the world to meet a deranged-looking man with a gun in the middle of a residential street. The officers could be seen speaking to Parnell, who began to slowly raise the pistol. It was an offhand gesture, much as though he was raising his hand to point at something, only in this instance the hand held a lethal weapon. The officers moved apart, positioning themselves on opposite sides of the man with the gun. They were unarmed, as are most British policemen. Parnell raised the pistol above his head slowly as though to fire a starting shot for the beginning of a race. A third officer who had come up silently behind him, probably the local beat patrolman, plucked the gun from his raised hand as easily as picking ripe fruit from a tree. Parnell turned to see where the gun had gone. As he turned, the other two officers stepped forward and pinned his arms behind him, then put him in the back seat of the police car. One officer sat in the back with Parnell, and the other started the car and drove off after retrieving the pistol from the third policeman.

There was no violence, no beatings with fists or a nightstick, no shots had been fired, no handcuffs were used, and nobody seemingly the worse for wear. It had been another instance of typical, smooth British police work.

They all watched as the remaining Bobby walked inquisitively toward the side of the house where Parnell had burst on the scene.

CHAPTER SIXTEEN

DEAD SOULS

Two widowed sisters, Mrs Kathleen Lockhart, aged seventy three, and Mrs. Beryl Donaldson, aged seventy-five, were simultaneously talking to the desk officer about the man they held propped up between them.

"He was standing in front of our cottage on Branward Close, you know, over by the new Sainsbury's on the High Street," Mrs. Kathleen Lockhart was explaining carefully. "He was looking around as if he were lost, so Beryl went out front and spoke to him."

"That new Sainsbury's is a waste of space if you ask me," Beryl responded from nowhere in particular. "In order to build it, they had to tear down that nice Mr. Ajani's news stand, as well as Mr. Cooper's butcher shop, and the old flats built in the reign of Queen Victoria. It was called Mansion House, which was a bit presumptuous even for the year of 1893 when it was built. But it was a tidy place, and the tenants were, by and large, acceptable people. Except for the musicians, naturally. They were a rowdy lot, always playing their instruments too loudly and too late at night. But I'm sure you know all about that, Sergeant, because you were always having to come and tell them to be quieter, weren't you?"

Sergeant Donald Crisp had been on desk watch for two years, and it was good duty. In to work on time and off from work on time, with a clean uniform each way. His wife appreciated not having to stitch up the rips caused by altercations when arresting drunks or thieves, and he enjoyed the orderliness of it all. These two old ladies had no one to talk to but each other, and bringing this elderly male foundling to the station would be a source of endless conversation for years to come. He waited while they wound down their story. The white-haired man between them seemed to be listening intently to their explanations, looking first at one and then the other, as though hearing the story for the first time. He looked a bit the worse for wear, but not as bad as some he'd seen. There was a reddish mark on his cheek where some stitches looked to have been recently removed from a cut.

". . . and Mr. Cooper always had the freshest chickens in his shop. He would cut them up any way you liked and his prices were less than Sainsbury's will ever be," Kathleen was emphasizing as she railed against the so-called Modernization of Britain. "I have always felt that Father was right. The things one must look out for. . ."

"Ladies?" Sergeant Crisp interrupted. All three of the people in front of the desk looked at him expectantly. "Might I ask the gentleman here a few questions?" They nodded in assent.

The sergeant turned his attention to the somewhat shabby man. "May I ask your name please, sir?"

"My name is Arlowe Peyton Cranmoore, officer," he responded instantly. "I am a retired thespian," embellishing the truth a bit.

"And how did you come to be standing in front of these ladies home, sir?"

"Well, I was kidnapped, wasn't I? They, no he, it was just one man, assaulted me most cruelly and took me to the embassy. No, it wasn't the embassy, it was a flat, no, a house. And he locked me in a tiny room and wouldn't let me out. And he asked me all sorts of ridiculous questions about where I had been and whom I had spoken to. He even hit me when I didn't answer him quickly enough." The man touched the reddish spot on his cheek warily.

"And who was this man, sir? Did you recognize him?"

"Oh, yes, of course I recognized him. His name is Reginald Parnell of the Foreign Office. Actually, he's with MI5, and I have done some odd jobs for him in the past. I have no idea why. . ."

A man in a suit that happened to be hurrying by the front desk stopped and stared pointedly at Cranmoore, "What name was that again, sir?"

"I said his name was Reginald Parnell, and in addition. . ."

The man in the suit grabbed a passing constable by the arm and said, "Escort this gentleman to an interview room and get a detective to take his statement. And do it immediately. I don't have time to explain, and I'm not going to ask you again."

The constable gulped and replied, "Right away, Guv." As the uniformed man led Cranmoore gently down the corridor, the "Guv" turned his attention to the two bright-eyed women.

"I am Detective Inspector Black. Are you ladies related to that gentlemen?"

Sergeant Crisp knew that he had to explain the situation quickly and succinctly before the two women started going on about Sainsbury's again. DI Black was always short on patience and long on nasty assignments for desk officers who earned his displeasure.

"These ladies found Mr. Cranmoore wandering aimlessly in the vicinity of their home, ascertained his confused state, and brought him directly to the station, Guv." Short and sweet.

"I would like you both to wait for a moment if you can. I'll ask one of our WPCs to escort you to the canteen for a cup of tea. Perhaps you can fill her in on the details of your finding Mr. . . . ."

"Cranmoore," they all piped up helpfully.

"Mr. Cranmoore, yes, thank you," the Detective Inspector responded quietly but intently.

"Mavis!" Sergeant Crisp barked. A stocky Woman Police Constable who happened to be walking past the desk area stopped in her tracks and was about to glare at him for shouting at her, but then she saw the DI stand by the desk and became all sweet and fluttery. "Yes, Sergeant. How can I be of assistance to you?"

"Would you take these two ladies to the canteen and get them each a cup of tea, please? And while you are there, ask them to give you the facts on the gentleman they just brought in to us."

"My, doesn't that sound exciting?" the WPC said unconvincingly. "Come with me ladies. We'll have some nice hot tea and you can tell me all about it."

Sergeant Crisp realized that he would pay for snapping at the WPC. Mavis would tell everyone that he had been sucking up to DI Black and she would make his life a misery. But it would go away eventually, and he would still have his nice assignment on the desk.

"Nice job, Donald."

It was DI Black speaking. He hadn't scurried away at the first chance like the busy man that he was, but was still standing in front of the desk, deep in thought and drumming his fingers on the countertop. And he had just complimented him on his work Would miracles never cease?

"Why don't you consider taking the Detective's Exam next time, Sergeant? You'd be a lot better at it than most of the lads I have now."

Strike while the iron is hot. "I would need a senior officer's recommendation to study for the exam, Guv. Desk Sergeants don't have much of an opportunity to. . ."

"Have someone write it up and send it to me. I'll be glad to sign it, Sergeant."

Sweet Mother of Jesus! It's a miracle. A letter of recommendation from DI Black. He was as good as promoted. Based on their new-found working relationship, the sergeant decided to do something that he had never, ever done before in his life. He asked DI Black a direct question.

"What's all this interest in Cranmoore, Guv?"

"It's not so much about Cranmoore, sergeant, as it is about that other name that he mentioned."

"Reginald Parnell, Guv?"

"Yes. Reginald Parnell is a Section head at MI5."

"And?"

"He is presently in Interview Room Three looking like a dog's breakfast. He was picked up by one of our patrol cars, standing in the street in front of his house waving an unlicensed firearm and babbling like a maniac. Among the unsolicited comments he made after being cautioned was one to the effect that "he had not been the man who had let him escape" or some such blither. The area PC, upon going to the rear of Parnell's home to assure that no one had been harmed and to make sure that all was secure, found the rear door standing open and an adjacent interior room in which it appeared that someone might have been held prisoner for a period of time. The Lab boys are going over it now, and preliminary indications are that someone may have been kept in the room for some time."

"Good Lord," the sergeant responded, wide-eyed.

"And, sergeant," the DI said quietly, "if someone that even faintly resembles a member of the Press Corps comes in that door, mum's the word, understood?"

"They won't even get the time of day, Guv. You can rely on me."

At about the same time at Prince Henry Barracks, a black Rolls Royce was being saluted through the main entrance. Inside were Major General Sir Hugh Frasier of the General Staff and an older gentleman in civilian clothes. "Damn nuisance, this," said the man in civilian clothes as the Rolls came to a stop and the door was opened by a ramrod-stiff corporal.

"Good morning SAH!" barked a heavily-ribboned older man in greeting as he saluted.

The general winced in pain at the sound of the booming voice. "This gentleman and I are here on the Queen's business, Sergeant Major, and I have a thundering hangover. If you bark at me again, I will have you shot. Is that understood?"

"Very good, sir," the Sergeant Major replied in a normal tone of voice. "Follow me, please." He led the two men directly to the colonel's office, glared the office staff out of his way and showed both men inside without a knock on the inner door.

Closing the door from the outside, the Sergeant Major spoke rapidly and softly to the two young troopers in the outer office. Both young men were standing stiffly to attention.

"The colonel is for the chop." he said softly to the two men at attention. "Ours is not to wonder why. Ours is to do as we are told. Anything you may hear through that door stays with you in confidence to the grave. If you breathe a word, I will have the both of you cleaning stables with your tongues until your enlistment expires. After that, I will personally beat both of you until a skilled pathologist will be unable to tell whether you are animal, vegetable or mineral. You may nod your heads once to indicate that you understand the gravity of the situation."

Both men nodded quietly and firmly, wide-eyed with apprehension.

Inside the colonel's office, everything seemed in order. "Please come in Sir Harold. Nice to see you again, General. What can I get for you? Sherry? Whiskey?"   The colonel was speaking from years of experience at dealing with influential people. His voice flowed calmly and evenly at the two men as he motioned them to leather chairs near the fireplace.

"Not this time, Tom. I'm afraid that we have brought some rather bad news," the man in civilian clothes replied stiffly. "It's about this situation with the injured greyhound that has been getting all the play in the newspapers and television."

"And it's all complete nonsense, Sir George. My people at the estate have given me solemn assurances. . ."

"Do shut up, Tom, and let's be done with all this," the General said sharply. "You are finished as of now. Whatever this mess was with your damn greyhounds, it started off looking bad and every minute that has passed has only made it look even worse. I want you into your mufti and out the side gate immediately. I expect no problems about this, Tom. Remember, you brought it on yourself. Starving an animal because he loses a race! Outrageous!"

"I did no such thing, General, and I will demand the right to clear my name. Where are all these lies coming from, and how could it become this serious so rapidly? I only first heard of it yesterday when one of my people at the estate telephoned and . . ."

"Tom, it's over. Now get out of uniform, get in your personal vehicle and get the hell off Prince Henry Barracks. Go anywhere you like, just stay quiet and let it pass like a good chap. If you make a fuss, we will drop you in it and help them drown you. None of this must be allowed to reflect on the Army or on any branch of the armed services. Do you understand?"

"Yes, but. . ."

"And be thankful that I am standing here in the present time rather than my grandfather standing here in 1945. If he were here, you would get a quiet room for no more than an hour, a desk, writing paper and envelopes, a pen, and an Enfield Webley service revolver with one cartridge in the cylinder, expecting that you would Do The Honorable Thing. You're actually quite a lucky man."

The colonel stood pale and shaken. His career was over, just like that. He was ruined.

The man that the colonel had called Sir Harold, opened the office door for the General, turned and said, "We'll see ourselves out, Tom. Good-bye."

In the outer office, the two troopers stood to attention.

Pausing in front of their desks, the General said, "One of you lads fetch Major Ross and the other get us some tea." Both corporals disappeared immediately, as if part of a magic act. The Sergeant-Major was almost bowled over as the two young men burst out the office door into the corridor.

He looked through the open door, and spoke directly to the General. "General, you can't be running these young lads about like that. They haven't been trained for the sprint races, and you'll wind-break them like foals." Sergeant-Majors have a wide degree of latitude in dealing with officers, and this man was not about to let the incident pass without comment. It was tradition, and he was bound to uphold it even if the man was a General.

"I sent the corporals to fetch tea and Major Ross," the General replied without looking directly at the Sergeant-Major. I say that the tea will appear before the Major gets here, and you have just bet me Five Pounds that the Major will appear first. Isn't that correct, Sar'-Major?"

"If you say so, General." Looking down the corridor, the Sergeant-Major saw the white-coated trooper pushing the tea-cart toward the office. As his gaze froze the man in mid-stride, John Ross passed on the outside and stepped into the room. The Sergeant-Major then nodded to the white-coated lad with the tea-cart to proceed.

"Major John Ross, gentlemen," he announced. "And the tea."

Ross' uniform was perfectly pressed, his shoes were brightly polished and every hair on his head was exactly in place.   "Good afternoon, General.," he said confidently, ignoring everyone else in the room except this very senior officer, and standing casually at attention. They shook hands.

"Major Ross, effective immediately you are Lieutenant-Colonel Ross, and I am putting you temporarily in command of the regiment," the General said evenly. "Colonel Reeves-Benedict has been relieved of his duties. Do you anticipate any problems carrying out these orders?"

"Sergeant Major?" Ross asked.

"Sir!"

"This word that the General just used: "problems". I am unaware of its meaning. Do we ever have any of these so-called "problems" in the Army?"

"Never heard of it, sir. I hear that "problems", as you call them, do occur from time to time in the Royal Navy and the RAF, but never in the Army, sir."

The General smiled slightly, as the tea was poured. Indicating the older man in civilian clothes, he said, "This is Sir Harold Rankin from Whitehall, Colonel Ross." The two men shook hands.

"Your father was in the Medical Corps, wasn't he?" Sir Harold asked.

"And my grandfather before him as well, Sir Harold," Ross replied easily.

"He won the DSO, didn't he?"

"As many other men did as well, Sir Harold. The family is very proud of him. He is ninety-one now and still quite active."

I like this young man, the General thought. His grandfather won the Victoria Cross as well, but he doesn't feel the need to push that fact in front of this civilian. Excellent judgment.

"We must be going, colonel, as we know that you have a lot of work to take care of. Perhaps we could play tennis at my club this Saturday?"

"I would be delighted, sir, although my game is a bit rusty I must say."

"Fine. That's settled. I'll send a car for you at ten."

The Sergeant-Major interrupted with a serious look on his face, "I believe that you owe me five Pounds, General. Cash would be preferred, if you don't mind, sir." The General fetched a banknote from his pocket and handed it over with a smile but no comment.

Ross and the Sergeant-Major then escorted the two men to their Roll-Royce, and both saluted as the car pulled away.

After the car was out of sight, the Sargent-Major turned to Ross and said, "My congratulations on your promotion, sir."

Ross thought for a moment and replied with just a hint of a smile, "Thank you, Sar'-Major. But we need to get this started off on the right foot with the men, if you know what I mean."

"That would mean that the colonel wants to inspect the entire regiment at 0600 tomorrow morning, rain or shine, and he wants them in full battle-gear with field packs, webbing, weapons and five-hundred rounds of ammunition per man. What about the officers and NCOs, sir?"

"Officers and NCOs as well, Sar'-Major."

"Oh , he's right bastard," thought the Sergeant Major to himself. "He'll do perfectly."

CHAPTER SEVENTEEN

HOME FREE

He struggled awake and sat up on the cot. Then he stripped off his grubby clothes and took a shower, shaving once more with the hand soap and the disposable razor. Then he put his old and fragrant clothes back on and walked to the embassy canteen.

He bought a cup of machine-made coffee and was in the process of choking it down when Wylie dropped two newspapers on the table in front of him. He had a brown paper bag in his other hand. ARMY COLONEL RETIRES IN WAKE OF DOG SCANDAL screamed the headline from The Sun. A teaser line lower on the page , referring to Parnell's detainment, said "Whitehall Figure in Drug-Crazed Police Encounter (see page 5)." Corresponding articles in The Times said only that an Army colonel had resigned under a cloud of intrigue over animal mistreatment and that an unidentified member of MI5 had attempted to assault a police officer while apparently under the influence of drugs.

"I see that they managed to keep both of their names out of the paper," Piper said sleepily.

"Don't make no never-mind anyway," Wylie replied. "They are both dog-meat as far as their careers are concerned. Their names are being whispered in every pub and private club in the country."

"One thing bothers me, Wylie, and I never even thought about it until now. What about the physical evidence that we left behind at Parnell's place? Don't those gas canisters and fractal transmitters make it easy for his defenders to say that he was framed?"

"You mean these gas canisters and fractal transmitters?" Wylie answered, putting the brown paper bag on the table. Inside it was a jumble of steel cylinders and wires.
"How did you get them out of his house?"

"None of your business, civilian," Wylie replied, almost smiling.

226

Marcus bubbled onto the scene as Piper chewed the dregs of the coffee in the paper cup. "Did I do it, or did I do it?" he gushed.

"Don't do it in the cafeteria, Marcus, whatever you do," Wylie answered. "Let's go to my office for some privacy."

Once inside, Piper asked for the details.

"Oh, man, it was beautiful," Marcus continued. "Those SAS guys really know their stuff."

There was a muffled thump as Wylie put his head on his desk and covered it with his hands. "Please tell me that you didn't call in the Special Air Service, Marcus," a pitiful voice croaked from beneath Wylie's armpit. "If it gets out that we laid on an illegal exercise to plant evidence at the colonel's estate, we will all go to jail. If it gets out that we did it using personnel from the SAS, we will be shot. I hate you, Marcus."

"Like Dr. Barker said, Never use a hand grenade if you have an A-bomb available. Anyway, what's the big problem? We're both on the same side, and they got to mount a clandestine insertion into terrain that looks a lot like Eastern Europe. They were happy and I was happy, because the thing went like clockwork. They landed the helicopters in a wood, completely. . ."

"Helicopters," Wylie rasped.

"As I was saying, the helicopters were concealed in a wood about a mile behind the colonel's country place, which is really a gigantic estate. It must be thousands of acres over on the border with Wales, and. . ."

Piper made Get On With It, Marcus, motions with his hand and Wylie let out another sigh.

Unfazed, Marcus continued. "They used civilian vehicles and rode right up to the place, announcing that this was a snap inspection by the Ministry of Agriculture owing to a suspected case of Rabies in the county. While the Brits held the attention of the people at the front of the house, the Russians went into the kennels and planted the bloody leash and the rest of the evidence for the others to 'discover' later."

Wylie's head popped up. "Russians? Did you say Russians, Marcus?" His voice sounded hopeful. Maybe all was not lost after all.

Maybe a small part of his career could still be salvaged, perhaps even his pension.

"Oh, yes. The SAS team has six Russians in it. These guys were Border Police KGB-types as far as I could overhear on the ride over in the CH-47s."

"God, Marcus, you didn't actually go on the operation yourself, did you? Please tell me. . ." Wylie's head fell to the desk again.

"Of course I went on the operation, Chief. Mr. Piper here told me that is the mark of a confident intelligence officer, that he will go on any operation that he plans. What's the difference? It all worked out perfectly."

"The problem, Marcus, is what the ramifications would have been if anything had gone wrong, such as a helicopter crash for example," Piper clarified.

"Well, that's the most ridiculous thing I've ever heard of," Marcus countered sharply. "Representatives of the US Government, in conjunction with the Special Air Services, lay on an operation to plant false evidence on a British colonel's property in order to incriminate him on animal-abuse charges in retaliation for having a US Naval officer jailed for life in an attempt to cover any possible links to the colonel and the IRA, and you're worried about the publicity fall-out from a possible helicopter crash? Are you out of your mind? Where's your sense of proportion?"

"He's got a point, Wylie," Piper said.

"Do please continue, Marcus," Wylie whispered, pouring himself a small handful of aspirin from a bottle and downing them with a swallow of Jack Daniels.

"Well, that's all there is, actually. The Russians planted the bloody leash and the dog poop in the kennel's store room, the Brits walked around back and discovered them in due course, they gave the evidence to the local police who linked it with the greyhound with the broken leg and the rest is history."

"If there's a stink, maybe we've at least got a draw because of the Russians," Wylie mused. "The SAS wouldn't mind dropping us in the soup if the operation were discovered by the newspapers. They'd say that we told them it was a raid on a suspected terrorist hideout, and that they knew nothing about any plot against the colonel. If only we had a way to prove that the men were really Russians, we would be in the clear."

"Here's the videotape that I took on the way over, Chief," Marcus volunteered. "Even though the background noise is pretty high, you can still hear that the guys were speaking Russian, and that the SAS guys were having a difficult time communicating with them because of the language problem."

Wylie looked at the 8mm video cartridge like it was solid gold. For his purposes, it was solid gold. "Thank you, Marcus," he said softly. It's called "Plausable Deniability."

"My pleasure, Chief."

Piper spoke up. "That little exercise that you two just went through helped to remind me for the umpteenth time why I don't like government work. Your whole life has to be consumed by making sure that all the paperwork is filled out properly, that no regulations have been knowingly overlooked, and that there is no possible way that anyone can come after you for anything that you have done."

"Or failed to do," Wylie piped in.

"Or can't prove that you did," Marcus added.

"I hate to admit that you were right, Piper, but you were right," Wylie said. "I see now what you meant by destroying their souls. The colonel and Parnell are both ruined men. Even if by some miracle the allegations against them were proven to be false, they would never live down the fact that they had been accused of the crimes in the first place. They could never return to public life, and that is where all their power and influence lay. The colonel is back on his estate wondering how a damn dog with a broken leg, a dog that he had never laid eyes on, could have gotten him dismissed from the service. From all reports, the psycho-gas really screwed Parnell up to the point that he may never be rational again. Cranmoore told his story exactly as we prepped him to say it, but the entire kidnapping-torture thing is being overshadowed by the fact that Parnell has been acting like such a raving maniac. Questions are being raised as to who it was that thought so highly of him, that is, who recommended him for such a sensitive post. There will be a lot of fall-out from this as people scurry to cover their behinds."

"You still gonna kill them, like you said that you would?" Piper asked softly.

"Probably not, I'm surprised to say," Wylie answered. "If Parnell is as messed up as we hear, he wouldn't know what was happening to him. So what's the point? The colonel has fallen so far in the power structure that it's wiped out everything that he ever did. There's even a rumor that his DSO is being investigated for authenticity. He'll most likely kill himself before I could get to him anyway, so again, what's the point?"

"That's the exquisite beauty of killing the soul first. It makes death of the body unimportant, almost a release from torment," Piper added.

The three men sat quietly, each thinking his own thoughts in silence. Wylie broke the spell first.

"Isn't it time that you went back to your lady friend, Piper?"

Nancy! He hadn't thought of her in days, not since the visit to the prison at Bournemouth. He was in trouble with women again, and for the same reason as always: his work.

They said perfunctory good-byes, the skinny Marcus anxious to go and play with his computers, and the harried black Station Chief. Piper thanked them for the chance to work with them, and for their trust in his abilities. He said that he could find his own way out, and they left him to use the office telephone in privacy.

They would never see each other again. That was the way these things went.

He took a deep breath, lifted the receiver and dialed. To his surprise, Nancy seemed happy to hear from him. Not knowing what to expect, he had expected the worst. She was up-beat, concerned with where he had been and what he had been doing. She even chided him about running around on her, but in a joking way. She asked if he could get there in time for lunch, but he had demurred, saying that he had an errand to run and would get there in mid-afternoon. She said she could hardly wait to see him again.

When he got off the train in Bexleyheath, he walked the mile or so to the town center. Suddenly, he was famished, so he popped into a small café and stuffed himself with fresh-baked scones washed down by mugs of hot tea with milk. They were delicious. Before leaving, he used the restaurant's Men's Room and smiled to see that the toilet with the overhead cistern mounted on the wall was a genuine Crapper, made famous by the noble firm of Thomas Crapper and Sons. He had crapped in a Crapper, and life was beginning to feel hopeful again.

He hadn't spoken to her in days. Truth be known, he hadn't even thought of her in days. She should be furious, and rightly so. He thought of chickening out, simply getting on a plane and going back to Dallas without going to see her. She would then burn his clothing and throw away his Comoy pipe. No, she was a practical woman, so she would give his clothing to Oxfam or some other charity, then burn his Comoy pipe and shaving gear, including the small pocket knife that his father had given him.

Sadly, she was a lost cause. He had destroyed their relationship because he had ignored her. From her viewpoint, it would be that he had come to see her, slept with her, gotten a more exciting offer, and forgotten about her immediately. There was no way to explain how intensely he felt about trying to help people that have been victimized by government bureaucracies. He would never be able to explain about the roadblock, or the Germans, Wylie, Marcus, Prescott, Parnell, or any of it She would never understand, because all women believe, with some correctness. that "you could have at least taken the time to phone."

One lousy phone call can change the World. And Sophia Loren is old and ugly. Yeah, right.

He stopped at a Marks and Spencer store and bought a new pair of shorts and a light blue tee-shirt. He changed in the men's room and threw the week-old set in the trash.

At least, if she killed him, he would die wearing clean underwear.   Every Southern mother's constant worry. He took a taxi the three miles to Nancy's house in Sidcup.

The door was answered by a pretty teenage girl. So the daughter, Amelia, was back from visiting her Dad. She had the

231

beautiful clear British complexion that made all American women feel that they had oily skin and enlarged pores and want to kill them on the spot.

"May I help you, sir?" she asked brightly.

"I'm Lewis Piper," he began hesitantly. "I'm here to see your Mother."

"Oh, Good Heavens!" she gushed.. "You are Mother's American chap, aren't you? You are even more extraordinary looking than her description. Please come in and sit down. I will tell her that you are here." She waved him inside with a smile.

Before he could settle himself on the couch, a tall young boy came smiling into the front room with his hand extended. "I'm Chris Carpenter, Mr. Piper. I'm pleased to make your acquaintance. Mother speaks very highly about you. Are you really from Texas? You don't look like a cowboy at all." He shook the young man's hand and tried to think of something neutral to say.

Well, her children didn't seem to hate him. That was something, at least.

"Hello, Sugah." It was Nancy. She was smiling as well. "Did I say it right? The word 'sugah', I mean." She gave him a hug and kissed him lightly on the lips.

Before he could answer, Nancy said, "We were about to go grocery shopping at Safeway. Would you like to come along?"

What was going on? Where was the explosion? Why were they being so nice to him?

They all got into Nancy's Honda and went shopping for groceries. Nancy bought some French wine and a bottle of blended Scotch whisky. Christopher and Amelia had followed along behind, whispering to each other and smiling broadly. When they returned home and all the groceries had been put away, they all four sat down at the little dinette table where he and Nancy had eaten breakfast so long ago.

"Can you tell us about it?" Nancy asked. The children were wide-eyed with anticipation. He noticed again how truly beautiful Nancy was.

I can't believe that this is happening. They actually LIKE me.

"If you can't, I'm sure we will all understand," Nancy offered.

"Mother, please!" Christopher pleaded. "We want so much to hear about it. Nothing like this has ever happened to us before. After all, he's a real Texan, and he's been off helping Uncle John with his questions about the Navy lieutenant. Please, Mother, let him tell us."

Nancy looked at him with sparkling blue eyes.

"I'll tell you as much as I can," he finally managed to stammer.

"Oh, golly. This is wonderful," Amelia gushed. "Wait until I tell the girls at school."

Before he could speak, Nancy said quietly but sternly, "You may not tell anyone anything, either of you. You must promise or Mr. Piper will not say another word."

The children were crushed, but they both promised to keep the secret.

So he gave them only the barest of an overview of what had happened. He included a moral about how men with power sometimes try to hide their mistakes by making even more mistakes. A vision of Richard Nixon, the league-leader in this category, flashed through his mind as he spoke. "There are articles in the newspapers today that address some of what was done. That will be the most that we can expect to hear from this," he added.

"Yes, I called John when I read that the colonel had retired, but he was unavailable to speak with me. I left him a message that I had called."

"Excuse me for being so blunt, Mr. Piper, but did you get to shoot anyone?" the boy asked.

"Christopher! Mind your manners," Nancy exclaimed.

"But, Mother," Amelia chimed.

Piper thought for a moment, realizing that he hadn't actually killed anyone for quite a long while, and shook his head.

The children looked disappointed.

"But I did get to run down a buxom young blond woman who was attempting to shoot me. Will that do?" he had added as an afterthought.

"Now you mind your manners, sir," Nancy said with mock seriousness.

"May I at least look at his hands, Mother? Please? I have never known someone like Mr. Piper."

Holding out his right hand, the steady one, Amelia took it and she and her brother examined the scars and marks carefully. Her eyes were wide with wonder. "Golly," she said.

"I think you have given my children enough excitement for one afternoon, Mr. Piper," Nancy said, again with mock seriousness. "Shall we think about dinner?"

Piper suggested that they eat out, and that it would be his treat.

"Can we have Italian, Mother? Can we? Please," Christopher said. Amelia nodded vigorously.

And so they took a taxi to a local restaurant called Primavera. A taxi was called so that he and Nancy could have too much to drink without having to worry about being stopped by the police and asked to take a Field Sobriety Test. He ordered Cannelloni, Nancy had Lasagna, Amelia and Christopher ate pizza from the buffet and drank Coca-Cola. Kids are the same the word over. He and Nancy split a bottle of Chianti. It was a wonderful, happy family meal. He had forgotten what they were like.

Once they were back home, Nancy excused herself and took the children aside, leaving Piper alone in the front room. She returned in a moment and said that she had told them that Mr. Piper was going to spend the night, and that that she was going to sleep in the same bed with him. She said that she had told them that if this was a problem for them, then she would send Mr. Piper on his way immediately.

"What was their answer?" he asked hopefully.

Nancy chuckled. "They said that their Father was sleeping with a Chartered Accountant named Dennis, and that Dennis was a certified twit as far as they were concerned. If I insisted on your leaving merely for the sake of appearances, they would prefer to go with you since I had obviously taken leave of my senses. Or, at least, that was the gist of our conversation."

"You have brilliant children," he said.

"They take after their Mother," she replied. "Shall we go to bed, Sugah?"

A little chill had run down his spine. She had gotten the word down perfectly.

Later that night, after they had made love, she was idly stroking his rumpled hair when she answered the question he dared not ask. Just what the hell did she see in him? Why was she so patient and loving?

"I'm forty years old, my ex-husband is a fruiter, my children adore you and I don't want you to leave. All I can give you is what I have. Just don't forget me, please." She smiled that blue-eyed smile that could melt a glacier.

The next morning after breakfast, he climbed the stairs one last time to pack his clothes for the flight to Dallas. An eight-hour flight and back into the August heat of the great Southwest, his cat, his house in the suburbs, his old Mercedes, and his ordinary bachelor life.

Then a horn was tooting in front of the neat white house in Sidcup to tell them all that the mini-cab for Gatwick had arrived. He shook hands formally with Christopher, gave Amelia a hug, gathered up his belongings, and shambled out the door. With the luggage stowed in the taxi, he turned for one last kiss, trying to think of what to say.

Nancy put her fingers to his lips and said it all. "Don't say anything, please, Lew." Then she kissed him and curled the hair in his ears. Placing her fingers on his lips once more, she said, "Just don't forget me, Sugah. OK? This memory is all I will have until the next time."

The next time. When? How?

The blue eyes misted and she pushed him gently toward the beckoning taxi door. He watched out the back window as he sped away toward Gatwick and Dallas. She continued to wave until the taxi made a right turn and she was gone from sight.

"You're a bit long in the tooth to be a newlywed, aren't ya mate?" the driver offered with a grin in the rearview mirror.

"Just drive the taxi, OK?" Piper grumped in return, wiping away a speck of something that seemed to have gotten in his eye.

CHAPTER EIGHTEEN

THE BROWN ENVELOPE

It was tough getting back into the routine of being in his own house again. The trip to the Post Office to re-activate his mail delivery had yielded a huge box of letters, papers, advertisements and small packages.

Daniel, his cat, had at first refused to come out of the cat-carrier in which he had been brought home from the veterinarian's, even though Piper had set him in the living room and opened the door wide. Daniel could see familiar objects and smell familiar smells, but like all cats, he knew that the entire thing was a trap. As in the Steven Wright joke, it was obvious to him that someone had stolen everything in the room and replaced them with exact duplicates. Eventually he had decided to make a break for it, and had roared out the carrier door and down the hall at top speed, ears back and tail straight out behind him. He was now hiding somewhere in a closet, building an impregnable defense perimeter. He would remain there forever, vigilant and watchful, or at least until he heard Piper open a can of cat food. Then everything would be back to normal.

He sat at the kitchen table and sorted through the mound of mail. All the advertisements got thrown into the Recycle Box, because the sales that they announced were long gone. His bills got paid by draft automatically from his bank account, but there were still notices that each account had been paid on time. There were letters from some of his consulting clients that wondered why he wasn't answering the emails that they had sent to his computer; he would deal with these later in the day.

There was a letter from his daughter which he opened immediately to see if she still blamed him for the breakup of the marriage to her mother. As he read the letter it became very clear that she still thought it was all his fault, and it was obvious that she was now into some new form of stylish solve-all-your-problems-with-my-$29.95-DVD-and-book-set crap that she had seen on daytime TV. Best to just let her lecture him and hopefully get it out of her system that way. Challenging her was never going to work; it would just make her more stubborn and convinced that she was right. It fascinated him that his daughter could find so many people to agree with her for only $29.95. At last count, this was the sixth different cure-all that she had found. Eventually, he had hopes that she would discover what he had learned the hard way: First, cure your own problems, then you can work on everybody else's failings.

There was a letter from an old Navy buddy that had been an alcoholic and had found God. Now he wrote everyone he knew trying to get them to come to church with him. He would write a noncommittal response later, but he wasn't going to go to church with a reformed alcoholic, that was for sure, old Navy buddy or not.

Finally, after working into the night, the mail was all dealt with and the plastic bin could be left out front for the postman to retrieve. He had sipped his way through half a bottle of Scotch and was feeling the effects of the smoky booze and the jet lag from the flight from London. Daniel had despaired of ever being fed again, so had left the security of his hiding place to come see if he might beg a meal. Piper took pity on the poor disoriented cat and fed him a small can of cat food with half a jar of turkey-flavored baby food on top like gravy. It was a Southern-style cat-meal for his friend and companion. Daniel stuck his face in the bowl and proceeded to eat and purr at the same time, which meant that he approved of the chef's choice of cuisine.

Since his day's work was now done, Piper went to bed and slept fitfully. Scotch always did that to him, but he still drank it when he felt like it without regards for the predictable consequences. He dreamed that all his clothes, sheets, pillowcases, towels and dishes needed to be washed and that there was no soap or water. It was a fitful night.

A week or so later, he had busied himself with laundry, re-stocking his refrigerator and filling his pantry after the absence. As he drove from the dry cleaner's to the supermarket to the liquor store, his mind wandered back to Nancy and the events of the recent past. In the process, he let down his guard. Everything in his background told him never to allow that to happen, but occasionally he did it anyway. Usually there were no consequences, but not this time. Staying on guard was the reason that his house had such an elaborate security system, complete with battery backup in case bad people cut the power off. Staying on guard was why there were two sets of video cameras at his house: the obvious ones that were non-functioning dummies and the hidden ones that actually recorded images. The real cameras were positioned opposite the dummy ones so anyone deliberately turning away from the dummies would be facing the real cameras. A video recorder was on a shelf in the hall closet behind some boxes where it could be found if someone really looked for it. The actual recorder was someplace much more safe and secure, and the camera images were transferred to it wirelessly.

So when the doorbell rang at 7:00 PM that night, he was smart enough not to blindly open the door to see who was there, but that was about the limit of his security skills. He looked at the monitor and saw that it was a mailman in a hurry who kept looking at his watch. He had a medium-sized package under his arm. The man rang the doorbell a third time. The automatic porch light had come on, the camera resolution was good, and he could clearly see a twenty-something black man in a Postal Uniform. Pressing the intercom button, Piper said, "Just leave the package on the porch, please. I'll get it later. I'm not dressed. I just got out of the shower."

"I have to get a signature on the Customs Form," he replied. "I can just leave you a Delivery Notice and you can come pick it up at the Post office the day after tomorrow."

"Oh crap," he thought to himself. Standing in line at the Post Office was almost as frustrating as standing in line to get a driver's license. "Hang on a second, I'll be right there." He stalled for a few minutes to give the impression that he was getting dressed. He also forgot everything he had ever been taught about Ingress-Egress Security as he concentrated on retrieving the package. He did remember one thing, and asked, "Who is the package from?"

"Somebody named N. Carpenter in the UK," the postman replied.

So it would be from Nancy. He wondered what wonderful surprise it might contain. Little did he know the extent of the surprise.

Opening the front door, he and the postman said their hellos. Piper pushed the screen door open and the postman handed him the box, placing a green US Customs card and a black ballpoint pen on top. As he tried to sign the card, the pen refused to write. He scratched the point on the paper wrapping of the box, but no ink came out. "You got another pen?" he asked. "This one doesn't work."

"I'm sorry, sir, I don't. But I'll hold the package for you while you get a pen if you'd like."

Piper handed back the box with a sigh, then turned and walked down the short hallway to his living room where there were several pens on a side table for just this purpose. He had subliminally heard some unfamiliar sound in the living room as he was talking to the postman earlier, but had assumed that it was Daniel screwing around with something. Another mistake. He also missed the fact that the postman had caught the screen door before it could close and was silently following him down the hall. Another mistake.

When he reached the living room, eight men dressed in black were there to greet him. Instinctively, his fists balled up and came up to his chest as he turned his left side toward the dark figures. A smiling man stepped forward and saluted smartly. "Thomas Gurney reporting for duty, sir! We have come to give you our personal thanks for a job well done."

The SEAL Lieutenant and his team has silently and effectively defeated all his defenses, personal and electronic, and were smiling at him as he stood there sheepishly.

"You look a lot shorter in person," Piper said, trying to gain back some of the initiative as he shook the man's hand.

" And you seem really slow and stupid, even for an old guy." The Lieutenant smiled brightly as he said it.

So much for gaining back the initiative.

Gurney began by saying, "My men and I came to thank you personally for getting me out of prison and returned to duty. None of that would have happened without your help and persistence." He went on to confirm how he had been arrested in his hotel while preparing to go on the non-existent parachute exercise the next day. He hadn't fought the arrest because he assumed it was all a mistake and would be easily cleared up. He was treated gently and politely by the police, but when they turned him over to the Intelligence Service, things changed immediately. He was handcuffed and gagged throughout the trial in the UK, then hooded and restrained until he got to the prison in the US, where he was immediately placed in solitary confinement.

"Did you ever suspect what it was all about?" Piper asked.

"Yeah, I figured out that it had to do with the pictures, because they really wanted to make me tell them what I had done with the film. They made all kind of promises that I would be set free once they had them, but I never believed them for a second. I figured they'd just kill me and dump my body in a ditch. But I never understood the details until I spoke to the Colonel."

"You spoke with the Colonel?"

"Yes, five days ago," Gurney replied

"Just before we killed the bastard," came a voice from one of his men.

Piper's shoulders slumped in disappointment.

Gurney saw his expression and immediately spoke up. "Mr. Piper, you are not the only one in the world that studies assassinations. We study them all, from Julius Caesar through Lincoln, Heydrich, Kennedy, all of them. We know all the ramifications, and we even studied Commandante Paulo's demise which we know that you were involved in. I had over a year to plan the Colonel's death, and it worked perfectly, thanks to help from my team."

Gurney explained that the Colonel claimed to have gotten involved in negotiating with the IRA at the request of a member of the Royal Family, whom he would not name. When he realized that Gurney had photographed him talking with O'Flynn in Belfast, he knew that he had to get possession of the photos and destroy them. He could not simply ask Gurney to hand over the film because he might get suspicious and refuse. Besides, as he said loftily, Senior Officers do not ask favors of Junior Officers and most certainly not foreign Junior Officers. The plan was to get Gurney out of London on a ruse, search his belongings for the film and destroy it. When they didn't find the film as they first searched his possessions, the decision was then made to get him locked away while further investigations proceeded. The rocket attack was simply a necessary part of the overall plan. The Colonel had told him that he could have avoided all the unpleasantness had he just told his interrogators the film's location. So, in the Colonel's view, it was all Gurney's fault from the beginning.

Gurney then produced a large brown envelope and withdrew some papers.

"To show you what an effective job we did, let me share some items with you. This is the Colonel's obituary, which ran only in the local paper. There was no mention of his death in the national or military newspapers."

It was a small three-line announcement that read, "Thomas Reeves-Benedict, a local resident, passed away suddenly on Tuesday the 4th. He was interred in a private ceremony attended by his family." There was no mention of military rank, no mention of his DSO, nothing.

Next, Gurney showed him a copy of a Police Report on the death. The colonel's body had been discovered by his wife, and the cause of death was ruled a suicide without an inquest. Not even the standard, "Suicide while the balance of his mind was disturbed" verdict from a Coroner's Court.

Gurney smiled proudly and said, "Now, here is a picture of the Colonel's body as found in his library." He handed Piper a large color photograph.

The Colonel was hanging by the neck from an overhead light fixture. He had a thin white rope looped around his neck. His feet touched the floor, and the knees were slightly buckled.

He was dressed in a white wedding gown in front of a full-length mirror. On his head was a red wig, and there were ringlets of curls cascading down over his ears. He was wearing full makeup consisting of mascara, rouge and lipstick. A sheer white net veil was in place, but the tiara had fallen to the floor due apparently to the tilted angle of the head. Lying near the tiara was a penis-shaped device, probably a vibrator.

This was an absolute textbook picture of Sexual Asphyxia gone very wrong. This is a well-documented practice of intentionally reducing the amount of oxygen to the brain during sexual stimulation in order to heighten the received pleasure from orgasm. The player dresses up in drag, ties a ligature around his neck, then bends his knees slightly to increase the strangulation pressure on the blood vessels in the neck in order to increase the sexual pleasure of manual stimulation of the genitals. If the player loses consciousness during the procedure, the result is often death by strangulation, as in this case. Clinically, it is a mental disorder, so the Colonel is now shown to have been a nut case in addition to his many other faults. Brilliant, simply brilliant.

"Damn, I'm impressed," was all Piper could muster.

"High praise indeed from the destroyer of the Commandante," Gurney smiled in reply.

"We have only one more item on tonight's agenda, and then we will be on our way," Gurney said. "We are going to make you an honorary SEAL. You have prior military service in the Navy, so all the better. I want to emphasize the word "honorary". As much as I appreciate what you did for me, as much as my team recognize your efforts on my behalf, nobody, I say again, NOBODY gets to call themselves a SEAL unless they pass BUD/S and SQT [Basic Underwater Demolition/SEAL and SEAL Qualification Training]. Do we understand each other?"

"Understood,." Piper answered.

"Take off your trousers, sir."

Piper hesitated, surprised by the request. Not, "drop your trousers" as if for a hernia or VD check, but "take OFF your trousers." He thought about it a moment too long.

"I can have someone help you if you like," Gurney said crisply.

Preferring to do it himself, Piper removed his trousers and handed them to an outstretched hand.

"Take off your skivvies and throw them away, sir" Gurney said tonelessly. "Undershorts," somebody said.

Whatever the game was, Piper was determined to play along, so off came the Jockeys and into a nearby waste basket they went. "You can put you trousers back on now, sir, but not your skivvies. Not now, not ever. No SEAL wears skivvies. If you are concerned about your dangling balls allowing a hernia to develop, my suggestion would be 100 sit ups a day for the rest of your life."

Producing a bottle of Tequila, Gurney announced, "And now, the obligatory toasts. We have only one bottle and ten people, so the toasts will have to remain smaller than Navy Regulation."

Piper was grateful because alcoholic beverages made from cactus made him really, really drunk – which was why he drank beer most of the time.

Small plastic cups were produced and charged with short shots of the alcohol. Gurney raised his cup and said, "To the President of the United States of America."

"The President of the United States of America," everyone responded and drank their cups dry.

The cups were re-charged, Gurney raised his and said, "To the United States Navy," and everybody drank as before.

Gurney then pulled a Trident badge from his pocket and removed the keepers from the pins that held it to the uniform. He poured the remaining small amount of Tequila over the pins, lined the badge up on Piper's shirt in the proper position, then hit the badge with the heel of his hand, driving the pins into his left chest muscle. It was a surprise and it was painful, but the pins were short and the Tequila was acting as a pain killer and the room had erupted into applause and handshakes and back-patting all around.

Then they said their good-byes and were gone as quickly as they had arrived.

It was over.

Standing in the middle of his disheveled living room he saw Daniel return from his hiding place, looking around curiously as he wandered toward his food dish. Piper removed the badge from his chest, examined it curiously, and reminded himself that it needed to be kept somewhere safe from prying eyes. Tired, excited and with a buzz from the Tequila, he decided that this was the perfect time to go to bed and catch up on his lost sleep. As he shuffled down the hall toward the bedroom, the telephone rang. He paused to let the answering machine pick up and to hear if there was a message.

The voice was low and metallic, the result of voice-disguising software. *"Lewis Piper, you have meddled in affairs that don't concern you for the last time. You have made some very powerful enemies who are now going to make it their life's goal to destroy you and everything that you touch. As you cower, waiting to be killed, remember: You brought this on yourself."*

Tomorrow. He'd work on this tomorrow, but there would be no cowering..

He had no intention of cowering for anybody.